# THE DAYS GROW COLD

# THE DAYS GROW COLD

By *Barbara Tunnell Anderson*

*The Macmillan Company · New York*

PRINTED IN THE UNITED STATES OF AMERICA

FOR

CALLIE DEAN AND SPENCER TUNNELL

In this story there are two characters who were developed from people I have known. These are Mittie and Cajy. All other characters, as well as places and incidents, are fictional and imaginary. Any names of actual persons or places that may appear here are accidental and wholly without intention. . . . However, the second theme grew out of the ideas and music-school experiences of

DWIGHT ANDERSON

who worked with me throughout the writing of this book.

# THE DAYS GROW COLD

## ONE

At the foot of the back steps Lucinda waited a minute. Her head turned slowly to the right, almost far enough, but not quite. Her neck tightened. She would not look yet. She would wait until she was in the tree. Even when she was in the tree she would shut her eyes and think about it for a while. Then she would open them and let them slide into the track that cut like a ray of light across the street and, narrowly through the trees, to the one big silver-gray column that told her where the house, with its forty-one other columns, stood.

Not looking, yet feeling it there, waiting for her to look, made a sweetness that blended with the sharp new smells the wind had brought into the yard and gave her a sense of something good about to happen. Her left arm closed hard around Adelaide. To hide the doll from Mittie, Lucinda had tucked her into the pocket under the crook of her arm made by the blouse of her half-buttoned red cardigan. A thin, cool stream of air trickled through the leaves and lapped Lucinda's ankles. She braced herself against a shiver and waded in, walking slowly, lifting her feet high.

"Jesus walked on the water," she whispered to the doll, "and we're walking on the wind."

3

But the wind would not stay underfoot. It swooped up to suck the bold words out of her mouth. Her long brown pigtails went straight out. Her skirt left her legs, a blue flannel umbrella, ribbed with pleat creases. She beat at it with her free hand but there was no stopping it. It went up until it slapped her face and blinded her. This was not the wind people talked about, saying it was from the east or from the west or in from the marshes or up from the Gulf. These were the Four Winds, and every one of them was bent on Lucinda. They whirled away with her and plunked her down at the high-peaked door of the tree.

She leaned against the big live oak to catch her breath. Then she sat flat on the ground and inched her way back into the tree. When the thin ridge of her bowed backbone touched the crumbly wall she drew in her feet. Her knees rose, and her long legs made a door that shut her safely in and left a triangular transom. She closed her eyes and pressed hard against the warm sweet-smelling wall until she felt herself filling the void. Her shoulders throbbed with the tremors that played up and down the trunk. Her arms reached out into the limbs and leaves.

"I saw it and I heard it," Lucinda whispered to the doll, "and part of it fell on my poor, poor tail."

Peering through the transom, she saw that out in the yard the wind, shrunk to cat-size, was sliding and squirming under the leaf rug. It bulged the rug here and there, lifted it, let it fall, carried it on its back as it crept along the ground. At last it plunged through and sent a handful of leaves somersaulting towards the tree. A maple leaf, red as an apple, fluttered through the transom and landed on Adelaide's tight-curled yellow mop. With the sight of it, Lucinda was resolved into herself again. She held the doll up to the transom, the better to see, and her delight cropped out in a song that followed, more or less, the pattern of "Three Blind Mice":

> You and me
> In the hollow tree;
> You and me
> In the hollow tree.
>
> Who brought us in?
> A big piece of wind.
> Who brought us in?
> A big piece of wind.

The door banged behind Mittie with her clothes basket. She dropped the basket under the line and padded over to the tree.

"Whachu doin not singin about Jesus?" she demanded.

Lucinda clapped her hands over her mouth.

"Donchu know Jesus save you? Howcome you alltime hidin in that rotten old tree and singin devil songs?"

Lucinda let down her knees.

"This is Tuesday," she explained. "I'm singing school songs."

"And don't Jesus save you ever' day? He don't wait till Sunday to save you, do He?"

"No."

"Then ain't you shamed to wait for Sunday to sing for Him?"

"I'll sing 'Jesus Wants Me for a Sunbeam' next," Lucinda promised.

Mittie searched her mind. "Callin it by the Jesus name don't make it no Jesus song," she said. She scuffled back to the clothesline.

"Will you tell me stories if I help you get supper?"
Lucinda called after her. Her thin voice was beaten down
by the flapping sheets. But Lucinda knew Mittie was always ready with stories about when she was a little girl
going to Castleton to help her mammy tote firewood for
the big wash pots in the back yard. Sometimes she would
be called into the house to dust under the chairs and tables that had got too low for old Kate. That was what
Mittie liked better than anything because when she crawled
around on all fours she could peep up at the big picture.
The big picture was in all Mittie's Castleton stories: the
one about picking out nuts for Selina when she baked a
shelf full of cakes for the parties; the one about the wedding of Miss Emma Cass and Mr. Tom Reeves when they
stood in front of the picture to be married and Mittie hid
behind the palms to see the bride. After the wedding Mittie had never gone back to Castleton. That was a long
time ago. She was soon old enough to have regular jobs of
her own, nursing or cooking. For a long time she kept
thinking maybe she'd learn enough to work at Castleton
some day, but things began to be different up there. Mrs.
Reeves was letting off servants instead of taking on new
ones. All the time Miss Emily Reeves was growing up
there was talk down on Gander, from this one or that who
was no longer needed at Castleton, about the stinting in
the kitchen and the collectors at the door. But Mittie
never forgot about Castleton and how things used to be
there. She could shut her eyes any minute and see it all
plain as day.

Now, since the Geography lesson, Lucinda had something of her own to add to the stories. Last night she had
tried to tell Mittie, but when she was ready to begin her

jaws went stiff with excitement. She couldn't move them. Later, in bed she went over and over it and heard herself saying calmly and eloquently the wonderful things that had made the Geography lesson.

"For our Geography lesson today," Miss Carley had said, "we're going to talk about our own town."

She had drawn down the map and pointed to the spot near the bottom that was Macklin. She measured the miles from the ocean and the miles from the Gulf and the longer miles from the mountains. Then she put up a map she had drawn with colored crayons. It was Macklin. She stuck it to the board with thumbtacks. She pointed to the straggling line on the edge of things that was Gander Creek and to the wriggling curve, on beyond, that was the river. She pointed to the red railroad station and the green square and the brown streets of the stores.

"But here," she said, and circled her pointer around the east side of the map, "is where Macklin began." She laid down the pointer and held up a big, old-fashioned photograph.

"This is Castleton," Miss Carley said.

The sharpest eyes could not pick out the outlines of the house. There was a forest of trees and a forest of columns, the two joined by a flare of steps that sprang widely out and up in a sweeping, fluted flight. On a circular driveway before the steps a horse drew a trap with a high-perched seat. A ruffled parasol bubbled up over the seat to touch one of the tassels of moss that hung from the branches of the live oaks.

"It isn't likely," Miss Carley said, "that many of you have seen this beautiful house. But most of you know the place." She hesitated, and her eyes ran quickly up one tier of seats and down the other. "How many of you know where Castleton is?" she asked.

Lucinda's hand went up. Miss Carley gave her a special smile.

"Lucinda is Castleton's nearest neighbor," Miss Carley said. She considered thoughtfully each of the other raised hands and the hands that were not raised. "I should think all of you would know," she said. "It's at the head of Cass Avenue. In the beginning Castleton was a plantation of four thousand acres, reaching back across Gander Creek and on to the river. Only thirty or forty acres are left now, but in the beginning all Cass Avenue was Castleton's driveway and the town was only the village that supplied Castleton's needs. That was nearly a hundred and fifty years ago . . ."

"We're Castleton's nearest neighbors," Lucinda whispered to Adelaide. The stone's-throw of street that lay between the tree and the high chained gates welled up to her, rich with Mittie's stories and Miss Carley's Geography lesson. She drew her feet a little farther in until only the smallest possible triangle of transom was left. Then she opened her eyes and set them on the track that would have been blocked if a single tree were moved so much as an inch to right or left. The elaborate gates stood in the clear. Castleton's own trees kept their distance. But every few feet the low iron fence was strained to bursting as if the whole thirty-acre mass of trees and shrubs and vines were pressing against it, determined to break bounds. There was no elbowroom for such antics as were going on in Lucinda's yard, and there were no maples or pecans or sweet gums to fling out leaves of red and gold. When Lucinda's trees bent double Castleton's trees only tossed their heads. And, instead of the silly whistling and shrieking that darted around now and then in Lucinda's trees, there was an incessant murmur that traveled from magnolias and live oaks, along wisteria and jasmine, through pines and cedars and elaeagnus. It flowed across the street and made its way into Lucinda's tree. Inch by inch, the darkness of the tree seeped out to meet it. The wind and the dark, the lesson and the stories came together. They moved through Lucinda and added her to their sum. . . . She knew how it had been. She could see how Castleton had gone on to the creek and, over the creek, to the river. She could see the white camellias, the miles of white camellias, that are more, maybe, than just japonicas. She could see the white azaleas, too. The flowers at Castleton, Miss Carley said, were always white. Everything at Castleton was green and white and white and green. The white pearls and diamonds on the ladies in the portrait. The green emeralds. The white dress. Lucinda could see the white satin flowing out. But there was a red dress, too, and a red chair and red curtains. She knew about the silver doorknobs, too, and the silver keys and the carriages trimmed with silver. There was silver on the horses' harness, and the ceilings were all over gold. She and Mittie could shut their eyes and see the gold ceilings. She could almost hear the singing Miss Carley's grandmother had heard. There were so many slaves singing in the cotton fields, and singing so sweet and loud that everybody could hear. Miss Carley said boats on the river ten miles away would hear the singing and stop to listen. And at night people in the town would walk to where they could hear the fiddles. Twenty slaves played the fiddles for the dancing that went on all night at Castleton, and

the people who couldn't go to the dances gathered in the
shadows of the trees along the street to listen. But Miss
Carley's grandmother was in the room under the gold
ceiling, dancing to the music. Lucinda would tell Mittie
about Miss Carley's grandmother dancing at Castleton, and
Mittie would tell her about the turkey breasts on silver
plates and the cakes as big as a washtub. Mittie would tell
her about the chairs from a queen's castle and the gold
harp like an angel's. Lucinda knew how it had been. She
would tell Mittie about when Miss Carley was a little girl
sitting in church on Thanksgiving Day and smelling the
tea olives that grew all along where it was Cass Avenue
now. Lucinda thought how it would be to smell tea olives
—a winter smell, Miss Carley had said, and sweeter than
anything on earth. . . .

A tingling in Lucinda's legs made her stretch them
out. The kitchen light had gone on. Supper smells drifted
across the yard. She kicked her heels against the ground to
wake her feet and legs. Darkness had cooled the wind and
whipped it up. It nagged the stiff green leaves of the magnolias and live oaks into a fretful chatter. It lashed at the
tall pecan trees until a hailstorm of nuts fell thundering
against the flat tin roof of the garage. Across the tumult a
sudden voice cut sharply.

"I can't stand it," the voice cried. "I tell you I can't
stand it. It's not as if I deliberately decided—"

It was a woman's voice.

A man's voice beat back, too close to the wind in tone
to be separated into words. It groaned and rumbled. Voice
tumbled on top of voice, pouring out anger.

An uneasiness stirred in Lucinda, rising from the pit of
her stomach. For a second it wavered between questions

and remembering. But as footsteps, muffled in wind, carried the voices away it ebbed to a vague discomfort, more disturbing to her stomach than to her mind. She pressed her mouth against Adelaide's back to stop the chattering of her teeth. It was long past time for her to go into the house. Mittie had forgotten about her. Any minute now she would be calling out from the kitchen door. Lucinda buttoned her sweater to her chin and summoned her courage for the dash into the yard. Before she had got to her feet a long rectangle of light fell across the back porch, and her mother, trim as a new doll, stood in it.

"Lucinda," she called. She still wore her hat and jacket. Lucinda's teeth dug at Adelaide's back.

"Lucinda," her mother called. "Lucy, darling." She turned back into the house, still calling.

Lucinda hunched out of the tree. She plunged into the black canyon that lay between the tree and the lighted windows, her feet bouncing like a rabbit's against the dry leaves. As she reached the steps the door from the back hall opened again.

"Lucy, darling." Her mother's voice was frightened.

One more step and Lucinda stood in the light. "Here I am, Mother," she said. The lattice door closed sharply after her. She lifted her face to her mother's but the anxiety in her mother's voice and eyes had to be appeased.

"Where were you, Lucy?" she cried. "Why didn't you answer when I called? Where were you? Don't you know what I've told you about staying out after dark?"

"I was playing in the garage," Lucinda said. Under her breath she added, "last week."

Her father was on the stairs. "How could you play in the garage," he said, "when the car was in there?" They had walked home. He looked straight at her and repeated, "How could you?" He did not distrust her. He only wanted to understand.

"I was playing in the car," Lucinda said.

Her mother's arm tightened about her shoulder. "You simply must not stay out after dark," she said. Her hand pressed the shoulder until Lucinda winced. "Promise me, Lucy, you never will again. Promise me," she urged.

Lucinda edged away. "I promise." Her mother's arm went out to her again.

Her father had reached the hall. He stood beside her and stroked the top of her head. "There, there, now." He stroked and patted to ease the tenseness under his hand.

Her mother said: "The child hasn't enough fear for her own protection. She must learn to come in before dark whether she's called or not."

Over her head, they looked at each other. Then her father turned and went into the living room. Lucinda followed her mother upstairs to get ready for supper.

"AIN'T I DONE said I can't do no tellin when I'm workin on these here peecans?" Mittie complained. "I ain't got no more wind than I need. Takes all my wind to bend my back up and down like a pump." Mittie turned her broad back on Lucinda.

"I'll pick up every one," Lucinda offered, "if you'll just sit here on the stump and tell me. You can rest while I do all the bending and picking."

"I ain't callin it rest to be alltime a-workin my mouth. I'm a-studyin in my mind. I'll pick up here, and you pick up over there." Mittie pointed to the other tree.

Lucinda turned to her basket. As she dropped the first nut into it the miracle happened. She was Miss Carley. The basket was the schoolroom. Under the tree was the playground where the pecan children waited for Miss Carley to call them into the Sixth Grade.

"Good morning," Lucinda whispered, dropping in a smooth brown nut. "Good morning, Jean. Good morning, Angela. . . ."

The basket had never filled so fast. Lucinda sat back on her heels and wondered at the quantity of nuts in it.

"Don't be settin there a-wastin your time," Mittie called.

13

"It's full," Lucinda said. She pointed to the basket.

"Then empty it out in the tub on the back porch and fill it up again," Mittie ordered.

Lucinda carried the basket to the porch and poured the nuts into the tub. That basket was Monday at school. The next basket could be Tuesday. . . .

At first Lucinda heard the sound only as a part of the pecan-children game. Then she heard it on the outside, coming from far away. She looked down Mimosa Street but could see nothing. It was a lazy, whining sound, the voice of a Negro singing. The song went up and up, broke in the air, dropped quickly and slowly climbed again. A ribbon of wind caught at it and flung it nearer. Then, suddenly, as if the voice had turned a corner, the song was filling the yard and overflowing it.

"H-i-p," the high, reedy voice sang. It made every letter into a word and sang it like a song.

Lucinda crossed over to Mittie's tree.

"P-o-p," the song went on.

"I think it's Cajy," Lucinda said to Mittie.

"O-t-a," the voice sang.

"It is Cajy," Lucinda cried. "He's coming this way. He's spelling a word."

"What's that poor crazy boy a-sayin now?" Mittie asked, her voice level with her knees. She pried herself up.

"He's spelling a word," Lucinda said. "Let's get him to spell for us. I haven't ever seen him, and I haven't ever heard him spell."

Mittie dropped nuts noisily into her bucket.

"Cajy thinks words are songs," Lucinda explained. "He'll spell for us if we'll let him."

"Howcome you tellin me all about Cajy?" Mittie asked.

"Don't I know Cajy? Ain't I been a-knowin that poor crazy nigger ever since he's been born?"

"Have you got any money?" Lucinda asked.

"I ain't got no money," Mittie said, "and had I money, I ain't a-givin it to no nigger to make out like he can spell."

"But he can spell, Mittie," Lucinda said. "He's spelling now. Everybody at school talks about the way Cajy can spell. Listen, Mittie, it's a long hard word he's spelling."

They stood listening as the song came nearer. Every letter was sung, drawn out with scales and turns. The letters fell into syllables to fit the pattern of the tune.

"I think he's spelling 'hippopotamus'," Lucinda said, a little too fast for her tongue.

"Huh," Mittie snorted. "That ain't no word. That's just slobberin. I know that Cajy. Cajy ain't nobody to be a-spellin. A-singin neither. Us down on Gander know that Cajy. Us ain't a-needin none of his spellin."

"Yes, it is a word," Lucinda insisted. "It's an animal. It's hard to spell. Let's get him to spell for us. Please, Mittie."

"H-i-p," the song began again. The tall thin Negro came in sight.

Lucinda moved closer to Mittie. She had never seen anybody so tall and thin. Cajy's head moved in and out of the branches of the water oaks that lined Mimosa Street. His swaying, shuffling amble brought him to the side gate. He saw the woman and the little girl and leaned against the fence.

"Cajy spell?" he offered. His taffy-colored face was turned to them, but his eyes stopped on the ground somewhere between the fence and the pecan tree.

"Go on away from here," Mittie ordered. "Us ain't a-takin our spellin from no nigger."

He looked at Lucinda. "Cajy spell?" he pleaded.

His face was like a little boy's, but he was taller than a man. He could see into the trees and maybe upstairs, if he tried.

"Cajy spell?" he repeated.

Lucinda shook her head. "I don't think we've got any money," she said. "My mother and father are not here."

"Cajy spell for taters," he wheedled.

"Let him spell, Mittie," Lucinda whispered. "Please let him spell."

Mittie turned her back on him. "He ain't got no sense, honey. He ain't like us. I guess his mammy drapped him. He don't know what he spell."

"But I want to hear him," Lucinda begged. "Flora says he can spell orang-outang."

Mittie grunted.

"Cajy spell for peecans." He pointed to the basket and bucket under the trees. "Cajy spell for peecans," he repeated. He drew a small measure, a pint, perhaps, in the air.

"Well, go on and spell," Mittie told him. "Give out what you want him to spell," she said to Lucinda. "He can't think of nothin to spell lessen you tell him. Cajy ain't got no sense. Ain't nothin but breath and britches."

"Spell 'orang-outang,' " Lucinda said. Her voice flickered with excitement and went out. But Cajy had heard her. He vaulted the fence and leaned against Lucinda's tree. His eyes rolled in his concave face like Andy Carter's agates in the hard-dirt marble ring.

"O-r
A-n-g
O-u-t
A-n-g."

The song was brief and definite, something to be finished with as quickly as possible and put out of the way.

"Oh, I know that's right," Lucinda cried. "I'm almost sure it is."

"You don't know nothin about it, and Cajy don't neither," Mittie said.

"Spell 'Mississippi,'" Lucinda said.

For a second Cajy's eyes hung, questioning, in Lucinda's. Then the shining marbles rolled again in the ring. "M-i s," he began. He made flowing motions with his long, double-jointed hands. He was spelling the river. His body swayed as he lingered over the *s*'s. He held on longest to the final *i*, playing it in his wide-open mouth against the back of his teeth.

"I wish I could think of some more hard ones," Lucinda said to Mittie. "Can't you?"

"I ain't got no time to be foolin around crazy niggers," Mittie said. "Wearin sacks for shoes," she added under her breath.

Lucinda had been trying not to look at the lumpy feet. If Cajy heard Mittie, he gave no sign. He was waiting for the next word. Lucinda was thinking, searching her mind for a hard one.

"I wish my daddy were here," Lucinda said. "He could think of lots of long ones, words harder than 'hippopotamus.'"

"H-i-p," Cajy began, reaching for the word even before

it left Lucinda's lips. He sang it softly, slower than before. Lucinda thought she would try to sing it to Cajy's tune sometime when she was alone.

"Hand me that little old paper poke a-settin by the steps," Mittie said to Lucinda, "so we can get shet of this here Cajy. Us got work to do."

Lucinda brought the bag. Mittie filled it. She was careful to put in only the smaller nuts.

"I've got another word now," Lucinda said. "Let me give him just one more."

"One," Mittie agreed.

"Peninsula, then. Spell 'peninsula,' Cajy."

Cajy dug his ragged toe into the leaves and squirmed slowly. A shiver moved upward along his scarecrow frame. The music began mournfully behind tight lips. Finally he opened his mouth and began to spell. It seemed he would never finish making the first *n* into music. Lucinda was afraid he did not know how to go on with the spelling, but at last the second *n* was finished too; and, with the *s*, he swung with a sudden flourish into the major key and threw out runs and wavers until the back yard and Lucinda and Mittie were caught up in the song. They stood waiting for more even after his teeth had closed on the final measure.

Cajy reached for the bag, lifted first one long leg and then the other over the fence, and headed for the corner, humming.

Lucinda gazed after him. "Look where he's going," she said, knowing perfectly well that Mittie was looking.

Cajy reached the gates and stood for a minute or two before them. Then he dropped the package of nuts on the ground and grasped an iron bar in each hand.

"Just like a jailbird," Mittie snorted. "Look at him lookin."

"What's he going to do?" Lucinda asked. "Is he going in?"

"No, he ain't a-goin to go in." Mittie's voice softened. "He just a-lookin. Thinkin maybe he'll see his pappy. Along about goin-home time, most always Cajy'll be a-hangin round at the back so he can trot home with his pappy. He'll be a-pickin up his bag and goin around back and a-waitin for his pappy to go on home and cook him up some victuals and wash him. Cajy ain't got sense to do nothin for hisself. He can't do nothin but kinder sing."

"I haven't ever seen Cajy's papa, have I?" Lucinda asked.

"Howcome I know what anybody seen or ain't seen? Maybe you is. Maybe you ain't."

"Do you think his papa is coming out the gates today?" Lucinda asked.

"Them gates? Abe? You ain't seen me a-goin out your mother's front door, is you?"

"No."

"And Abe ain't no better'n me, is he?"

"Tell me about when the gates were open," Lucinda said, "and Miss Emily was a little girl and people going in and out all day."

"Night, too," Mittie reminded her. "Look like them folks didn't know night from day. Them days."

The tub on the back porch was full of nuts. The November sun had settled on the top step. With her hands on her knees, Mittie let herself down, her broad bottom reaching out to test the warmth of the steps with the gesture of her spit-wet finger trying the heat of her iron.

"It ain't to-say cold," Mittie said, "if you'll get your sweater on, I guess we'll call us a-restin a little right here."

Lucinda sat beside Mittie and squirmed into her sweater, hardly moving her arms. A breath too deeply drawn could break the mood of Mittie's remembering.

"Is the big picture as big as this back porch?" she asked, holding on to her voice.

"You say this here back porch? You say this little old back porch, here?" Mittie demanded.

Lucinda nodded, ashamed of her measure of the picture.

"Ain't no wall in this here house big enough for that picture," Mittie declared.

"Is it as big as the front porch wall?" Lucinda asked.

"Bigger, honey; bigger'n that. Reckon you couldn't think of a wall big 'nough lessen you seen that picture."

But Lucinda had already found a wall. She was seeing the picture hung in the air before her, stretched across the back yard.

"Are there chairs in the picture, and tables?" she asked, just to get Mittie started.

"Chairs? Ain't I done told you they's chairs? Ain't I done told you them chairs is big as the preacher's, and all over gold?"

"Not gold. You didn't tell me gold."

"Yessir. Gold chairs. And the folks a-settin, big as life."

"You said gold for the harp," Lucinda said.

"That's right. Solid. Solid gold from top to bottom. And the pretty young lady a-settin in her red dress and her hand all ready to play on it."

"And her father standing by her, looking at her."

"Yessir, the old man standin straight as a stick. Never a-movin his eyes. Just standin there a-lookin like he wouldn't take nothin for her. And the big boys standin around they mother like she was a queen or somethin."

"With her white skirt spreading all around her and out to the door. And the young lady's skirt all over the other side."

"Yessir. I reckon they must be moren a hundred yards of silk in them skirts. But don't ask me about they waisties. Look like they waisties was nekked as jays if they didn't have all them diamonds on, and pearls."

"Bracelets and necklaces and rings," Lucinda said. She slipped imaginary rings up and down her fingers.

"All of them a-settin so pretty," Mittie said. "And they little cat."

"But you didn't tell me about the cat," Lucinda cried. "You never did. Tell me now about the little cat."

"I done told you about that little cat a-sleepin by the chair."

"No, Mittie. No, you didn't. And the little chair. You didn't tell me that."

"Well, now, it ain't nothin but a little old black chair. Ain't gold. Just a-settin in the picture. Ain't nobody in it. Little cat just roll up by it."

Clearly against the sky Lucinda set the little chair, its short fat legs, its arms reaching out, its coziness beside the cat. *I love little Pussy—* Her own hand held the brush that gave the chair and the cat their places in the portrait.

Mittie leaned forward, her elbow on her knee, her cheek against her hand. As she talked her breath made little winds on the top of Lucinda's head.

Sometimes Lucinda thought her mother began being unhappy back in August when they had to leave her grandmother's house in North Carolina. Or maybe it had begun weeks before that when her father drove away in the car to the new job in the new town. That was the first time she had ever seen her mother cry. After a while the furniture rode off too, heels in air, in a big truck, and she and her mother went next door to her grandmother's house to wait for the letter.

Her mother had cried again when the letter came, and that made Lucinda cry. But a little later, when they were alone in their room, her mother threw her arms around her and kissed her and said: "Aren't we glad this dreadful month is over? We'll be in our own home again with our own things. We'll manage our own life and we'll be all together again."

But there had been a great deal more crying the day they left, the day that began before it was light with Lucinda's grandmother coming in to clap her hand down on the alarm clock. "If you must go," she said, "I don't want you to miss the train. I'll be back to help you after I see that breakfast's started."

She was back before Lucinda was out of the bathroom. "Look, Ethel," she said, "your slip shows when you don't stand up straight. If you can't yank it up enough I'll pin it for you."

"I always stand up straight unless I'm dressing," Lucinda's mother said, "and I don't dress in public. See if you can help Lucy finish."

That was the very minute when Lucinda was about to be sick. She was afraid to be touched. She backed off gingerly, taking care not to jostle herself.

"Well, I don't seem to be needed in here," her grandmother said, and went out of the room so fast that Lucinda and her mother looked at each other.

Her grandmother had got over being mad by the time they went into the dining room to have breakfast. There was a little fire in the grate. The leaping flames and the widening red streaks at the windows were so beautiful and so dizzying Lucinda didn't dare look at them. She looked at the table instead, and there in the center was the little rabbit vase that was always called Lucinda's rabbit. She had a secret name for him. It seemed cruel to go away and leave the rabbit without telling his name to somebody.

"Hurry up, Lucinda," her mother said. "Think who it is we're going to see this very day."

The thought of seeing her father again in the wonder of a new house, a new town, even a new state, moved through her. The sadness and the happiness churned in her until there was no room for food.

Her mother and grandmother talked about the fire. "That's one thing you won't miss tonight," her grandmother said.

"Clifford says the nights are always cool, always a breeze."

"Yes, I know about those cool nights down there. If only he'd let you stay until time for school to open."

"You know, Mother, it's not a question of Clifford's letting us stay. You know how generous and unselfish he has been. He's been there alone a month. He's done everything for us, found the house, moved in the furniture, found a cook."

"I know all about that. I know all about everything he's done. It's what he can't do that worries me. He can't change the climate. It's a risk for anybody used to our nice cool summers to go into that heat right in the middle of August."

"But we're going, Mother. That's all settled. Let's not get upset about that again, now when we're practically on the way to the station."

Lucinda made herself eat a little after that to keep her grandmother from feeling too badly. Then the taxicab came and there was more crying until all the expected fun of getting on the train was lost. Lucinda thought she could have managed her own tears if it hadn't been for her mother's. They sat side by side on the train crying into their handkerchiefs until Lucinda said, "I'm sorry we have to go away and leave Grandmother."

Her mother turned from the window and dried her eyes. "I'm not sorry," she said. "I want to go. We've all been nothing but parts of her life. It's going to be our life now. She left her mother and made her life. I have a right to do the same. It's just that it's so pitiful to see her getting so old." That set her to crying again and, of course, Lucinda too.

Then, before Lucinda knew what was happening, she was being sick right there on the seat beside her mother. That kept them busy for some time. By the time it was over and the cleaning up done, they both were ready for a nap.

At two o'clock they got off the long cool train and had a sandwich and peppermints in a little junction station while they waited for the train that was to take them to Macklin.

"Haven't you any ice cream?" Lucinda's mother asked.

"No'm," the boy behind the little counter said. "Ice melts so fast we can't hardly afford to fool with it out here so far from town."

"I'd think you would plant some trees around the station," Lucinda's mother said. "Wouldn't that help a little?"

"We had a chinaberry once," the boy said, "but it didn't do no good. Reckon it needed a flock of hens to roost in it, or something. Didn't do no good, so we chopped it up for firewood last winter. Looks like, if you've got a place down here that trees'll like, you can't stop them; but if you've got a place that sets out to be bare you can just give up and let her be."

At last they heard the train. Lucinda and her mother backed into the little station to escape some of the cloud of smoke and dust that rolled in ahead of the gasping engine. It was a short train that had come for them. Something had happened about the chair car. It had been left off. There was nothing to do but get into a day coach. Lucinda and her mother, with the junction man carrying the big bag, clambered up the steps and brushed dust and cinders out of the only one of the dirty red plush seats that was empty. As soon as they were under way, stinging showers of cinders poured in the open window. Lucinda's mother pulled and tugged at the window and, between efforts, sent a look sideways at the man across the aisle; but he refused to see her looks. The window would not budge. After a while the conductor came along, and she asked him to put it down. In less than five minutes the woman behind them had it up again.

"That makes it a lot dirtier," Lucinda's mother said, looking back, "and I can't see that it makes things any cooler."

"Well, I can," the woman said.

Every now and then Lucinda's mother went to the end of the car and held two or three handkerchiefs under the water spigot. She wiped off her face and Lucinda's, and sometimes she folded one of the wet handkerchiefs across her forehead.

"Of course it will be too dark by the time we get there to see what anything's like," she said, "but I'm glad nobody will be able to see what wrecks we are. I'd have let your father drive to the junction to meet us if I hadn't thought we'd have the air-cooled chair car."

At eight o'clock they still had reached neither the new town nor the dark. Lucinda watched for both until her eyes gave out. When her mother's voice and her hand on her arm said, "Wake up, Lucinda, we're almost there," the train was moving through walls of solid night. It was too late to see what it was that lay between being there and not being there. The tired people were gathering up their belongings, sending out sweaty smells.

"Only ten more minutes," Lucinda's mother said. She stood up to take their hats off the rack above them. The breath was leaving Lucinda's body. She felt it going, sliding down as if to ooze out through her feet. She could not raise herself from the hot scratchy seat.

"You're not going to be sick again, are you, Lucy?" her mother said a little crossly. She bent over Lucinda.

"No," Lucinda said. It was a new kind of dizziness, not very different from the other, but safer.

"Wait a minute," her mother said, and she made another staggering trip down the aisle. She came back with the wet handkerchief.

"I see the lights of Macklin," she said as she sat down, and began sponging.

It was her words, rather than the cool handkerchief, that made Lucinda feel better. She reached for her hat, held up her nose for a touch of her mother's powder puff, and walked down the aisle like everybody else.

The station platform, crowded with lights, bells, voices, moving people, and trundling baggage carts, came forward to meet the train as it shuddered to a stop. As Lucinda followed her mother down the steps, her father's face and voice loomed through the din, and she was caught into his strong arms. Back and forth, he kissed her, then her mother, many times. Between kisses, he shouted orders right and left, quite the center of things. He told Lucinda to look out for this and that; he explained to her mother about the part of town they were in; he called out to some near-by Edward that, thank God, he was not a widower any more. Already he knew about what was inside the strange darkness beyond the station. Macklin was his home already.

"My, it's hot!" Lucinda's mother said as they got into the car.

"Is it?" he said. "I hadn't noticed. I guess the breeze has

died down a little. The nights are always cool down here. It won't be long before you'll feel the breeze.

"We're on Magnolia Street, now," he said. "I wish you could see it. Twice as wide as the widest street at home. I tried to write you about the wide streets down here, but you'll have to see them. You will tomorrow."

The street had seemed exactly the width of the car, a narrow foot-log of a street swung over a river of darkness. But, with her father's words, Lucinda saw the darkness take the shape of Magnolia Street. The support under the car widened, stretched out and out, to tall bouquets of trees that were blacker than the darkness in which they were set. The trees did not move, but shadows moved slowly under them. Still farther away, and a little lower than the street level, strands of lighted windows trailed along cushions of darkness like old necklaces that had lost most of their stones.

"Get that smell," Lucinda's father cried, and brought the car almost to a stop. "It's Mrs. Aldrey's butterfly lilies."

Lucinda breathed it in and swallowed.

"It's overpowering," her mother said, as the car moved on. "It's really pleasanter now that we're not too near."

"I wish you could see the houses. Up one street and down the other. Big old Southern Colonials. There're at least thirty or forty of them finer than the Groves' house. I can't wait for you to see the crape myrtles tomorrow. And the moss. You never saw anything like this hanging moss."

"I see some of the moss," Lucinda said, her face thrust through the window.

"I guess not," her father said. "There's no moss along here. These trees are mostly water oaks. We're on the Square now."

"Cobblestones?" her mother asked.

"No, just brick, but old. They're rough, but they give an air. Isn't the Court House a honey?" he cried. "Front and back exactly alike because at the time it was built not one person living on either street was willing to have its back turned to them."

"All I can see is a lot of white columns," Lucinda's mother said.

"That's right, eight on each end. This is really the front we're passing now, and tomorrow you'll see the old Hardin house there on the corner. It's the only good one left on the Square, really. The two that stand beside it, in front of the Court House, have gone to pot. Everything's stores now across the back and along the other side. On this side, on the corners, are the Presbyterian and Methodist churches. You can see them. But you can't see what's in between."

"What's between?" Lucinda asked.

"You'll probably think they're playhouses," her father said. "It's the cutest string of little one-story, one-room brick houses you ever saw. Four of them. Each a little different, but all the same size. The town's first office buildings. A lawyer's, a doctor's, a dentist's, and an apothecary shop."

"I'd think one room would be pretty cramped for a doctor," Lucinda's mother said.

"Of course it would now. They were built a hundred years ago. One's a shoe repair shop now, one's a dry cleaner's, and one's a quick-lunch joint. The other's just about falling down, so the pigeons have taken it over."

"The Square isn't very well lighted," Lucinda's mother said. "The lights can't seem to penetrate the shade of the trees. They really should take out some of those lower branches."

Lucinda leaned forward and touched her father's arm. "Isn't that the moss out there?" she said, pointing. "It looks like the post card you sent me."

Her father laughed. "No, that's nothing but mist. There's lots of mist down here. It does look a little like the moss. You know we have miles of marshes not far to the southeast."

He turned a corner and cried out, "And this is our street. Cass Avenue. We live on the corner of Cass and Mimosa."

Cass Avenue was not as wide as Magnolia and the streets of the Square. The trees came closer. The lights, when there were lights, were nearer, too.

"You could see the house now," her father said, "if it were not night."

"I simply can't wait to see it," her mother said. "I loved everything you wrote about it except that there was no place for flowers in the back yard."

"That's because there is so much shade. But there are crape myrtles and japonicas in front and oleanders on the side. And here we are," he cried.

Lights shone from half a dozen windows, upstairs and down. Lucinda and her mother ran ahead while he dragged the bags out of the back of the car. He dropped them on the front porch and took out a key.

"Wait a minute," he said. "I've got to carry both my girls over the doorstep."

"Oh, Clifford," Lucinda's mother cried, "you'll break your back." But he had an arm around each of them. He lifted them high and set them down in the hall.

Lucinda saw the little table first of all. Her mother had

picked it up in a secondhand store one day because it was the right height to fit under the dining-room windows and hold the Boston fern. From the minute Lucinda had seen the little drawer tucked in between the dropped leaves she had thought of it as her table. Sometimes she kept the smallest things in the back of the long narrow drawer. With the front of the drawer empty, nobody would think that in the back there might be four-leaf clovers and gravel diamonds.

Somebody had come in one day who knew about the table. It was a treasure, an antique. It was too fine to be hidden by the fern. So it went to a shop to be scraped and refinished and came back to stand in full view, chestnut-smooth and glowing. Lucinda hardly dared to keep things in the drawer after that, but sometimes she put them there until she could find a good place for them in her own room.

Standing now beside the front door, the table was more important than ever before. It had to do with the coming and going of people, themselves and the mysterious people out there in the dark town. As her father explained about things Lucinda stood near the table to feel against her leg the height that made it just her size. Behind her back her right forefinger found the silky strip of inlay. She felt for the little brass button of a knob and opened the drawer an inch or two. It would be a good place for the pink slip the Pullman conductor on the first train had given her.

"It's not one of the old ones," her father was saying, "and it's not new enough to have any clever modern gadgets; but I liked the size of the rooms, and I liked the trees and the general location."

"It's perfect," Lucinda's mother said, "absolutely perfect. . . . I've always wanted to have the bedrooms upstairs where people wouldn't be running in and out all day. We don't need as many rooms as the old houses have, and the new little ones hardly ever have an upstairs. It suits me exactly."

"Good! I thought it would. And, see, every room's been papered and the woodwork painted. They didn't much want to do that, but when I said I'd sign a lease for two years, they came across."

"Well, I should think so," Lucinda's mother said.

"I'd promised you a new house or one good as new. You like it, do you?" He knew she did.

"Oh, I love it. It's just right." He caught at her hand and drew her into the living room.

Lucinda stood in the hall, forgotten. She opened her pocketbook and took out the pink slip. The drawer was empty. She put it so far in that it touched the back of the drawer. For the time being she had finished with the table. She turned her attention to the stairs. They were almost exactly like the stairs at her grandmother's. The only difference was that there was a window on the landing and a small window seat. After the first disappointment she realized that this was an advantage and would not interfere in the least with the game. The more she looked, the better she liked the seat. She decided that it would probably fit into the game and add something to it.

They were in the dining room. "What wonderful windows!" her mother cried. "Perfect for flowers. I must get some new plants. Come, Lucy, and see the lovely windows," her mother called.

Lucinda put out her long leg and gave the lowest step a good-bye touch with the tip of her toe.

"Pretty nice. Pretty nice." Her father was still gloating.

"They're just beautiful," Lucinda said of the windows, and followed her mother and father back to the living room. Her mother moved the green armchair closer to the gate-leg table. She turned on the radio. It sounded exactly as it had sounded on the bookshelf at home.

"I've kept it close for company," her father said. "You'll probably want it back on the bookshelf, Ethel. Put it any-where you like. I guess it's really too big for that table. Doesn't leave much room for anything else."

But she liked the radio, too. "I think it looks very nice there," she said. "We'll turn it on oftener this way."

Arm in arm, they started upstairs. Lucinda trailed them and counted the steps.

"A lighter wallpaper in the hall might have been bet-ter," her mother said. "In daytime this hall will be dark in spite of the window. Don't you think we could have that heavy vine cut away to give the hall more light?"

Lucinda saw the steps shut in by the daytime darkness for herself and the game. She lagged behind, imagining it.

"Come quick, Lucy," her mother called, "and see your darling room."

Lucinda ran to see. There stood the pink-painted furni-ture against walls strung with blue and pink morning-glories.

"I wanted to put the curtains up," her father said, "but I couldn't figure them out. I couldn't match up the pairs, somehow. I guess there weren't this many windows in your old room, Lucy."

"That's the trouble. There are only two windows in the room at home. Lucy and I'll figure out something in a day or two."

Their room was across the hall. There were pansies on the wall, and there were two pairs of windows. The bathroom was at the front of the hall, between the two bedrooms.

They ran back and forth, examining first one room and then the other. Lucinda turned on the water in the bathroom basin. She felt a little silly doing that, but when her mother came in she did the same thing. Whenever there was a good opportunity Lucinda opened her closet door to look again at her winter clothes, already hanging there, already wise in the ways of the new house.

There was no telling how late it was, but when they had finished seeing things upstairs they went down again. Nothing was said about Lucinda's bedtime. They went out to the kitchen. Sliced chicken and salad and milk were waiting in the icebox. Lucinda's father put everything on a tray with a plate of crackers and cookies and carried them into the dining room.

"Tell me about the neighborhood," Lucinda's mother said.

"You couldn't beat it. The Carters, next door, did everything you could possibly think of to help me get settled. Let me have hot water. Let me use the telephone. Sent me half an ice-cold watermelon the first day. Invited me over for supper. Gosh, they've been nice."

"Have they got a little girl?" Lucinda asked.

"No. There's a daughter who has a job at the Court House and two boys, one sixteen and one fourteen or fifteen. But there are a couple of little girls not much older than you who live on the street."

"We're right in town, aren't we?" Ethel Darby asked.

"Close enough for me to walk to the office. You can

have the car most any day I don't have to make a country trip."

"The Carters live on our right. Who lives on the left?"

"We're on the corner, you know. Mimosa Street runs along there and the old Cass place takes up everything on the left as far as you can see. Cass Avenue runs right into their front gates. The monogram of the Cass who built the place is in the iron work over the gates—R.C.—and the date, 1802."

"That sounds very grand," Mrs. Darby said.

"People seem to think it was pretty famous in its day."

"What's it like?"

"Can't see the house. It's way back up in the trees. You never saw such trees. It's like living across the way from a big park, or a forest."

"Have you met the family? Did you say the name is Cass?"

"No. There's nobody left up there but Mrs. Reeves and her daughter. They keep pretty close, I guess. Mrs. Reeves was a Cass. She must be getting on. Not equal to going out any more, I suppose. From what people say, the daughter must be pretty devoted to her mother. Nobody sees them any more."

"Listen," Mrs. Darby said. She turned an ear to the windows.

"It's the breeze. You can always hear it when it comes up because the leaves on the trees down here are so stiff: magnolias, live oaks, japonicas, and the like. The pines, too. Makes you feel cooler just to hear it."

"It hasn't got into the house yet," Mrs. Darby said. She fanned herself with a folded newspaper.

Mr. Darby pushed back his chair. "Come out on the

porch," he said. "I want you to see the way the moss swings when the breeze comes up. The moon ought to be up by now." They followed him through the hall. "There's no moss around this corner except over at the Cass place—Castleton, they call it. But it hangs like curtains from the big live oaks on both sides of their driveway. It's funny about the moss. It will be on one tree and not on another, and nobody can tell you why. We've got a live oak in our back yard as big or bigger than any of theirs. But we haven't got a hair of moss."

"Is it hairs?" Lucinda asked.

"Hairs, threads, strings. I don't know what. There's some up in North Carolina, but shorter and not near where we lived. Down here it's as long as your arm or leg, and longer. It makes you cool just to see it blowing. And in the moonlight—"

They were on the porch, staring into blackness.

"But there isn't a moon. It's cloudy," Mrs. Darby said, "and the breeze has already died down. You can't hear a sound."

Lucinda closed her eyes against the pressure of the blackness and listened. There was nothing to hear.

"No. It's a cloudy night. Gosh, I'm sorry. The moon was wonderful last night. I figured it would be rising about now, right through there. I sat here and watched the moss swinging over there. It swung back and forth like big fans, and the iron gates made shadows like the pictures in the book of New Orleans. I thought about you and how we would see it together tonight."

They were standing together, a little apart from Lucinda.

"You could cut the darkness with a knife," her mother said.

Lucinda reached over the banister and pushed her first finger into the darkness.

"I'm afraid it's no cooler out here than it is in the house," her father said.

"When it's as hot as it's possible to be, there doesn't seem to be much difference between inside and out," Ethel Darby said, "and there's a smell out here. Can't you smell it, Clifford? It's like something dead."

"There's been a lot of rain lately. I guess there's a good deal of muck under those trees. Nothing worse than that."

"It's bedtime, anyway," Lucinda's mother said. They went back into the house, blinking at the lights. "I was wrong about the heat," she said as they mounted the stairs. "It is hotter in the house, and we are adding another degree for every step we go up."

"That's what we pay for having the bedrooms where people won't be running in and out all day," Clifford Darby said.

"You may have the first bath, Lucinda," her mother said, "and until we get used to having a hall between our rooms we'll sleep with the doors open."

They called back and forth to Lucinda as they undressed, and when she was ready for bed they came in to kiss her good night and turn out the light. Her father held up the mosquito net while she crawled into bed.

After the first night Lucinda slept with her door closed. It was one of the reasons that Macklin marked the line between being a little girl and a big girl. Sixth Grade was another thing. And the school skirts coming out of the closets so short that letting down hems didn't make enough difference.

AFTER CHRISTMAS, Sue Brown sat in front of Lucinda. "My governess had to go back to England," Sue explained, "and Mother decided to try public school."

Lucinda was awed by this turning of the tables on school. Before the end of the day, she saw that school was in danger of failing to pass the test. She slipped her spelling pad through the crack in the seat so Sue could copy her words, and sometimes Sue passed the hard arithmetic problems back for Lucinda to solve for her. But usually Lucinda needed help with the arithmetic, herself. Every now and then Sue's fat black curls gave a wide sweep and sent Lucinda's pencils rolling onto the floor. But when Sue felt Lucinda twisting the silky corkscrews around her pencil, she kept obligingly still. At recess they turned their backs on the other girls and walked off together, their arms around each other's shoulders. Sometimes, on Saturday, Lucinda went to Sue's house to play in the Swiss chalet playhouse in the garden. On the Saturday that was Sue's twelfth birthday she went to spend the day.

"Come quick and see," Sue called down from the upper hall. "I've never had so many beautiful presents. Aunt Kit's come back from Paris and brought me four new dresses and coats and hats and everything. All from Paris."

Sue's bed was covered with boxes marked with strange-looking names in flowing gilt letters. Mountains of pale tissue paper lay about on bed and chairs. Yards of narrow ribbon littered the floor, already trampled as if it were no better than ordinary twine.

Jessie was knocking on the door across the hall. Lucinda saw the door open, and Jessie went in, followed by Dora May, carrying a breakfast tray.

"Oh, Sue!" a high silvery voice called through the open door.

Sue dashed across the hall. The voice ran out to meet her. "Jessie's ready now."

"May Lucinda watch, too?" Sue cried.

"Of course. Lucinda," the voice called back lightly, saying Lucinda's name very fast.

Lucinda, cold with excitement, followed Sue.

Sue's Aunt Kit lay against the pillows of her bed. She was an exaggerated, grown-up Sue. Her curls were shorter than Sue's, and blacker. A short-sleeved coat of heavy blue satin fell back from her throat and showed the lace of her nightgown. She had taken a crimson japonica from the breakfast tray and was pinning it on the quilted collar of the blue coat. The bed was a throne, rich with lacy pillows and monogrammed linens and taffeta puffs. Mrs. Brown sat beside it, neater than ever in her blue sweater and the skirt that was the color of her short, gray-shot hair.

"This is Sue's little friend, Lucinda Darby," Mrs. Brown said, taking Lucinda's hand and drawing her nearer the bed. "And this is my sister, Mrs. Bogart."

Mrs. Bogart put out her long white hand. A wave of fragrance came with it and swallowed up Lucinda. Sue ran around to the other side of the bed and flung herself against her aunt's shoulder.

"Oh, I love my pretty presents, Aunt Kit," she cried. She kissed the cheek that was a promise of what her own would be after thirty happy, luxurious years.

Mrs. Bogart's eyes turned from Sue to Lucinda and back again. "What perfect foils for each other," she said to Mrs. Brown.

Lucinda looked at Sue to see if she was understanding. She was studying the arrangement of her aunt's curls, not listening.

"You had better run along now," Mrs. Brown said to Sue, "and let your Aunt Kit finish her breakfast."

"But we can stay in the room," Sue begged. "Didn't you say, Aunt Kit—"

"Of course I did," Mrs. Bogart said. "I told Sue they could watch Jessie do my unpacking," she explained to her sister.

A big trunk and a little one stood before the door of the dressing room. Jessie was snapping locks and opening drawers. Sue beckoned to Lucinda, and they crossed the room to a little chintz-covered sofa that Jessie had drawn to the side of the trunk.

"Mind you ain't touchin nothin," Jessie cautioned. She lifted a long white coat from a trunk hanger and transferred it to a padded silk hanger in the closet.

Lucinda's ribs felt Sue's arm trying not to reach out to the fuzzy coat.

"Of course," the clipped, sparkling voice was saying, "I know I'll not need the evening things until we go down to New Orleans."

Mrs. Brown laughed. "I'm glad you're not expecting to be very gay here," she said.

Mrs. Bogart laughed, too. "Your letters have been preparing me. I suppose we'll have to look in on Cousin Perk. But there's nobody left that I want to see, except Emily, of course."

"Seeing Emily's rather difficult, you know," Mrs. Brown said. "I haven't been able to get her here for five or six years. They don't go anywhere, and they make it perfectly clear that they don't care to have their old friends come to Castleton. They can't bear having us know how things are."

"They can't hide it any longer?"

"Heavens, I should say not!"

"The last time I was here," Mrs. Bogart said, "all of the rooms were closed except the drawing and dining rooms. But there everything seemed about as usual. There was no reason to suspect that the other rooms were closed because they were empty."

"That was nearly ten years ago," Mrs. Brown reminded her. "Now there isn't anything left but a few scraps. As for Emily and her mother, they've dressed out of attic trunks for years. But one can't very well wear attic shoes. So they stay at home."

The cloudy skirt of a chiffon dress brushed the knees of the children. Sue whispered against Lucinda's ear, "I'm going to have a pink dress with a train and a pink veil when I'm a bride."

"And blue ribbons like that?" Lucinda asked.

"They're aqua," Sue said; "but I won't have aqua on mine. It will be all pink. The veil, too, and the slippers."

Jessie was hooking gold slipper heels over the rod on a

slanted shelf. Silver slippers came next. Then black, blue, green, brown. Straps and pumps and ties.

"I counted them," Sue said against Lucinda's ear. "Eighteen."

"Nine pairs of slippers," Lucinda said.

Words were rising out of Jessie's humming:

> "I got shoes, you got shoes,
> All God's chillun got shoes."

It was a funny thing to make a song about, Lucinda thought. Jessie sang the words slowly, dragging them up by the hardest, one at a time. Over and over, straining and groaning, she brought them up:

> "I—got—shoes,—you—got—shoes,—
> All—God's—chillun—got—shoes—"

She was sorting the slippers now, shifting them so that the low-heeled black and brown shoes stood on the lowest shelf. The middle-sized heels stood on the middle shelf. On the top shelf were the thin high heels and narrow toes of the evening slippers.

> "When I get to hebben gonna put on ma shoes—"

Lucinda saw her own flat heels, six of them, set against the closet door at home, hanging half out of the pockets of Aunty Clare's red cretonne Christmas present. "And already smeared, Lucinda, with mud and shoe polish." . . . In the closet across the hall her mother's tiny shoes were standing on heels as high as Mrs. Bogart's evening-slipper heels. "They're as tall as they're long, my dear." On the top shelf of the closet, between two hatboxes, they stood as if on stilts, neatly set in shining pairs, carefully toeing the mark. . . . On the floor below was her father's other pair, looking as if his feet were still inside. Sometimes there was only one shoe, and her father down on all fours reaching back into the dark corners. "Where the hell has that God-damn shoe gone? Who's made away with it this time?" "Don't swear, Clifford; and tell me, please, who in this house would have any use for your shoes. Just tell me that. If you would only—" "And if you would only do your God-damn straightening on your side of the closet." "But don't you see, Clifford, how much time and trouble you would save if you would simply put your shoes where they belong instead of kicking them into the closet from wherever you happen to be when you take them off? Don't you know there's no telling where they'll land? I leave the whole floor of the closet for you and your one pair of shoes—" "And the laundry bag and the electric heater and half a dozen boxes and—" . . . The yellow shoes that brought Mittie up from Gander Creek, squeaking all the way from the corner, bulging with corns and bunions. "Look like that little new moon ain't never comin round to charm them corns away." The spreading black shoes with the flapping soles that waited for her in the kitchen closet. "Good old shoes. Come here, shoes, and ease the misry in your poor old Mittie's dogs." . . . Miss Carley's shoes with the laces. Miss Carley standing by your desk, and you seeing the darns in the laces and the shiny places where the iron had pressed them. "Anybody'd know she's not poor when she's got a job teaching school. I bet she's just too stingy to buy shoestrings." . . . Miss Crutcher's

Principal-shoes letting her come in the door without anybody knowing it until she was behind Jack Davis' desk. "This young man, Miss Carley, should have been in my office half an hour ago. He has managed to construct what appears to be a rabbit trap without let, hindrance, or detection." The person who detected wore rubber soles so that she wouldn't be detected. That's why the boys called her Detective Crutch Rubbers. . . . John Fowler's cardboard patch slipping through the sole of his shoe. "Look at old Johnny with his foot under him. Looks like his leg's cut off at his knee. Looks like his knee's the end of his leg. One-Leg Johnny. Hey, look at One-Leg Johnny." . . . Cajy's big lumps squirming in the dusty leaves. "Niggers that wear sacks for shoes." . . . Attic shoes. "One can't very well wear attic shoes." What are attic shoes? Maybe just a name, like saddle shoes, saddle oxfords. Why are oxfords shoes? Maybe it didn't mean the attic in the house. Maybe it didn't mean the attic in the house any more than saddle meant the saddle for a horse. . . .

The song was coming out of Jessie easily now. It was high and light, seeping out through her eyes and ears and nose. You couldn't see her move her lips but you could hear the words:

> "When I get to hebben gonna play on ma harp,
> Gonna play all over God's hebben."

There wasn't room for another dress in the closet, for another shoe on the slanted shelves. Jessie lifted a big box out of the bottom of the trunk. It was full of hats, nested in tissue wads and rolls and twists. One by one, she took them out. She held each hat at arm's length, turning it admiringly in her hand. One after another, she placed them on the cunning stemmed cushions of silk and velvet until the hat shelf was a garden in full bloom.

Over by the bed the voices whispered like the swishing of skirts from trunk to closet, like the leaves of the live oaks rustling in the windy night.

Sue's fat legs shot out. She was on the stairs before Lucinda was out of the room. "Last one in the playhouse is a rotten egg," she called.

"Sue!" her mother cried, but Sue was gone.

Lucinda stretched her long legs and ran after her.

At one o'clock Dora May brought the birthday lunch out to the playhouse. At half past three she came with a message. Mrs. Brown and Mrs. Bogart were going to call on their cousin, Miss Perk Folkes. Sue was to come in and have her bath at once so she could go with them. Lucinda would be taken in the car as far as the foot of Cass Avenue.

"I don't want to go," Sue said. "I want to stay here, and I don't think it's nice to make Lucinda go home when it's not time for her to go."

"Don't make no difference who don't want to go nowhere," Dora May said. "That's what she say, and she say to give this place a good cleanin up while I'm here." Dora May threw open doors and windows and went for the little stove with a great rattling of coals and poker.

Mrs. Brown called from upstairs, "Just wait down there, Lucinda. I want Sue to dress as quickly as possible."

Lucinda sat stiffly in the hall and waited. When, finally, Sue came down, following her mother and aunt, she wore the new green velveteen coat and the brown hat with the green feather. She had on brown shoes and gloves and carried the brown bag with the lamb's head clasp. But she was buried somewhere inside her new finery. She didn't smile. She didn't even look at Lucinda. She stalked doggedly through the hall, her eyes on the floor.

"If you're not feeling more cheerful by the time we get to Cousin Perk's," Mrs. Brown said to Sue, "you'll have to sit in the car while we make our call."

Sue sent a look of sullen appeal to Lucinda.

"No," Mrs. Brown said, "Lucinda will be getting out at her street. Jessie has already called to tell her mother that she is on the way home."

Sue stared out the window. Mrs. Bogart was talking.

"It's too unbearably depressing," Mrs. Bogart said. "As soon as Eric and I decide on the place we want I'm going to begin looking around for you. A place near New York but—"

Mrs. Brown stopped her. "Don't be ridiculous, Kit," she said. Some of the irritation left over from her conflict with Sue sharpened her voice.

"Stay away as long as I have," Mrs. Bogart said, "and come back. You'll realize then how much has happened. And not happened. The town's dead, done up for its burial." Her hands went out to left and right. "Look at the Dalton place. Laid out. Ivy wreaths in the sweet old yard to mark the spot. Camellia sheafs beside the Barkers' doorway. Dingy white columns looming up everywhere like shafts in a cemetery. Look at their epitaphs: *Boarders; Tourists; Rooms.* It's tragic to think Castleton's going to pieces, too."

"I'm afraid Castleton set the pace," Mrs. Brown said. "And there nothing is being done to stop the ruin. Mrs. Alben puts up a car full of tourists overnight, and mends her roof. The Dalton place doesn't look as you remember it, but you should have seen it before they filled the house with boarders."

"Didn't you write me years ago about a plan to take over Castleton for the Woman's Club?"

"I suppose I did. We worked out a plan when we thought Mrs. Reeves had to sell the place. The Club was to use the four big rooms on the first floor and close off everything else except the west wing. That was to be reserved for Mrs. Reeves and Emily."

"But nothing came of it?"

"Mrs. Reeves wouldn't hear to it. She said there was no wall in the west wing large enough for the portrait and she could not think of leaving it for the eyes of riffraff and hoodlums. That's when we found out that the portrait means more to her than the place. If we could have carried out our plan Castleton would have been repaired while there was time to save it. But she refused to be separated from that canvas full of Cass splendor. Now it would take a fortune to restore the house. Not to mention the grounds."

"And Emily humored her mother?"

"We thought that, in her heart, Emily was for our idea; but she didn't have the courage to come out and say so. When her mother got pathetic she backed down."

"She always spoiled her mother," Mrs. Bogart said.

"The worse things get for them," Mrs. Brown said, "the more Emily's knees weaken. She gives in to her now about everything."

"Including Curtis."

"Yes, finally, including Curtis."

"How she's tortured him," Mrs. Bogart cried. "I suppose she did, even from the first."

"But not any more, I think," Mrs. Brown said. "She had

finally to choose between him and her mother. She chose
her mother. I think it's Emily who's suffering now. He's
doing wonderful things. After the last break with Emily
he didn't come back here for ever so long. But when I saw
him in New York this fall he said he expected to spend
more time here. This is where he finds the best subjects
for his work."

"Perhaps," Mrs. Bogart said indifferently. She lighted a
cigarette. "I wish," she said, "I had known that Mrs.
Reeves was selling mantels and paneling. I wonder if
there is anything left."

"Not now. I tell you they have sold everything but that
seven-league canvas."

"And they've dug in behind it for the duration?"

"For the rest of Mrs. Reeves' life, at least. By that time
Emily will be worse than dead."

"So long as the walls stand," Mrs. Bogart said, "it will
be the most beautiful house in this entire country."

"There is one near Natchez," Mrs. Brown began, but
her sister wouldn't let her finish.

"No, Susan. I know the one you mean, but the columns
are too heavy. Every proportion at Castleton is perfect."

"Yes, even the wing is right. And the colonnade—"

But Mrs. Bogart's eyes were changing the subject. She
was leaning forward, looking over Clyde's shoulder through
the windshield. "Well, whether Curtis ever lives here again
or not, it's good to see how beautifully he cares for the
house."

Lucinda's eyes followed Mrs. Bogart's. There, directly
ahead, was the Hardin house, the bricks that actually were
pink rather than red; the tall, narrow, double front doors
that, people said, were whiter and harder than marble; the

shutters that were as shiny green as magnolia leaves. The shutters spread more widely as the car moved nearer. Lucinda could almost see the brass knocker that was shaped like a woman's hand and marked Two PALMETTO STREET. Maybe in another minute she could see it.

But the car had reached the Presbyterian Church corner. It drew over to the curb. Only Mrs. Brown said a proper good-bye to Lucinda. Sue was still pouting. Mrs. Bogart's hand fluttered absently, and she went on talking as Lucinda got out of the car. "It has a towny, sophisticated look that gives tone to the whole Square in spite of what's happened to the Green and Archer houses. You could show it to strangers, foreigners even, and say this is what Macklin was once. And they would know."

Mrs. Bogart's words, strange as they were, gave Lucinda the Hardin house—the Curtis house, people usually called it. She didn't stop seeing it after she had taken the dozen steps beside the church and turned away from the house, to follow Cass Avenue home. The things she had heard people say about the Hardins and the old Curtis house and the Palmetto Street side of the Square were falling into place like the parts of a picture puzzle. As she walked, in a dawdling zigzag, along the brick sidewalk she saw the house even more plainly than when her eyes had been fixed on it. It had a clean, complete look standing there on the corner, separated from the dilapidated Green house by the brick wall and the hedge of crape myrtles and japonicas and azaleas. It was the high hedge that managed the separation rather than the wall.

There were stories about the wall. Mrs. Hardin's heart was broken when Reuben Morris turned the Green house into a tenement and ripped off the little Ionic entrance portico so there would be room to build his clothing store in the front yard. At first she only cried. For days she lay in bed, crying. Then she began having her garden wall made higher. Anybody could still see where the old wall had stopped and the new one had begun. The old wall was silvery pink and almost covered with ivy and moss. The new wall, that rose for three feet above it, was different. The bricks were old, people said, but they didn't look old. Year after year Mrs. Hardin had had them coated with manure water but they wouldn't look like the rest of the wall, no matter what she did. And the ivy wouldn't grow on them. In some places the ivy and moss went all the way to the top of the old wall, but there was not an inch of either on the new part.

The Hardin place filled exactly one-third of the Palmetto Street side of the Square. The Green house took another third; the Hotel Palmetto, that had been the Archer house, another. Each of the houses was three stories high. "Fine Georgian types," people said.

Mrs. Hardin had died of a broken heart before the Darbys came to Macklin. People said she had talked all the time, just before she died, about the beautiful boarded-up doorway. She would talk about it and call it a corpse. "Nailed up like a living corpse in its coffin," she would say, "stifling for breath." Thinking about it had brought on her own death, some people said.

But Miss Letha said it wasn't that at all. Miss Letha sewed for some of Mrs. Hardin's friends, and they had told her it was something else that broke her heart. They said being married to Fred Hardin had done the same thing to Thalia Curtis that the Morris clothing store did for Dr. Green's doorway. Miss Letha said she had her own ideas about it, too. Her look, when she said that, made you remember how much she must have known about things at the Hardins', going there as she had done, every first Thursday for twenty years, to sew or mend. Miss Letha said it was the struggle that took Mrs. Hardin, the strain of standing between a boy who wanted to paint pictures and a father who wanted him in the road-contracting business; that, along with knowing the Hardin business was no fit place for her son. Miss Letha said Mrs. Hardin never spent a cent of her husband's money until she found her son would not inherit it. After that she never spent any of her own money.

Talk about the Hardin Brothers road-contracting business went on in whispers. Old Mr. Hardin was a person to wonder about. But Mrs. Hardin was a person to try to see when she drove through the streets. Or so the stories made it seem. She never wore any color but blue, and nobody would have dreamed there were so many kinds of blue in the world. Her dresses always came from Paris. She never went to Paris, herself, after her marriage, but her hats and coats and dresses were made there every season by the same dressmaker who had made her trousseau. Her writing paper came from Paris, too. It was marked, like the knocker, Two Palmetto Street, and underneath were the words, *On the Square.* Lots of people thought that was a funny thing to have on her writing paper, but Mrs. Hardin didn't think it was funny. She thought the Square was a nice place to live because her mother and father had lived there, in the same house. She'd had the wall to keep her from seeing what happened at the Green house and people said she had closed her mind to the state of the Archer house after it became Hotel Palmetto. That meant she didn't think about the kinds of things Lucinda's father had found out about Hotel Palmetto.

When Lucinda's father first came to Macklin he thought he would like to stay there while he looked for a place to live. He had written a letter to Lucinda and her mother about what he had thought when he saw the handsome old house that had been made into a hotel. He thought that by staying there he would come to know more about the real Macklin than by staying at the ugly little new hotel called Magnolia Terrace. But he said he couldn't sleep on fluted columns or eat carved panels so he moved to the Terrace. He had written a long letter full of things like that that made people laugh. Lucinda's mother had read it to all of her friends. Nearly every time she read it Lucinda's grandmother would say, "No doubt he found out about the real Macklin, all right." Sometimes, when she said that, Lucinda's mother would laugh and sometimes she would look unhappy.

There were not any stories about the houses on Cass Avenue. Lucinda's father said they were neither good enough nor bad enough to make stories. They were built by a man named Ferris at the wrong time. Some of them, like the Dentons', wore a cupola over one eye. Others, like the Carters', were bungalows that looked a little squashed, as if they had been dropped in a hurry. Mr. Ferris had had nothing to do with the Darby house, and that, Lucinda's father said, was why it was just a good honest house with a decent front porch and a nice back one and six comfortable rooms. Mr. Ferris had made Cass Avenue, with all of its houses, out of half of Castleton's front yard. Castleton's gates and fence had been moved up to where they were now, and then Mr. Ferris began to make room for the new houses. The first thing he did was to cut down the live oaks, all but the one that was now Lucinda's. The Dentons had a magnolia left from Castleton, but that didn't seem as important to Lucinda as her tree that was exactly like the big live oaks up and down Castleton's avenue, except that her tree had no moss and the Castleton trees, so far as she could see, had no doors in them.

As she got to Flora's yard a smothered giggle came out to Lucinda. It was the slow teasing laugh that meant Flora was thinking about something she would talk about but would not tell you really. Lucinda didn't look up, but she listened for the laugh to come again. Perhaps she would call to Flora and ask her to go home with her. Maybe she could persuade her to talk about the secrets that made her laugh. Flora would say she was such a baby she would not understand, or something like that. But the coaxing and the almost-telling were exciting.

It came again, loose and gurgling. Lucinda's eyes followed back along the way the giggle had come until they reached the bamboo screen of Flora's side porch. In summer the screen hung low to help the low wall of scrawny oleanders keep out the sun. In the fall it had been rolled up, but something had broken, letting down one end, so that now it cut a sharp diagonal from the railing to the narrow band of beading at the top of the porch. Through the oleanders and the broken slats of the screen Lucinda saw Flora's white sweater. Flora and Donald Cate were sitting on the rail, their feet caught around the spindles. Flora was huddled between Donald and the wall of the porch. Donald was one of the big boys. He sat all afternoon in the back of the movie with High-School girls. Donald's head moved and touched Flora's. Another giggle burbled across the yard. It shut Flora in behind the oleanders with Donald. Lucinda walked on, taking care that her heels made no sound on the uneven pavement.

HER MOTHER was having breakfast in bed. Her father had just gone downstairs. That meant there would be time for the steps. In the new game Lucinda was Betty practicing scales. The idea had come one day when she was sitting in Betty's hall waiting for the end of the practice hour. "Up, up, up, up, up, up, up, up," something inside her sang with Betty's flying fingers. "Down, down, down, down, down, down, down, down." She had made words for Betty's pieces, too. There was the piece that went, "No, sir; No, sir; No, sir; No, sir; No, sir; No, sir; No, No, No. When I tell you No, Sir; No, sir, why don't you get up and go?" And the piece that said, "Good morning, Good morning, Good mo-orn-orn-ning, I'll bring you a bouquet of flowers in the spring."

The special thing about the steps was that there was exactly the right number for one scale on each side of the landing. Beginning at the top, she would sing a *down* for each step and when the scale was finished she was exactly where she should be, on the landing. The *downs* held her back. She never wanted to take them on the run. It was right to do them slowly, almost stopping on each step, letting her whole body sink into her heels. But the *ups* were different. She soared on the rise of the scale. Everything about it was up. If nobody was looking or calling out to her to hurry down she always turned on the landing to reverse the scale. Sometimes when she took the up scale very fast she was a bird or a kite by the time she reached the upstairs hall.

The newspaper rustled slowly in the dining room. If she didn't take the *downs* too slowly there would be time for at least one of the up scales. She kept her footsteps quiet and sang softly, "Down, down, down, down, down, down, down, down." The last *down* was so low in her throat she almost choked when she reached it, but she managed to swallow it and turned on the landing to do the *ups*.

As she turned she heard Mittie's sliding step move through the pantry and into the dining room. A low snort told her Mittie had seen her. She hurried to finish the scale while Mittie placed her father's coffee beside his plate. The loose-soled shoes came towards the hall doorway. Lucinda crouched low, her stomach hugging the steps. Mittie's eyes pierced her tense shoulders. Lucinda knew she had done the wrong thing. She felt herself running innocently and casually down the steps. If she hadn't tried to reverse the scale Mittie would never have caught her. But to have stopped then would have been like holding her breath. She strained against the steps. Her back winced under the pricks of Mittie's eyes.

"Whachu call yousef a-doin on them steps?" Mittie demanded, her voice low with severity. "How many breakfusses has I got to fix? Oughta done been done eatin. Alltime scuttlin on them steps."

Lucinda turned, cringing. Then she saw Mittie's face. Mittie's eyes did not match her voice.

"I'm coming, Mittie," she said with a carefully docile tone.

Mittie waited. As Lucinda passed her in the hall her hand went out and found Mittie's hand, half buried in the bolster-rolls of fat massed at the belt of Mittie's apron. It was a small hand, shorter than her own, the only thing about Mittie that was not fat and slow.

"Git on to your breakfus now and leave me go," Mittie ordered under her breath.

Lucinda turned to the breakfast table. Her father did not look up. "I'll finish this column," he mumbled. But he went on reading. She watched his eyes move from the bottom to the top of the page. Lucinda rattled her fork against her plate to remind him, but he didn't look. He didn't wink or grin as he usually did when he kept her waiting. The distance between their places widened. She decided she might as well play the table game.

The table was Cass Avenue, and her plate was home. The knife was her father; the fork, her mother; the spoon, herself. The glass of milk was the tree. The bowl of flowers in the middle of the table was Castleton. Her father and mother went into the plate-house to see the bacon and eggs, but there was no way for the spoon-child to get in. If it had been a cocoa morning the child could have had a fine time in the cup-and-saucer tree. But on a milk morning there was nothing to do but stay outside and wonder how she could manage to get inside somewhere. The easiest thing, she decided, would be to pretend that she was still such a little girl that she used her spoon for eating eggs. She watched through the side of her eye to be sure her father wasn't looking as she scooped a spoonful of scrambled eggs. And there they were, mother, father, and child, together in the house.

"Lucinda!"

His voice blasted the breath out of her body. As the breath went, a sickness, mixed with remembering, came in to take its place. It was the same angry voice that had come across the hall last night, nudging and prodding her out of sleep, making her know the thing she had tried not to know. It had been so much worse than ever before that rolling herself into a tight ball and drawing the covers over her head had done no good. At last she had crept out of bed and gone to the door to listen. Her door had come open in the night. That was why she had had to hear words this time as well as voices.

Her mother had been crying. "I hate the very sight of it," she sobbed. "It's doing things to me. No decent person could stand it. It hangs over me."

"You're making up things," her father had said. "Have you no sense at—"

That was what had brought the cry, a sharp, broken cry that had set Lucinda to shaking until there was nothing to do but sit on the cold floor. It was the cry that had made him say "My God," over and over and louder and louder. And then the dreadful thing that had brought her own tears in such a deluge that she had gone back to bed and the muffling protection of the covers. She was hearing them now as plain as they had been last night through the cracked door. . . . "Sometimes, I swear to God, I think I'll clear out, catch the first train and get out for good and—"

"Lucinda!"

Lucinda managed to look up.

"Do I have to tell a great big girl like you that you are old enough now to eat with a fork?"

"No, sir." She grasped the seat of her chair to stop the trembling.

"Then will you please be good enough to eat now, or would you rather spend the rest of the day in bed?"

"I'll eat," Lucinda said.

"Then do it," he shouted, louder, angrier than ever.

Her hands didn't dare let go the steadying chair seat. She looked up to see if she could tell him she would begin in a minute. He was staring at her, unable to believe she was not obeying him. Suddenly he pushed back his chair, giving the table such a violent shove that the dishes clanked against each other. His glass of water emptied itself into his plate and, discolored with egg and jam, trickled over the cloth. In the next breath the front door slammed with a bang that set the pineapple picture at a crazy angle and brought Mittie trotting from the kitchen.

Lucinda was holding on hard to the chair. She took no notice of Mittie. Mittie stood in the door, her eyes shuttling between Lucinda and the attitude of the chair at the head of the table.

"Gonna set all day eatin, I guess, tell I ain't got no time tall to make them 'lasses teacakes," she said finally.

Lucinda did not hear her. Her eyes had not left her plate, but she had seen him. He was almost running when he passed the living-room windows that were exactly opposite her place at the table. Whatever it was that was wrong, she had made it worse.

Out beyond Gander Creek a whistle tooted dimly. It was the breakfast-time train. In another minute it blew again, then again, declaring its rate of speed with a booming crescendo. He was running to catch the train. *Sometimes, I swear to God, I think I'll clear out, catch the first train and clear out for good and all.* She had reminded him. If she had eaten breakfast properly he would still be sitting there. She had made him go. She would never see him again. He must be already halfway to the station. The whistle, shrill and near, cut through the room as the train split Gander Creek.

Lucinda sprang from the table, past Mittie, and out of the house. If she ran every step of the way, maybe she would be in time. She would say she was sorry about the spoon. She would beg him not to go. She would tell him it was just a game she was playing until he finished the paper. She would promise to stop all the baby things and leave Adelaide on her bookshelf.

Joe Carter and the Underwoods were on their way to school. They yelled at her as she dashed by them. Her long hair rippled after her like the clouding smoke that trailed the locomotive.

"Don't come, don't come," the swift clap of her feet prayed to the train. "Not yet, not yet." The town quivered under the lightning streak of the train. The alternating steps of her feet slowed her down unfairly. To save time she cut catty-corner across the Square.

"Hey, Sister," a cracked old voice cried out. "Not so fast, there. Not so fast."

Lucinda looked up. The four old men were at their game of checkers in the Court House yard: two playing, two waiting to take their turn at the board. "Must be trying to catch a train," another old voice croaked. The town shook with the pounding of the train. There were three more blocks to go. She loped ahead.

A wall of laughter stopped her. Her father's laugh, gay and easy, separated itself from the wall. He stepped out of the group of men standing in front of the Corner Drug Store and held out his arms. "Under the wire," somebody cried. Lucinda felt the roughness of her father's sleeve against her cheek.

"I'll bet she's set a record, Cliff," somebody said. The voices chuckled and teased. Lucinda tried to draw away, but the hand that seemed to be only stroking her back held her fast. "Or maybe just running away from school," another voice was saying. They laughed again. The group broke up.

"What are you up to, Lucy," her father asked, "so early in the morning?" He had turned back with her in the direction of home.

"I wanted," she began, and stopped.

"Yes?" her father said. He was not hurrying her, just letting her know he was listening.

"I wanted to ask you if I could have a nickel for a new drawing pencil."

His hand was in his pocket.

"I thought maybe I'd catch up with you," she said. She really did need a pencil, so it wasn't exactly a lie.

"Couldn't your mother help you out?" He was slipping a quarter into her hand. "It's not good for you to run like this right after breakfast."

"Mother was asleep," Lucinda said. "I peeked in her door." There it was, really a lie. And just when Jesus had answered her prayer.

Her father stopped stock-still. "Bless me, if we aren't forgetting that pencil," he said. "Wasn't that the store where you get them?" They turned back.

When the pencil was bought her father said: "I'll write an excuse for you. You'll need a few minutes to get back home for your books. Might be a good idea to do something about your hair, too." He took a notebook out of his pocket and wrote half a dozen quick lines. "I told Miss Carley you would be about thirty minutes late," he said, "so take your time." He leaned over her as he said that, and pressed his lips against her ear.

THE LINE broke up at the fountain, and the boys took to their heels. Seventh Grade had already marched out. Flora and Betty, who were at the head of the Sixth Grade line, were lagging at the corner, giving Lucinda time to overtake them. Flora looked in all directions. Most of her crowd was in High School. She never walked with Betty and Lucinda when the older girls and boys were within reach.

Sue said to Lucinda: "I see Mother and Aunt Kit. Let's get them to take us by your house to see if you can go home with me."

They turned to the line of waiting cars. Mrs. Brown leaned from the longest, blackest car, the only one driven by a chauffeur.

"We're going up your street, Lucinda," Mrs. Brown called. "Won't you let us take you home?"

Clyde held the door open, just as he did for the ladies. Lucinda felt Flora and Betty watching as she turned her back on them. She smiled feebly in their direction. They tried not to look as the car swept by them.

"Your aunt and I," Mrs. Brown said to Sue, "are going to Castleton to call." Then, "Don't you think, Lucinda,

63

you can sit in the car with Sue for the few minutes we'll be there?"

Sue said, "Why can't we go to Lucinda's house and play while you're there?"

"Make her say No," Lucinda prayed.

"We won't be staying long enough for that," Mrs. Brown said. "I think you'd better just sit in the car. You can wait with her, can't you, Lucinda?"

"Yes, I can wait," Lucinda said.

They headed up Cass Avenue, the car pointing straight at the gates. "I'm going in, I'm going in, I'm going in," the voice inside Lucinda said.

But, when they reached Mimosa Street, instead of continuing to the gates Clyde made a sharp turn to the right and they drove along Mimosa Street between the Castleton fence and the row of little houses until they came to the corner of Castleton, which was also the corner of Mimosa and Pine streets. The car turned left. Pine Street ran along the side of Castleton and on down to Gander Creek.

"Only the box gate is used now," Mrs. Brown said to her sister.

What would a box gate be?

The car stopped beside a low, narrow iron gate smothered in uneven masses of boxwood. As far as Lucinda could see the shoulder-high shrubs walled a path that ended in the same darkness the front driveway ran into.

"Drink it in," Mrs. Bogart cried. "It's the most divine smell in all the world. Breathe enough of it and you're anesthetized against everything that's happened since 1860."

"All the other boxwood was sold," Mrs. Brown said to

her sister. "There's no telling how soon this will go, though most of it is so scrubby I doubt if any one would want it. Four trucks came from Montgomery a year or two ago and went away loaded. It's the only place I know of so far south that ever had luck with boxwood."

The path made Mrs. Brown and Mrs. Bogart walk single file. Lucinda and Sue sat in the car.

"Let's play Rummy," Sue said. She took the cards out of the car pocket. They moved to the back seat and used one of the folding chairs as a table.

Lucinda saw that, in distance, she was little nearer Castleton than she had been when she was in her own yard. But she felt much nearer. It would be so easy now for something to happen. That very minute Mrs. Brown or Mrs. Bogart might be telling them that Sue and Lucinda were out at the gate and maybe Miss Emily would come to invite them in. Lucinda divided her attention between the cards and the path.

Sue said: "Aunt Kit is going to send me six dolls. All different. Peasant dolls. They're not to play with. She says they're to put on my window seat. They're all different sizes."

Maybe, Lucinda was thinking, she would have a chance to touch the cat, just enough to see how a cat in a picture would feel.

"Two of the dolls have got on cute little aprons, Aunt Kit said."

"Did you ever see a cat in a picture?" Lucinda asked. "One as big as a real cat, but a painted one?"

"What good's a painted cat?"

"They've got one." Lucinda pointed up the path.

"Shoot!" Sue said. "They haven't got anything. I've

heard Mother and Aunt Kit talk about how poor those people are. Aunt Kit's going to give them some money, maybe."

"They've got the biggest place in town," Lucinda said.

"What's big?" Sue demanded. "Look how messy it is. Just big's not anything. It's not nice like ours. Look how messy it is."

"They've got the biggest picture, too," Lucinda said. "I guess it's the biggest picture in the world. The cat's in it."

"Well, I don't care if it's just a painted cat. I'll bet it's not a Persian like Mother's real one."

"They've got a harp in the picture, too," Lucinda said. "You haven't got a harp," she added boldly.

Sue searched her house for half a second. "But we've got a grand piano," she said.

The game was no good. Sue put away the cards. She leaned luxuriously against the deep cushions and spread out her accordion-pleated skirt.

"Aunt Kit's going to write out the names for the dolls," she said. "Some of them are from the countries where the war is. One is Olga and one is Sigrid, but Aunt Kit says she's going to throw Olga away if the Russians don't go back home and leave Finland alone. I can't remember the other names. I'll learn them when she writes them."

"Olga and Sigrid," Lucinda said. "I never heard Sigrid. Is that the Finland doll?"

"There they come. There they come," Sue cried, "and we haven't had any fun yet."

Lucinda leaned forward. It was only Mrs. Brown and Mrs. Bogart. They walked side by side so they could talk.

They pressed against the boxwood, not careful as when they had walked in, single file.

"If only I'd known they were being sold," Mrs. Bogart said as they got into the car.

Mrs. Brown said: "None of us knew until it had been going on for years. Trucks would come in the night. The gates were opened in the middle of the night and chained again."

"Of course the portrait will have to go, sooner or later."

"You would think so. I don't know what will happen, Kit, but I don't think that portrait will leave Castleton while Mrs. Reeves lives."

"I'd forgotten how much of the background the painter managed to get in," Mrs. Bogart said. "It's a grand period piece, as busy showing the room as showing the family."

"He did better by the room, I think, than by the Casses," Mrs. Brown said, "better by the materials and fabrics than by the flesh and blood."

Mrs. Bogart laughed. "For that matter, so did God. The portrait has outlived the people. The chairs and sofa and secretary, wherever they are, will probably outlast the paint."

"I believe those were the first pieces of furniture Mrs. Reeves sold. The story was that somebody on Jekyl bought them for enough to pay a stack of debts and keep Mrs. Reeves and Emily going for a year. Before that, she'd sold jewels and silver, less conspicuous things."

"Wasn't it eerie the way we sat, making a circle with those five life-size zombies! She saw to it that we turned our backs on the bare room."

"It was easy enough," Mrs. Brown said, "to imagine the illusions they've built up."

"Not for me," Mrs. Bogart cried. "I couldn't think of anything but what's happened to Emily. I was seeing her and Castleton as they were the night of her debut. Twenty years ago. Was there ever such a party in the world? Music and food from New Orleans. Dresses from Paris. Curtis and Ted and half a dozen youngsters ready to die for Emily."

"And within the week Tom Reeves was dead, and they knew the strain they'd been under for twenty or twenty-five years was nothing to the poverty that was ahead of them."

"Castleton's finished," Mrs. Bogart said, "and so is Emily. But Mrs. Reeves manages to identify herself with those painted Casses, sitting forever on Chippendale chairs, blazing with jewels."

"Yes," Mrs. Brown said, "Emily's done for. The light's gone. It was her radiance that gave the effect of physical beauty and mental brilliance. Without it, she's a little on the dull and faded side. Poor old Abe carries the years better than either of them."

"I wonder why that wheezy old man was the one of all that tribe of servants they chose to keep?"

"Probably because he was the only one who was willing to take on all the work and do it for nothing."

"They never get too poor down here," Mrs. Bogart said, "to hold on to the loyal retainer, bowing and scraping for nothing but his bed and keep."

"Not Abe's bed, though room is the one thing they have to spare. He has to live down on the creek so he can take care of his half-wit son. Remember that gangling Cajy who spells and sings? Mrs. Reeves won't have him on the place, so Abe has a little shack down on the creek and goes there nights to look after him."

The car was stopping in front of Lucinda's house. Mrs. Brown laid her hand on Lucinda's. "Have you ever heard Cajy spell?" she asked.

"One time I did," Lucinda said.

"Wouldn't it be fun some time to have him spell for one of Sue's parties?" Mrs. Bogart asked.

"Oh, Cajy's no novelty around here," Mrs. Brown said. "Besides he's likely to have one of his fits any time. He's epileptic. I rather sympathize with Mrs. Reeves' feeling about having him around."

As soon as she opened the front door Lucinda knew there was nobody in the house but Mittie. A storm of water was pouring out of the kitchen faucets, and Mittie was singing at the top of her voice. Lucinda stood in the pantry door and waited for a lull in the singing or the water. When she saw both were likely to go on for some time, she joined Mittie at the sink.

"I'll help you," she shouted, eyeing the pan of spinach.

Mittie reduced the deluge. "Just look at it," she cried, pointing to the round green clock on the shelf between the windows. "Whachu think I'm gonna say when she asts me did you come right straight home from school? Whachu think I'm gonna tell her?"

Mittie held her ground at the middle of the sink. Lucinda reached over and fished a leaf of spinach out of the pan.

"I was with Sue and her mother. And her aunt from Paris," she said impressively.

Mittie turned a skeptical eye on her. "Think you're mighty uppity off with them rich folks. Mighty uppity and not mindin what your mother says about comin home."

"If you'll move over, I'll help you," Lucinda offered.

70

"Help ain't sometimes whachu calls its," Mittie said. She turned a fresh sluice of water into the pan. Lucinda drew back from the spattering. "Ain't got no time for help," Mittie said, enduring the spray of water against her arms and bosom in order to keep Lucinda at a distance.

"If I tell you something," Lucinda shouted, "will you cross your heart and hope to die?"

Mittie managed to make less noise. "Ain't crossin nothin," she snapped. "Ain't hopin nothin. Just waitin my time. When He's ready for Mittie, He'll come and take her home."

Lucinda leaned against the wall and considered how to attack this complacency. She couldn't think of a ruse, so she decided to come out with it. "I've been over there," she said. She pointed in the direction of Castleton.

Mittie gave the faucet a wrench and turned her full attention on Lucinda.

"Howcome you goin there?" she demanded. She collapsed into the chair with the sagging bottom.

Lucinda mounted the stool her mother sat on to make mayonnaise. "I went with Sue," Lucinda said. "Mrs. Brown and her sister went to see them."

Mittie said, "Reach me them apples and that there little knife and the white pan." She peeled a long thin curl, taking her time. "Howcome they takin you?" she finally asked.

While she was making the long curl, Lucinda and the stool became a totem pole. Keeping her eyes on Mittie's knife made it easy not to move. The knife turned round and round in one spot. Mittie's left hand brought the apples to it. They turned over and over under the narrow blade.

"Reckon you didn't see nothin much noway," Mittie said.

A totem pole could talk, just so it didn't move. "I didn't see the picture," Lucinda said, setting her voice carefully in the front of her mouth so as not to disturb her balance.

Mittie snorted. "Reckon not," she said. "Ain't got no business a-goin noway." The apple crackled juicily as she cut thin slices.

"I didn't see anybody," Lucinda said. "We sat in the car by the little gate."

Mittie let knife and apple drop into the pan. She drew herself up as straight as she could in the cowering chair. "Howcome you call it goin when you just set in the street? Howcome you tell me what ain't so about where you ain't never been?" Her voice shook.

"Mrs. Brown said could I go to Castleton with them and sit in the car," Lucinda explained.

"And you makin out you think that was goin? Makin out you don't know no better'n that?"

Lucinda quaked. "Well, I told you I didn't see the picture or anybody. Didn't I tell you? Not anything."

"You told you went," Mittie insisted, "and you know what that is. And I hope you'll get down on your knees tonight and pray the Lord to save your soul from all them lies. Never seen a child so full of what ain't so."

On the sunny steps of the front porch Lucinda sat huddled in her warm coat, waiting for church to be out. She cupped her hands around her eyes so that she could see as far as possible, but the street was empty. Everything was waiting for the benediction and the burst of the organ. She dropped her head on her folded arms and gave herself up to the nearness of Castleton. She had only to shut her eyes, and there it was, an arm around her shoulder, making her know what was beyond the trees at the end of the avenue.

A rattling of mudguards told her the Brents' car was passing. Half a dozen cars followed, more sedately. The Methodist Church was out. The Carters turned into their driveway—Miss Winnie, as usual, talking loud and fast, the others roaring with laughter.

"He said if I'd bought the Dee Lux model it wouldn't have this squeak; and I said, Brother, do you mean to tell me that the beauty of this Standard job of yours is that you put it out, complete with squeak? And he said, Well, the Dee Lux sure won't squeak, and I said, Well, the one thing you high-powered salesmen did not drop in Winnie's ear about your little number was that it had a squeak good

73

for more miles than the carburetor. So we jawed back and forth like that until . . ."

Heavy wheels and clanking harness sounded a block away. It was the Arctic Ice wagon coming up Cass Avenue with the last chance for Sunday ice-cream freezers. The Darbys' freezer stood, already packed, on the back porch. The wagon droned lazily past and turned into Mimosa Street, dribbling as it went. The next sound was the familiar whir she had been listening for. The car nosed to the curb and settled beside it. When they opened the car door she would pop out like a jack-in-the-box and run to meet them.

But they were in no hurry to get out of the car. They hadn't seen her. Her father sat humped over the wheel. They were talking hard about something. She sat back to wait, and almost at once both doors opened. With one leap, Lucinda's long legs cleared the steps. Then she saw their faces. They were strange and frightening. Her father and mother were mad at each other. They saw her and twisted their faces, trying to smile, but they did not want to smile. They did not want to see her. They wanted to go on being mad and talking about it.

Before she knew what was happening, Lucinda's legs had turned and were running as fast as they could go around the house. She heard her mother call out to her, but she could not turn back. At the oleander corner she pushed in behind the clump of trees and hid her face against the hard white clapboards of the house.

Her mother called again. Her voice was nearer. She was following. Lucinda slid out and made for the back porch. She flew across the porch, through the hall and up the stairs to the bathroom. She turned the key in the lock and stood with her back against the door. Her father was following, too. They were coming up the steps, first one, then the other, calling her name. She flushed the toilet to gain time. When the noise of the water let up she knew she had to answer.

"I'll be out in a minute," she said through the locked door. She was saying under her breath: "I got here first . . . I beat you . . . I beat you . . . You can't get in . . . I'm in and you're out . . . I won't let you in . . . I hate you . . . I hate you . . ."

"Lucinda," her mother called, "let me in. Let me in this minute, baby. I must see what is the matter with you." She pounded on the door.

"In a minute," Lucinda said. "I can't just yet."

"But you must, Lucy. What is the matter?"

Lucinda reached for the handle and brought down another rush of water. "Hate. Hate. Hate. You can't get in. You can't. Can't. Can't. Can't." She pressed both hands over her mouth to keep the words from leaping out.

"Are you sick, Lucy?" her father asked in a voice she could hardly hear. She felt him there beside her mother. Her heart rose in her throat.

"Not much," she said over the lump. "I'll be out in a minute."

They were whispering to each other. She heard her father say, "Don't try to force her now." She heard him turn and go downstairs. Then she heard her mother moving about in the bedroom.

Lucinda stood at the high, bathroom window, her elbows on the sill. The littleness of the bathroom folded her in. The tree feeling began. "Nobody can come in. Nobody. Nobody. Nobody. I'm here by myself. Me, me, me, me, me, me, me." Her lips made a popping, snapping sound as they mouthed the word. It was a sound like the dripping of the cold-water faucet in the bathtub. "Me," the drip said. "Me," Lucinda's lips answered. "Me." "Me." "Me." "Me." The bathroom was almost as good as the tree. And she could almost see the place. She pressed her face against the window pane. She *could* see it. Out of the corner of her left eye she could see a length of driveway rippling with moss shadows. A rippling answer stirred inside her. She had the bathroom now. When she couldn't go to the tree there would always be the bathroom.

"Lucinda!" Three sharp knocks struck the bathroom door.

"Yes, Mother."

"Open the door." There was no begging in the voice now. "Open the door at once."

Lucinda turned the key.

"Tell me just exactly how sick you are, Lucinda."

"I was sick at my stomach," Lucinda said.

Her mother put a hand under Lucinda's chin and lifted her face. "Did you—" She substituted a look for the unpleasant word.

Lucinda nodded. (Maybe it wasn't exactly a lie since neither of them had said real words.)

"Open your mouth, and let me see your tongue."

Lucinda put out her tongue.

"It's perfectly clean, and your breath is sweet and fresh." Her eyes made Lucinda's eyes look straight into them. "Lucinda, did you really throw up? You had nothing for breakfast that could have made you sick. I think you'd better tell me what is the matter."

"Maybe it was the candy," Lucinda said. Her eyes fixed themselves on the toothbrush holder.

"What candy?"

"Madge's candy." Her neck was burning as it always did when she told a lie. "Madge had her birthday candy."

"Candy at Sunday school?"

"Yes, in a bag. I ate six pieces."

"Six pieces! Lucinda, you know better than to do a thing like that."

"I'll not do it any more."

Her mother took her hand away, but she stood looking down at her. After a long time she said: "I think you'd better go to bed for the rest of the day. And of course you'll not want anything more to eat." She went into Lucinda's bedroom.

Lucinda turned to the bowl to wash her hands so she could think about what to say. Her mouth watered until the glands of her throat ached for the taste of the crisp wishbone, the rich bits of liver, the praline sauce on the ice cream.

"Come on, Lucinda," her mother called from the bedroom. "Hurry up and get undressed." As she helped with the buttons, she said: "I'm not punishing you, Lucy, for eating the candy. You know that was wrong, but I'm not punishing you. I'm putting you to bed so you'll get well more quickly."

"I think a little ice cream would make me feel better," Lucinda said. Her mother hadn't heard. She was smoothing Lucinda's sheets, plumping the pillow. Lucinda tried again, a little less certainly. "Don't you think a little bit of ice cream might make me feel better?"

Her mother turned from the bed. "Why, Lucinda!" she cried. "After vomiting?"

Lucinda knew what that tone of voice meant. Her mother went into the bathroom and came back, stirring a mixture in a glass. "This is all you should have for a few hours," she said. She held the glass to Lucinda's lips. It was hateful bicarbonate. Lucinda drank it down. Her mother went to the drawer and took out a fresh nightgown, the pretty new one with the square-cut neck and puffed sleeves. Lucinda pushed her arms through the little sleeves. The long skirt fell softly against her feet. It was an evening dress. She got into bed and closed her eyes.

"That's right, baby," her mother said. "Go to sleep. It will do you good." She kissed Lucinda lightly on the cheek. Already Lucinda was sweeping into the ballroom under the gold ceiling, her long skirt stretching out into flowing yards of train.

Some time later, after dinner surely, she heard her door open a cautious crack. She kept her eyes shut and didn't move a muscle. The door closed again. When it opened the next time there was no secret about it. Her father's step and the squeak of the knob were open and aboveboard. So was the delicious smell. Lucinda sat up, sniffing. It was a smell like apple pie. But Sunday was ice-cream day, and apple pie was never known to come in cereal bowls.

"Think it's settled?" her father asked, and laid his hand on his own stomach.

"Yes," Lucinda said. "I'm all right now."

"Hungry?"

"A little," she admitted. She hoped there was enough, whatever it was.

"When I was a little boy," he said, pulling up a chair, "they used to give me milk toast after a stomach upset." As soon as the tray was safe on Lucinda's knees he went after the lock of hair. It always fell over his eye when he bent his head or even moved it very fast. It was red-brown, like his eyes, and was always doing something, standing up or dropping over or curling at the ends if rain was in the air.

"I had milk toast after the measles," Lucinda reminded him, "but it didn't have the smell."

"That's the cinnamon," he told her.

The cinnamon made the taste good, too. She held the tray on her legs and, under her father's eye, ate slowly, deliberately. She longed to lift the bowl and gulp the warm, buttery, brown-flecked milk.

"How would you like to get up now?" he asked when he took the empty bowl.

"I don't mind staying a little longer," she said. The story had been at a wonderful point when he came in and she had just thought about bringing Adelaide into bed with her.

"If you don't feel like getting up," he said, "what would you rather do than anything else?"

Lucinda hesitated. His eyes were shining with what he wanted her to say. "Have you tell me stories," she said.

"Or read to you?" They both knew it didn't matter which. "See what I brought." He drew the fairy-tale book out of his pocket. Before he opened it he leaned over and took her hand. The long lock fell down and made him look as if he were winking at her. But his wide mouth drew a quivering line across the lower part of his face. His full lips strained against each other to keep from saying something. He looked hard at her and squeezed her hand. The hair flopped lower, this time covering his eye entirely. "Damned fetlock," he muttered, and raked it back. There was no danger now of his saying it. A lump swelled like a balloon in Lucinda's chest and crowded into her throat. He squeezed her hand again and dropped his eyes to the book.

He was finishing the bell story when her mother came in. "They ran toward each other and clasped each other's hands in that great church," he read, "and above them sounded the unseen holy bell."

"How close the room is!" Ethel Darby said. Her little feet on the glistening high heels barely touched the floor as she hurried across the room to the front window. "Winter has hardly started," she said, "but already it's warm like spring." She pushed the window up and stood, looking out, her back to the room.

The cozy attic smell was gone. One breath from the window had cleared it out, taking the story with it. At the window Ethel Darby's shoulders rose and sank on a long fluttering sigh. "There's something terrible about not having any winter," she said, still looking, waiting for the polished leaves to drop from the trees, waiting for frost to burn the bright green grass.

"Still a little homesick?" Clifford Darby said in a half-question.

"Of course I'm not homesick, Clifford. You know it isn't that." She went on talking without turning. Her voice seemed to come from out of doors. "I told Mrs. Graham yesterday I'd never understand why she, or anybody else, did not like a normal winter."

"The people who've lived down here all their lives call this a normal winter," Clifford Darby said. He leaned forward in his chair and rested his elbows on his knees. He forgot about the lock, and his hands turned the pages of the book back and forth. Lucinda waited to see which story he would pick. Over and over he turned the pages, his left hand holding the book between his knees, his right thumb catching and twirling the pages. His eyes were on the book, but he was not seeing it, not hearing the sound the pages made.

The funny feelings started in Lucinda's legs. She drew her right foot up and pushed it down. Then her left foot. She wished she were double-jointed like Betty, who could make herself into a frog whenever she liked. Or Cajy. She saw Cajy writhing and coiling against the air as he spelled. It would feel good to stretch and squirm like that. She drew her right foot up and pulled her toes to see if that would help.

A freshness at the window stirred the frill of her mother's collar. For a minute she didn't look so lonely. The breeze picked up the cover of a magazine on the table and dropped it, lifted and dropped it with patient irregularity. The flapping of the paper on the table fell into place between the rolling chords of the book, as her father turned its pages, and set a ruffled syncopation against the silence of the room. So far down the street that the thin tones could hardly be heard, a limp hand touched a piano. Slowly the inert fingers toiled up the scale, stopped for breath, and staggered back to middle C. Up and down, up and down, the hand that was without muscle and without bone made the same stumbling journey over the same tedious track. At last it gave up the scale and tackled a hymn, still using only one hand. The waits between notes were long, but after two false starts the tune came through.

"Jesus, Lover of my soul,
Let me to Thy bosom fly."

Ethel Darby turned from the window and drew a rocking chair into the doorway between Lucinda's room and
the hall. She opened her round sewing basket and took out
a scrap of green pin-dotted silk, left from her new dress.
She held it up for Lucinda to see, waving it lightly. In the
other hand she held Adelaide. She draped the silk around
the doll to show how becoming it was. Adelaide was going
to have a new dress after all. Yesterday she had said:
"Surely you don't want to dress up that dirty old doll.
Aren't you old enough to give your dolls to some poor
little girl?"

Lucinda couldn't see what was happening while her
mother held the silk flat against her lap to cut it out. Her
eyes went back to her father. His Adam's apple was moving up and down in his throat. Sometimes she thought it
was lodged at the top, but always it came down again,
sometimes very fast.

"Will I have an Adam's apple, too, when I'm grown
up?" she asked.

Her father looked at her. He was not sure she had
spoken. After a minute he said, "I hope not," replying to
the echo his mind's ear had heard. "But I can't promise
you," he added. "You had a great-aunt who went around
all her life with a whopping big canary she couldn't quite
swallow."

"Of course you won't have an Adam's apple," her
mother said.

Her father had found the story. "There was once a
King's son who had all sorts of picture books," he began.

The silk was taking shape behind the quick snips of her mother's scissors.

"Hailstones bounded about the floor, and snowflakes floated in the air," her father read.

Lucinda slid more deeply into the warmth of the bed and wrapped herself against the snowflakes that floated between her eyes and her mother's hands; between her ears and her father's voice.

Down the street the Court House clock gave a mighty gasp and set its teeth in the back of the afternoon. One by one it gnawed the hours away.

"It's four o'clock," Clifford Darby said. He half closed the book. "Perhaps your mother will read to you now. I think I'll run down to the church and practice a little."

"I thought surely you'd take us for a drive," Ethel Darby said. "I can't read today. I promised to read to Mrs. Graham again tomorrow, and I'll not be able to hold out for three hours if I don't save my voice today."

"Lucy doesn't feel like getting up, do you, Lucy?" her father said. He had closed the book. Lucinda knew, whatever she said, he was going to the church. He went every Sunday afternoon. He had to go. Nothing could stop him. Nothing. "Go, go, go," the voice inside her cried. All week he waited for Sunday afternoon. Sometimes Lucinda went with him, but not often. He liked better to go alone.

"I thought we might drive out to call on the Gardeners," Ethel Darby said. "It's been more than a month since they came to see us. You'll never get anywhere, Clifford, if you're determined to put in all your spare time at that organ."

He was in the hall. "Maybe I'm already somewhere," he said. His voice rang out with a sudden lift. He ran back

and gave Lucinda two boisterous kisses on her right eye.
"Maybe I'm already there," he cried, and his voice rang
again. His happiness flowed over Lucinda in cool streams.
He ran down the steps singing,

"Oh-h-h, he flies through the air with the greatest of ease,
  The daring young man on the flying trapeze."

  "Do you suppose your father's taking lessons from Miss
Reba?" Lucinda's mother asked, half to herself.

  "Why, he can play lots better than Miss Reba," Lucinda
said, surprised.

  "No, Lucinda, your father plays only by ear," her mother
said. "He would never be able to play for a service."

Her mother didn't really know about this. She had
never gone to the church with him. Lucinda closed her
eyes and followed him down the street, around to the low,
ivy-framed side door of the church and along the dark,
damp-smelling corridor. He mounted the high organ
bench, reached carefully for this stop and that, flung out
his legs, and the music sprang from the organ, taking the
shape of familiar words as it swelled and poured over the
pews and down the aisles until the corners were crowded
with it and the windows threatened to give way:

    Thy gardens and thy goodly walks
    Continually are green
    Where evermore the angels are
    And evermore do sing.
    Jerusalem, my happy home . . .

  "Lucinda, do you hear?"
  "Yes, Mother, I'll just stay in bed."

"You're sure you don't want anything?"

"Nothing but a little supper."

"What are you talking about, Lucinda? I just finished telling you that unless you feel well enough to get up you shouldn't eat anything more today."

"Oh," Lucinda said, keeping surprise out of her face and voice, "I thought you only said did I feel like getting up."

"You couldn't have, Lucinda. What are you talking about? What are you thinking about?"

"Not anything."

Her mother was looking at her again. She had finished the dress and was putting it on Adelaide. She was massaging the doll, pushing cotton down to make her legs fatter where they would show. But she didn't look at the doll. She looked at Lucinda. Lucinda began to count morning-glories in the wallpaper. There were three bunches in the border and two in the clusters that ran up and down the walls.

"I think I'll leave you while you decide whether you'll be well enough by six o'clock to dress and come down for supper," her mother said. She laid her hand on Lucinda's forehead, moved it questioningly along her cheek. "You certainly haven't any temperature," she said. She propped Adelaide up on the bookshelf. "Of course you're too big now to play with her, but in this new dress I think it will be nice for her to sit on the shelf with your books."

"How sweet she looks!" Lucinda cried as Adelaide's curly head rested against the "Swiss Family" and her legs dangled from the narrow shelf.

Ethel Darby crossed the room to the window, stood looking out for a few minutes, and came back to the bookshelf. She was waiting for something. She picked up the doll, straightened a sleeve, and put her back on the shelf.

"It's too late now, I guess, to expect callers," she said. "I suppose if they had any idea of coming they'd have been here long ago."

Lucinda knew, but that didn't keep her from asking. "Who?" she asked. "Who did you think was coming?"

"Oh, nobody; nobody in particular. All the neighbors have been to call except Mrs. Reeves and her daughter. Of course I don't expect them any more, and I don't really care whether they come or not. It just seems strange that they don't. It's not polite to let us live under their very noses like this for months without knowing we're alive."

"But if they don't go anywhere?" Lucinda began.

"Well, they should. That's what's the matter. It's uncanny and unhealthy to live like that. If they'd leave the place once in a while maybe they'd realize how depressing it is for people to have to live under the shadow of their reeking jungle."

She stood beside the shelf. Her hands were busy with the doll, but her eyes had gone back to the window.

"Can you imagine living in a wilderness like that and still being such a snob you couldn't even notice your neighbors?" Her eyes turned to Lucinda's. "I don't suppose you have ever seen them, have you?"

"Mrs. Reeves and Miss Emily?"

"Naturally. Who did you think we were talking about?"

"I haven't exactly seen them," Lucinda said, "but Mittie tells me about—"

"Yes, I know all about that. That's hardly seeing them, Lucinda." She leaned over and shifted two books on the bottom shelf. "I thought maybe you'd seen them walking in their driveway."

"No," Lucinda admitted, "I never have seen them. Not Abe or anybody."

"That doddering old man. I saw him the other day down by the gate. A fine servant, he must be."

"He's Cajy's papa," Lucinda said.

Her mother moved towards the door. "The japonicas are loaded with blooms," she said. "I think I'll cut a few for the house."

She stood between the shelf and the door. She was waiting for Lucinda to say something, but Lucinda didn't know what it was. She had to leave her there in the floor with nothing to hold to.

"I'll get the big scissors," she said. That started her. In another minute she was going down the stairs. Each little foot touched the steps twice, a padded tap and a sharp click sounded on every step.

Lucinda listened until her mother passed the landing. Then she swung her feet from under the covers and tipped across to the bookshelf.

"We're going back to the party," she whispered to the doll, "and you're going to wear your beautiful new dress."

She settled Adelaide on the pillow beside her and drew the sheet over their two heads.

TWO

As Miss Carley passed out the drawing books she said, "I wonder how many of you know who Curtis Hardin is?"

Sue held up her hand. "My Aunt Kit wrote him a letter when she was here," she said, using her most proper voice.

Miss Carley looked at Sue. She was thinking of something to say, but she did not say it. She looked away from Sue and said, "Curtis Hardin is a great artist, and Macklin is his home."

"Why do we always have to draw in these old books?" James Givens grumbled.

Miss Carley pretended not to hear. "Macklin is very proud of Curtis Hardin," she said. "He has spent very little time here in recent years, but now he has come home. He wants to paint more of our region. A few months ago one of his pictures of Gander Creek Negroes won first prize in the most important exhibition of the year. And last week the Metropolitan Museum in New York bought another one of his pictures of Negroes down on Gander. I have brought a print of it for you to see." She held up a small picture. "I'm going to tack it to the board so you can look at it often. Notice the faces of the Negroes and the colors of the tree and its fruit. You can almost smell the pomegranates. Almost taste them."

"Cuckoo," Cator Randall whispered behind Lucinda. "Cuckoo Carley."

In front of Lucinda, Sue's plump shoulders gave an exaggerated heave to tell Cator she had heard and was laughing.

"Do you realize," Miss Carley said, "that it is this same Mr. Hardin who gave the Sixth Grade its beautiful piano?"

Sue's hand went up. It was nice to see Sue want to answer questions. "And all the other grades," she said.

"Yes, every room in the public schools has a piano exactly like this, and the High-School auditorium has a grand piano—all gifts from Mr. Hardin. And this is a very good time for you to copy the inscription that is on the bronze plate." She pointed to a small square of metal on the side of the piano. "Turn to the front page of your drawing books, and copy exactly what I write on the board. Put it in the center of the page, directly under the title." She took blue chalk and wrote on the center board:

> All things return to dust
> Save beauty fashioned well;
> 　　The bust
> Outlasts the citadel.
>
> The gods, too, die, alas!
> But deathless and more strong
> 　　Than brass
> Remains the sovereign song.

"Some day," Miss Carley said, "we'll talk more about this inscription and what it means. When you finish copying it, turn to page eleven of your books."

At the supper table Lucinda said, "We had about the painter today."

"Oh," her father said, "Curtis Hardin. I've been meaning to tell you. He's in town." He was talking to Lucinda's mother. "He came in yesterday to talk about insurance on that big family portrait they have up at Castleton. Seems to think it's not insured. Wanted to know if they had a policy with me. It seems there's a firm up East in the market for the picture. He heard about it up there, and it set him to wondering about insurance on it. He says they're thinking about sending a man down to see Mrs. Reeves. They want to make her an offer. If Mrs. Reeves hasn't got a policy he wants to take one out himself without letting her know, but can't quite decide whether he dares do it or not. I guess the old girl's pretty proud."

"Her place looks like it," Lucinda's mother said, bearing down hard on *place*.

Over Lucinda's head their eyes were locked. Their look was a bar pressing against the back of her head where her hair stopped and her neck began. It kept her from raising her head to look at their faces. It made her neck ache. Her eyes could not leave her plate. They were fixed on the stripped chop bone, already ugly garbage beside the snowy mound of potatoes.

Without lifting her eyes she knew the looks, the darting blue eyes and the slow brown eyes holding each other somewhere on that plane above the supper table where they met day after day in messages that were not for her. Without moving her eyes from the plate, Lucinda could see the arc of brown crepe that rose above the table and the round white collar held by the buckle-shaped blue enamel pin. She knew where the pin touched the short round column of throat, exactly under the dimple in the little pointed chin. She knew that now the mouth was shut so tight there were no lips at all and that the round bird eyes could look longer than the brown eyes. *Her place looks like it—her place looks like it—her place looks like it.* The eyes were repeating what the voice had said. Up there, above Lucinda's head, the blue eyes were saying it to the brown eyes. The brown eyes said nothing back. The wild red hair stood up with things to say. The wide mouth opened and shut and said nothing. The clock took it up. *Her place—looks like—it her—place looks—like it—her place—looks like—it her—place looks—like it . . .*

Lucinda's hand let go the fork. It slid to the plate without a sound, as if the life had gone out of the china and silver, too. A key had turned, and the spool was running backward, clicking with the rhythm of the clock as it ran off the reel of the months in Macklin, bringing back words that had broken through doors and walls and darkness and night and sleep, fitting them together to make a meaning. Her place—looks like—it her—place looks—like it. . . . "How can I help it if the odor makes me positively sick?" "And how can I help it if I've signed a lease? How can I expect people to keep their contracts with me if I don't keep mine?" . . . "Some day you'll know. I can't help myself, I tell you." "Sometimes, I swear to God, I think I'll catch the first train and get out for good and all." . . .

"If they would only clear the place out and be normal, maybe there wouldn't be those disgraceful people in the middle of the night creeping in." "And if you would stay in bed where you belong, and go to sleep, maybe you wouldn't be spying on what's none of your business." . . .

"Rot and decay under the filthy tangle, under your very nose." "Tell me why your imagination's all centered in your nose, Ethel, all centered in your nose." . . . "Can't you smell it? Can't you smell something dead?" "Just muck. Just a little harmless muck. Nothing but muck. Nothing but muck." . . . Her place—looks like—it her—place looks—like it. . . .

"Listen," Lucinda's father said. His wrists pressed against the edge of the table. The fork in his hand lifted its tines to hear. "Listen," he said again. The brown arc of her mother's blouse rose ever so little. The honey sweetness of Mittie's voice drifted through the light pine panels of the kitchen door.

> "Oh, Lord, oh, Lo-or-ord,
>  Whachu gonna do about me?"

Lucinda's ears stirred. They were bigger suddenly than her head. They wagged away on either side, heavier than a cocker's, sharper than a rabbit's. If only her hair were hanging loose so nobody could see how funny they looked, twitching there in the open in front of her skinned-back braids.

"Listen," her father said again. His voice shivered.

> "I ast you, please, Sir, Jesus,
>  Whachu gonna do about me."

"Mittie's warming up for prayer meeting," Lucinda's mother said. "And look at Lucinda's plate. You don't want to make Mittie late for prayer meeting, do you, Lucinda?"

"Oh, no," Lucinda said. She filled her mouth with cold potato. Mittie was still singing, but they were no longer listening.

Lucinda's father laughed a chuckling, remembering laugh. "The first thing I thought of when Hardin came in yesterday was the pianos."

Her mother said, "I wonder how much truth there is in that story, anyway."

"Oh, it's true, all right," Clifford Darby said. "I guess those old Hardin men were pretty mean. People have a way of saying they were so tight they never sat down all day at their plant for fear they'd wear out the seats of their pants. Harry has a good tale about them. He said one day an explosion that took the roof off the building took half a dozen men with it. And the poor devils were docked for the time they were up in the air."

"People like to make up tales about them."

"Well, the piano tale wasn't made up. One reason the Macklin schools are no better than they are is because old Joe Hardin sat on the Board for fourteen years. He used to say things like music and French were for children who could afford to go away to school. He said they just put notions in the heads of poor people. The pianos were the logical memorial to him." Clifford Darby could hardly talk for laughing.

"I consider the whole thing very disloyal," Lucinda's mother said. "After all, he was his uncle."

"All the more reason for Curtis to try to atone for some of the old man's meanness. He'd voted down buying pianos for the schools for years. Half the Board was under his thumb; so, year after year, the request was voted down."

"Miss Carley said the painter gave the pianos," Lucinda put in.

"He certainly did," her father said. "Thirty-two of them. With what little he got of old Joe's money. He didn't get a dime of his father's, you know."

EVERY DAY Lucinda went to school expecting to see Curtis Hardin. He was up Miss Carley's sleeve. Any day she might produce him, his arms full of pictures for the children to see. She did say his name nearly every day.

"Governor James Arthur Cass was Macklin's greatest hero," Sara Hardy read from the composition her father had helped her write.

"Governor Cass was our celebrity then," Miss Carley explained, "just as Curtis Hardin is now."

Perhaps that was why he didn't appear. One never saw heroes.

"Cotton is the principal crop," Paul Storey recited a few days later and Miss Carley said, "The pictures in the series called 'Cotton' were the first to bring fame to Curtis Hardin."

"My father says those artists don't know anything about farming," James Givens announced. "He says they're like some of the rest of the people who won't let folks tend to their own business."

Miss Carley didn't look at James. "The artists," she said, "have the gift of insight. They help our hearts, as well as our minds, to understand the world we live in."

The big feet in the back of the room scraped the floor impatiently.

Miss Carley looked at the boys. "You must listen to what I am saying," she said. "You are old enough to begin to think about the world you live in." She looked up and down the room, daring a hand or foot to move. She fixed her eyes on Kirk Stevens' face, warning him that this was no time for his sarcastic laughing. "Our South is not all silver moss and fried chicken and azaleas and watermelons. It is starvation and rags and pellagra for too many people. You've got to begin thinking about these things because when you're a little older you'll have to do something about them. We haven't been very good citizens here in Macklin, or anywhere else, for a good many years. We've been on the wrong track, too blind, too selfish, too indifferent to the evils in the world. Before long it will be your job to make Macklin a better place than it is today. Your great-grandfathers built our beautiful houses and planted our fine trees. They founded the college and brought scholars here to teach in it. Today the college building is a warehouse owned by men who have never seen Macklin. We're not even holding on to what is ours. Dozens of our big trees are dying of neglect. Our streets are fringed with weeds. A stream of filth stands in Gander Creek. We let these, and worse, things happen because we don't care enough about goodness and justice and beauty—"

All at once the thought of it was too much for Miss Carley. Her voice gave way, and she turned quickly to her desk. She groped in the drawer for a handkerchief and blew her nose. But that didn't help much. She had to keep her back turned. Her hand went up to one eye and then the other. She blew again.

Out of the corner of her eye Lucinda saw Kirk pushing his pencil box. With his forefinger he pushed it the long way, little by little, towards the edge of his desk. He sat perfectly still with his head down. But one eye was on Miss Carley. His hand did not move but the box moved, and the finger against the box. It reached the edge of the desk and stopped. Kirk looked at Miss Carley's back with careful examination. Then the box began to move again, more slowly than ever. An inch hung over the edge; and another. Lucinda stiffened herself for what was coming. The children stared at nothing. Her back still turned, Miss Carley fingered pens and pencils as if she were looking for something. The room had never been so still. The box moved again, hung on the edge, balanced, and went down with the most deafening crash Sixth Grade had ever heard. The pencils rolled hilariously in every direction.

Miss Carley wheeled just in time to see Kirk dive after a pencil. "Cator and James," she said, "will you please help Kirk pick up his pencils?" She shut her lips together tightly for a second. Then she said in the usual way, "If you would keep your pencils inside your desk, Kirk, you could avoid that kind of accident." She turned to Mary. "Now we will hear Mary's composition," she said.

EVERYTHING WAS different at Mrs. Graham's. Some things were different because Mrs. Graham's real home was up North. Others were different because something was wrong with her. The northern winters were too cold for her, and the Florida winters were too hot. So she came to Macklin every year after Thanksgiving and stayed until her son wrote that it was warm enough for her to come back home. Lucinda and her mother went to call on Mrs. Graham because Lucinda's uncle worked for Mrs. Graham's son. After that Lucinda's mother got in the habit of going every Saturday when Mrs. Graham's nurse had the afternoon off.

Mrs. Graham's house was not far from Sue's. When Jessie said it was time to stop playing Lucinda would walk down the hill to Mrs. Graham's so she could ride home with her mother. On the Saturday Sue went to New Orleans with her mother, the playing had to stop an hour early. Lucinda made the time longer as she walked down the street by looking for gravel diamonds beside the pavement. She didn't like to sit in Mrs. Graham's hall until the reading time was finished.

Mrs. Graham's differentness began with the hedges and

went down the smoothly set concrete blocks of her front walk to the shining copper screen that enclosed the big yellow portico, columns and all. Nobody's hedges, not even the Browns', were so neatly trimmed. Always there were two men at work, measuring and clipping, clipping and measuring. Nearly everybody had front walks of slick, greenish bricks, bulging and breaking over roots, sinking and stumbling between them. Or, if they were not brick walks, they were sand and gravel, best of all places for finding diamonds.

Mrs. Graham's was the only yellow house on Magnolia Avenue. Mrs. Graham told Lucinda's mother about the shocking condition the house had been in when she bought it. "You'd think the neighbors would have been glad to see it fixed up, but they actually had the nerve to stop in and ask the painters if they weren't making a mistake. They said it had always been white. The painters stopped work until they could come down to the Terrace and ask me if I really meant for them to make it yellow."

Even the doorbell was different. Lucinda pushed the little pearl button and listened just as she always did. As usual, there wasn't a sound. Then, when she had decided she must push it again, the door opened so suddenly she almost jumped out of her skin, and there stood Rosa in her white uniform that had never been sat down in, holding out a little silver plate. She lowered the plate when she saw Lucinda and looked questioningly at the big hall clock. The voice of Lucinda's mother, reading, came from the bay window two rooms to the left of the hall.

"I'll just wait," Lucinda said. She sank into the chair nearest the front door. Rosa disappeared through the back hall. Lucinda wished Rosa had asked her to go to the kitchen with her. Her mother had told her about the kitchen that was as white and clean as an operating room. You have white kitchens, Lucinda supposed, if you have white maids in stiff white uniforms.

Something was wrong with Lucinda's chair. The seat was hard and slanted. Lucinda felt as if she might slide off any minute. The back was so heavily carved that when she leaned against it the uneven lumps hurt her shoulders. When she did not lean the sliding feeling started again. She peered into the front parlor. Her eyes traveled from chair to chair. Each one seemed on the point of backing out of the room. Nearest the hall was the chair she had sat in last week and the week before. She knew it by its position and considered it briefly, but it didn't look as if she had ever sat in it, as if it had anything to do with her. She decided she would be no better off for changing to it now. Across from it and almost as near the door was a chair with arms. Lucinda eyed it. She felt her arms resting on the arms of the chair, her hands fitting over the curved ends, anchoring her. The grooved rhythm of her mother's voice made a wall between her and the two women by the window in the back parlor. Behind that wall she could make a quick dash for the chair without danger of being seen. She held her breath and reached out with her right foot as far as possible. She brought up her left foot and stood, balancing, relieved to have made the first step without sound or mishap.

"What's that?" Mrs. Graham said in a clear, strong voice that set Lucinda to wobbling again.

"Why, Lucinda," her mother said. "So early?"

"Sue had to go away on the train," Lucinda explained.

"Come over and speak to Mrs. Graham," her mother said.

Lucinda steeled herself for the journey to the bay window. Her legs always seemed to grow longer and thinner with every step towards the big couch. Inside, she felt herself closing against the moment of standing over the mountain of perfumed corruption. Her hand cringed from the touch of the handful of hard cold flesh, tightly stuffed into slippery skin. Her eyes refused to fix themselves on the high dais where Mrs. Graham lay like the effigy on the tomb in the history book, covered with shawls and scarves, cast in lavender bronze.

"How do you do, Lucinda?"

"How do you do, Mrs. Graham?" Her eyes had to look then, and Lucinda saw that Mrs. Graham was in a new position. She was flat on her back, as usual, but her knees were drawn up. Her arms, from the elbows, stood at right angles to her body and her fingers wiggled stiffly above her. She looked like an elephant of a dog playing dead with everything but her forepaws.

"And how's the girlie, today?" Mrs. Graham said, rolling her head and wiggling the sausage fingers. "Hungry, no doubt, and nobody with sense enough to give her so much as a cookie."

Lucinda's hand went out and gave itself up to the sausages. They were not greasy; just slick and tight and cold.

"Ring that bell, will you, Ethel?" Mrs. Graham said.

Lucinda's mother touched the pearl button set between the windows.

"They never hear it," Mrs. Graham said. Her chest rose and she called, "Clara, you Clar-oo."

It was a trumpeting call. Her voice was not sick. It had gained in volume as disease had throttled her body. The vitality of her legs had been transferred to her voice. She sent it on journeys her legs could never undertake again.

"Clara Gordy," she boomed.

Somewhere at the back of the house doors were slamming, footsteps running. But Mrs. Graham heard only her own voice. She gave Clara up and sent out a ringing call for Rosa.

"You Rosa," she cried. "Where are you, Rosa?"

Everybody but Mrs. Graham heard Clara as she ran from the kitchen repeating, "Yes, Mrs. Graham—coming, Mrs. Graham."

Rosa was on the stairs. "Yes, ma'am—sure, ma'am," she panted.

But their voices were no match for Mrs. Graham's. She threw out first one name and then the other with mounting impatience. The girls, stuffed into their uniforms like Mrs. Graham's hands into their skin, met at the back parlor door. They stood for a minute, drooping and muttering, red with haste and chagrin, before Mrs. Graham saw them or heard their truckling duet.

"Why are you girls always as far away as you can get when I want you?" she said, gathering her voice back grudgingly.

The girls tried to look at each other. Everything in the house, everybody, was always as far away as it was possible to be. Only Lucinda's mother came close. Sometimes she would lay a hand on the lavender shawls, would let it lie there as she read.

"Why can't you girls get cookies for Lucinda? One of you get her a plate of cookies. Don't we always have cookies for little girls? Get her some cookies now. And a glass of milk. Sit there in the rocker, Lucinda, and one of them will bring you some cookies. Maybe they'll be animal cookies with raisins."

Mrs. Graham couldn't get a good look at her from that position, Lucinda thought. That was why she always talked as if she were such a little girl.

Rosa and Clara were looking at each other, asking each other which should go for the cookies, knowing that whoever went would be the wrong one. They went out together.

Lucinda sat in the rocking chair that tilted her so far back she was sure she was going over. She wondered how she could manage to hold a plate of cookies and a glass of milk and keep the chair level at the same time.

Rosa had the good fortune to return to the room when Mrs. Graham was too busy talking to notice her. The cookies and milk were on a small tray that sat securely on Lucinda's lap. Lucinda munched and counted the triangles in the border of the rug and forgot about the voices in the window until she heard her own name.

"Lucinda ought to know," Mrs. Graham said.

Lucinda swallowed a mouthful of dry cookie.

"Eva Carley's your teacher, isn't she, Lucinda? Has she got Curtis Hardin's pictures tacked up all over her room at school?"

"She's got one," Lucinda said.

"I told you, Ethel," Mrs. Graham said. The fingers were hanging stiffly from the hands now like the prisms from the chandelier above her. "She's as bad as ever. Whenever Mrs. Reeves broke things up with him and Emily he seemed to turn to Eva for comfort. She almost landed him the last time. Everybody'd always thought she was one of those shy, timid girls, but she went after him then for dear life. Then all of a sudden he pulled up and went away. He's never been here more than a few months at a time since he went away to college. Stays around here a little while painting, then puts out again. But they say he's come back for good, this time."

"Maybe Eva will get him this time," Lucinda's mother said.

"Everybody says he won't marry anybody now. He's too full of his painting. But the last time he was here he really gave her a rush. The Wilds told me they'd see him drive up every day to take her home from school." The head rolled again towards Lucinda. "You don't see Eva Carley driving off these days with Mr. Hardin, do you?"

"Sometimes," Lucinda said. Her heart was beating so loud she barely heard her voice. She hadn't meant to tell a lie. She had no other way to let them know about Miss Carley's happiness when she was saying the name of Curtis Hardin for the Sixth Grade.

"Was Emily Reeves ever really in love with him?" Lucinda's mother asked.

"The affair went on, people say, off and on, from the time they were children. What I think is that Emily Reeves never loved anybody but her mother. She had a lot of beaux when she was young and going around. The Reeveses never were what you'd call intimate with Macklin people. They went to more parties in New Orleans and Savannah and Montgomery and places away than here. Weren't many people here good enough for Emma Cass Reeves and her daughter. When Emily was a little girl sometimes they'd ask Macklin children to her parties. Once they even took Eva Carley to Europe with them. But as Emily grew up nobody here was good enough to go to Castleton but Kit Greshem and Curtis Hardin. Kit married Eric Bogart and went to Paris to live about the time Tom Reeves died and the family's troubles began to come to light. Then, the first thing you knew, they had cut themselves off from everybody but Curtis. First you'd hear Emily was going to marry him, and then you'd hear it was all off. Nobody ever saw either Emily or her mother, but things got out. I'll bet those two women haven't left the place for years. Looks like they can't face being less than the richest, let alone being the poorest."

"Have you ever seen Emily?" Ethel Darby asked. "Is it true that she's so beautiful?"

Mrs. Graham's shoulders heaved, and she almost raised her head. She wanted to send a look along with her words. "Of course I haven't seen her, Ethel," she said sharply. "You know I haven't. I wasn't able to go around, even when I first came here. Everybody else came to see me. But you know those Reeveses would let you rot before they'd notice you, don't you?"

"I know they haven't called on me," Ethel Darby said, "and I'm sure I should not want to be put in the position of feeling there's any reason for me to set foot on that place. I only hope it won't be long before I won't even have to see it." Her voice went high. She had to stop for breath. "I suppose they won't come now," she added.

Lucinda looked up to be sure that the strange voice was her mother's.

"Never fear," Mrs. Graham said. "Of course they won't." The clicking scabbard of her false teeth closed down on the sword of her tongue.

Anger boiled up in Lucinda. "I hate you, I hate you, I hate you," the inside voice was saying. She kept her eyes on the mountain of Mrs. Graham to make sure the hating was all for her.

"Well, I must say," Lucinda's mother said, pouring out Miss Carley's unhappiness to dilute her own, "Eva Carley doesn't strike me as the marrying kind. And she's certainly not a beauty."

"I should say not," Mrs. Graham gloated. "I'd call her plain."

"Oh, no, not plain," Lucinda's mother cried. "I'd never call her plain. There's something about her—I don't know what, but something."

In a flash the hating was gone. Love flooded through every vein and alley of Lucinda, loosening and warming her, pouring over her mother and father and Miss Carley, gathering the three of them to her.

"What's the picture like?" Lucinda's mother was asking. "What's it like, Lucinda, the picture Miss Carley has up in your room, Mr. Hardin's picture?"

"I can tell you," Mrs. Graham put in. "It's dirt and darkies. I'll bet on that every time. It's all he thinks about. Am I right, Lucinda?"

Lucinda nodded. She was trapped. "And a tree," she added, "a tree with pomegranates."

"It's always the same," Mrs. Graham said. "Perfect libels. Beautiful as it is down here, that's all he can find to paint."

"Some people are like that," Lucinda's mother said. "You'd think he would want to paint the flowers, the oleanders and azaleas."

"No flowers for Curtis Hardin," Mrs. Graham said. "Plenty of white trash, though, and Negroes and razor-back mules and slat-ribbed pigs and gullies you could stand up in. He's got it in for the South."

AT SUE'S, in the long narrow sun room where the windows were full of white and purple hyacinths, Lucinda saw Curtis Hardin for the first time. Two men appeared at the door, piloted by Jessie. Mrs. Brown jumped up from the card table where she was helping Sue and Lucinda start a puzzle.

"Curtis," she cried, "I had almost given you up."

She moved down the room. Hands were shaken, names spoken, chairs dragged over the marble floor.

Lucinda's eyes were good at the trick of looking up while her head looked down. They were quick at seeing without being caught in the act. After two or three stolen glances they were satisfied that the tall handsome man looked exactly as Curtis Hardin should look. His hair was as gold as Flora's and as deeply waved. He spoke with rich, broad *a*'s and ringing *g*'s and *r*'s. He tried to keep his voice from being too loud, but when he saw the hyacinths it got away from him.

"Ah, white hyacinths," he cried. "White hyacinths."

He bent over the curled clusters and lifted himself on deep-drawn breaths.

"Who would want two loaves of bread?" he asked. His

shining eyes turned to question the eyes beside him. Before they could answer, his smile hurdled the room and landed at the sunny table where the little girls sat. Lucinda tried to smile back, but her face felt as if it were breaking to pieces. He gathered his attention back to his end of the room, and Lucinda twisted her eyes and mouth so they would be ready for the next time.

"Do begin at the beginning," Mrs. Brown was saying, "and tell me all about it."

"I was deeply moved," he said. "Moved and touched beyond words. Shall I tell you all about it?"

"Oh, do, please," Mrs. Brown urged.

The little man had nothing to say.

"I was in a trance, in another world from the moment I entered the boxwood path. Do you know that camellia tree?"

"The only one of hundreds that's left," Mrs. Brown said.

"Loaded with white blossoms," he said, "and lighting, somehow, the gorgeous and tremendous gloom of that great park."

The little man moved to another chair.

"I'll always remember that camellia tree in the ruined park as the counterpart of the beautiful woman in the gaunt house with its raw and bleeding walls." The rich voice was halted by a sigh.

"Emily is still pretty," Mrs. Brown said, "but a few years ago—"

He could not wait to set her right. "It is the mother I speak of. I grant you the daughter has a certain beauty. But one feels that Mrs. Reeves has come into a loveliness that transcends the beauty even of her own youth. Her snow-white hair and the finely traced lines of her face add distinction without subtracting anything. I shall never forget that manner. She received me like a queen and talked brightly as pampered ladies talk at parties, cleverly holding off my proposal."

The little man wasn't even listening.

"If you could have seen the look she turned on her daughter, then on the portrait, when I finally brought myself to speak of my errand. I felt like a marauder. What are thirty thousand dollars to a woman like that, a daughter of a hundred earls?"

Nobody spoke. After a minute he added, "Miss Reeves had very little to say."

"I can believe that," Mrs. Brown said. "It was like that when we called several weeks ago. My sister and Emily Reeves were close girlhood friends. My sister's interest in finding a market for the portrait dates from that afternoon. She was convinced that Emily is sick of humoring her mother, that she is perfectly realistic about their plight, but lacks the courage to take a stand about it."

"I should think their friends—er—might arrange something tactful. Perhaps—"

"All that kind of thing has been tried," Mrs. Brown said. "Mrs. Reeves makes it impossible for their friends to help them simply and normally. But she is so vague about the details of business that my husband once managed to pay off one of the mortgages on Castleton without being discovered. Even Emily didn't seem to suspect, though she must have known that, more than once, another friend has reduced the amount of a mortgage or paid the interest."

"I doubt if she knows any more about business than her mother knows," the little man said.

"You see," Mrs. Brown said, "we all love Castleton.

There is a great deal of pride in all that the place has stood for. There is no longer any general prosperity in Macklin but, even so, there have been attempts from the Woman's Club and other organizations and individuals to undertake the restoration of Castleton. Every plan has been most considerate of Mrs. Reeves and her daughter. They would have been comfortable and secure in a portion of the house reserved for them. But Mrs. Reeves has been unwilling to share Castleton with the community and just as unwilling to let us share her problems. She has met every emergency alone, simply by selling another treasure or another van load of furniture—and withdrawing a little farther from us. That's how it has gone from year to year."

"And now there is nothing left to sell," the big man said, "except the portrait." He leaned forward. "Can't you see how that enhances for her the value of the portrait? It is the sum of so many of the treasures she has had to give up. If I had realized the full import of the situation I doubt if I could have brought myself to come on this mission."

"My sister," Mrs. Brown said, "has not seen, as we here in Macklin have, the gradual sacrifice of Castleton and those two women to the portrait. We have come to accept it. It was an overwhelming shock to her to find Emily imprisoned behind it. I believe I share her conviction that it was right for her to try to find a buyer for it."

"You do not feel that Miss Reeves shares her mother's emotion for this symbol of what the family has been?" The rich voice filled the room.

The little man jumped up. "No," he cried. He strode across to a window. He was not so little when he walked about like that, when he spoke in the loud voice and didn't have the big man looming over him. "That portrait is a symbol of nothing but arrogant indulgence and display, the kind of showing-off that finally wrecked the family. There's a lot in Castleton's past," he said, still in the loud voice, "that we need to be reminded of today. Richard Cass and his sons helped to build the nation and the state, as well as Castleton. Mrs. Reeves' father, the youngest son in the portrait, freed his slaves before the South seceded, and came back from the Civil War to cook and wash and iron for his invalid wife. He worked in his own fields and brought the plantation back to prosperity. But Mrs. Reeves has forgotten those things. She's let the good things go out of her memory as well as out of her house. Don't think she cherishes that picture because of its artistic value. Years ago she parted with half a dozen of the finest portraits Thomas Sully ever painted, any one of them more valuable, simply as art, than this gaudy collection of Cass trappings." He sat down again and finished more calmly: "If it is a symbol of anything, it is of what we do not want and do not need in this country today."

Lucinda had been fingering the colored scraps clumsily, trying to hold Sue's interest so she could stay in earshot of the talk. With the last quiet words her concern for the portrait was lost in the realization that she had not put names and faces together correctly. The little man was Curtis Hardin. His outburst had shocked Sue. She made a wry face in his direction for Lucinda's benefit.

"I think Mr. Hardin's lovely," Lucinda whispered across the table.

Sue slanted her eyes towards the other man. "I like *him*," she whispered back.

Lucinda shook her head. "Mr. Hardin's just like Miss Carley," she said.

"He is not," Sue hissed, a little too loud. "He is not. And besides Miss Carley hasn't got a mustache." Sue held her mouth to keep from laughing.

Lucinda leaned across the table to explain what she had said, but she had to give up. The likeness had shown itself in a flash and gone as quickly as it had come. She looked again at the thin, narrow face and small, dark mustache and wondered why she had said such a thing.

Mrs. Brown had summoned her resources for keeping a smooth surface. "Sorry as we all would be to see the portrait leave Castleton," she said, "I think you have found the perfect place for it. My sister says there will be no handsomer building in the East, that it will be suitably hung."

The rich voice became crisp and efficient. "There is no more distinguished club in the world. My clients are men who will value the portrait for all that it is and all that it represents. Hung in the great hall, it will complete the style and period of the architecture."

"Of course we appreciate your sympathy for Mrs. Reeves," Mrs. Brown said, "but I hope with all my heart she will decide to accept your offer."

"I have given her until the first of August to let us know," Mr. Griscom said. "The new building will not be ready for it until fall."

EVERYBODY KNEW about the man who came from New York to try to buy the portrait from Mrs. Reeves. Somebody said it was a thousand dollars he offered her. Somebody else said it was a hundred thousand. Nearly every story had its own figure. The picture got to be different, too.

"It's a painting of General Cass signing the Declaration of Independence," Betty said, "and it's so big they'll have to get twenty men to take it down from the wall."

"Have you ever seen it?" Lucinda asked.

"No," Betty said.

"You've lived right here on this street ever since you were born and you haven't seen it?"

"No. I don't want to see it. I wouldn't look at it if I was right in the room where it is."

"Oh, yes, you would," Flora said. "Anybody would look at anything somebody wanted to buy for ten thousand dollars."

"It's more than that," Lucinda said.

"How do you know?" Flora asked.

"The man was out at Sue's and I heard him say, but I've forgotten how much."

Flora and Betty declined to go further into the matter.

They made a point of pretending indifference to the things that happened at Sue's.

"The Carter boys said the portrait had already gone. The man from New York paid fifty thousand dollars and drove off in a van with the picture. They saw him go off in the van. They saw the picture in the van."

Lucinda asked how they knew it was the picture if they'd never seen it. But they swore they knew. They hadn't seen the van coming through the gates either. The van was in front of the gates before they saw it, but there was no being mistaken about a picture so big it had to be moved in a van half a block long. It was the biggest van ever seen in Macklin.

The president of the Parent-Teachers had a plan. She called Lucinda's mother on the telephone and told her about it. It would be a shame, she said, for such a work of art to leave town when so many people, particularly the children, had never seen it. She thought it would be a fine thing for the Association to co-operate with Mrs. Reeves in arranging a day when Castleton would be open to the public. The Association would sell tickets at fifty cents each and divide the proceeds with Mrs. Reeves. Mrs. Baird wanted Mrs. Darby to work with her on the idea. Mrs. Darby told her she would help sell tickets, but she would not think of going with Mrs. Baird to Castleton to submit the plan to Mrs. Reeves. She could not go, she said, because Mrs. Reeves and her daughter had never called on her. It made no difference, she said, that they had never called on Mrs. Baird. Mrs. Baird had lived in Macklin all her life. She wasn't a close neighbor, anyway. Mrs. Darby said she wouldn't go to see the picture, either. She would buy a ticket to help the Association, but she would not think of going to Castleton under any conditions.

Lucinda knew that meant she would not be allowed to go. But she hadn't really thought of seeing the picture that way, going into the house with crowds of people. She had thought of seeing it with Mrs. Reeves and Miss Emily. And she had thought of herself alone in the room with it. To feel herself in the little chair, to touch the cat, she would have to be alone.

Mrs. Baird reported to Mrs. Darby that Mrs. Reeves refused to discuss the plan. So that was finished.

To cancel the Carter boys' story about the portrait in the van, there were dozens of stories about why it was still at Castleton, why Mrs. Reeves would accept no amount of money for it. There was the story that she sat all day talking to the five painted figures.

"She won't even speak to her daughter. She just talks to the people in the picture and never leaves it day or night. She thinks people are coming from all over the world to try to take the portrait away from her, so she never leaves it, not even to sleep."

"Sometimes she calls it *the portrait* and sometimes she calls it *the family*. She doesn't know the difference."

"But if nobody goes there, how does anybody know what she does and what she says?" . . .

"Our cook says it's not just a picture. Our cook says they're people, real people in the picture. She says she's seen them plenty of times walking at night up under the trees. She says they walk down to the gate and stand and look out and try to unfasten the gate, but they can't unfasten the chain because people like that, that are dead, haven't got any strength in their hands."

"Our cook says it wouldn't do any good to buy the picture. She says the man would pay his money and take it off, but when night came you'd see them right back there, walking down to the gate."

"You wouldn't pay any attention to what niggers say about things like that. They're talking about ghosts. Nobody but niggers believes in ghosts." . . .

"I bet Sue's seen the picture. Haven't you, Sue?"

"I guess I did when I was too little to remember. My mother's seen it, I guess. Maybe I could remember about it if I thought hard enough." . . .

Every day there were stories at school. Even at Sunday school people talked about the picture. But at Lucinda's house nobody spoke of it, not even Mittie.

Ethel Darby did not wait now for Saturdays to go to Mrs. Graham's. She went two or three times a week. They did not read any more but talked all the time. Mrs. Graham knew what everybody was saying about the portrait. They were saying it was Mrs. Bogart who had started everything. She'd gone to see the Reeveses when she was in town and had got all worked up over their condition. This business about the portrait was all her doing, they said. Eric Bogart belonged to the club that had sent Mr. Griscom down with the offer of thirty thousand dollars. Mr. Hardin, being a painter and knowing the people in the Griscom galleries, had helped determine the value of the portrait. But that was all he had had to do with it. Mr. Griscom had wanted Mr. Hardin to go with him when he made the offer, but of course he didn't know how things had been with Mr. Hardin and the Reeveses. He wouldn't have asked him if he had known. It was Kit Bogart who was engineering the whole thing.

"Some people think," Mrs. Graham said, "Kit Bogart got it into her head when she was here that Emily's as much in love with Curtis Hardin as she ever was. Maybe Emily said something to her. Miss Perk Folkes said the

120

other day she wouldn't be surprised if Emily's as gone on him as ever."

"Miss Perk's a cousin of Mrs. Brown and Mrs. Bogart," Ethel Darby said, "but I hear they don't have much to do with her."

"Maybe not, but they went to see her when Kit was here. She said so when she was talking about Emily and Curtis. She said any affair that had been off and on as many times as theirs had been was likely to flare up again any day. She said just let Emily get rid of her mother or get her mother to come to her senses and the whole thing would be on again hot as ever. She said that a flame that has life enough to flare up as many times as that one has takes a long time to burn out."

"Sounds like an old maid's talk," Ethel Darby said. "So far as I'm concerned, I don't care what becomes of any of them if only I can live through what's going on now. If I can get Clifford to break our lease, that's all I care about. I can't tell you how I hate the sight of the place. Sometimes when I'm driving home I have to shut my eyes to keep from seeing it. Sometimes I think I'll go raving mad if I can't get away from that sour smell and the creaking sound those trees and big vines make. You don't know how funny it sounds to me when I hear people saying that the most beautiful house in the South is up there behind all that. And talking about what aristocrats those women are. Imagine it. And living like that. I tell Clifford it doesn't matter so much about us but we owe it to Lucinda to get her away from an atmosphere like that. It's not safe, now that the old man's running around with a gun."

"Gun, nothing," Mrs. Graham said. "That old man

couldn't hit the side of a house. If he's got a gun it's probably one that hasn't been fired since the Civil War. What
makes you think he has a gun, anyway?"

"I know it," Ethel Darby said. "Don't ask me why,
because I can't tell you. But I know it." She lowered her
voice, almost to a whisper. "Mrs. Reeves thinks the whole
world is after that portrait. You'd think so, too, if you
could see how people have taken to walking and driving
by. Strange-looking people, most of them. Curiosity
seekers. They've heard about the offer. I don't know how
Mrs. Reeves knows about them if she and Emily never
leave the house, but she must know. She thinks everybody's after the picture. That's why she sends the old
man out to snoop. He'd shoot any of us on the slightest
provocation."

She had drawn her chair closer to Mrs. Graham's as she
talked, gradually hitching it along. She was talking louder
again. She had forgotten Lucinda was in the hall.

The tension in her mother's voice held Lucinda. She
clutched the seat of her chair with both hands. Her feet
strained against the round of the chair until her sharp-
jutting knees quivered.

"Pooh, Ethel," Mrs. Graham said. "Don't let yourself
get so worked up. Just because you feel as you do about
the Reeveses, don't let your imagination run away with
you. I don't think much of them, myself, but I'd say they
have sense enough not to set their servant on people with
a gun."

"You don't live under the shadow of it," Ethel Darby
said. "You'd see for yourself if you did."

WINTER HAD finally come—the coldest winter, people said, Macklin had ever felt. It lasted only a few weeks, but Ethel Darby thought it was much more disagreeable than the North Carolina winters. Macklin houses weren't built for it; that was the trouble.

But, through it all, spring must have been just under the surface. On the first warm day it came oozing up through the dark sandy soil that was too loose to hold anything back, and one night of warm, damp wind, with the trees swaying and moaning like Negroes at church, was enough to blow the jonquils open all over town.

"Have you seen Magnolia Avenue this morning?" Miss Carley asked the Sixth Grade. "My grandfather used to say Magnolia Avenue was Macklin's field of the cloth of gold. But every year now there are fewer jonquils. Tell your mothers it is necessary to divide the bulbs. Leaving them year after year in tight little clumps strangles the life out of them."

In Mrs. Graham's deeply manured borders crisp-frilled fat-trumpeted blossoms stood thickly on the longest, juiciest stems in town. At Mrs. Brown's they tumbled headlong down the green slopes in ruffled yellow skirts. The dozen

or two small clumps in Lucinda's yard had short stems
and small, pale blossoms, but over at Castleton narcissus
and jonquils had popped up everywhere. It had been
many years since careful hands had touched them, but
some prod in the rank leaf mold had kept them stirred
up, just as it had lit the little candles of jasmine that strung
the tallest pines. Under the trees forsythia hovered like
swarms of fireflies, and the big elaeagnus clump in the
fence corner had taken another cedar under its green and
silver tent.

Already the column was shut away from Lucinda. Her
mind's eye quickly found the path her sight had worn
through the trees but, for days, now, it had not been able
clearly to penetrate the mass of smothering green. When
she sat in school wondering how she could manage to see
the picture, or lay in bed wondering, she would think that
if only she were in the tree she would be able to think of
a way. But being in the tree was no good either. Maybe it
was because the tree was too small for her now. While
the weather had been too cold for playing in the yard her
legs had grown until now her knees pushed against the
top of the tree door and cramped dreadfully. The tree
was no fun with her legs spread out on the ground outside.
Unless she could draw them up to make a door there was
nothing secret about the tree.

It wasn't simply that her mind's eye could not see the
picture. There were things she couldn't keep from thinking about. She couldn't keep from remembering what
the Carter boys had said about the van that carried the
picture away. Maybe they were right. Or maybe if it had
not gone that way it had gone as the furniture and mantels
and doors had gone, in the middle of the night when

everybody was asleep. Or maybe it would go tonight. Perhaps she could stay awake and watch.

A running shuffle of feet sounded in the street, and Lucinda drew up her knees as far as she could. A voice cried, "Cajy." The feet pounded closer. Single voices darted in and out of the running voices of the pack, calling, "Cajy, you Cajy."

A body flung itself against the tree and shouted, "Where that Cajy go?"

"Shake him down," another cried. The body struck the tree again.

"Ain't seen no Cajy treed," another called.

"Shake him down."

"Ain't no Cajy up."

Feet and voices had gathered on the walk beside the tree. Cold with fright, Lucinda wound her arms around her knees. She had forgotten again about the dark. It had slipped up on her. Bodies and half-grown voices beat against the street wall of the tree. She didn't dare look out. She twisted her aching knees to force them inside the peaked door.

"I seen shadder long like Cajy. Lookee."

"Lookee where?"

"Lookee."

"He ain't up. Lookee off there."

"Man. 'At's him."

The feet made for the corner in a tiptoed run.

Lucinda's head, cautious as a turtle's, came out of the tree. She saw the figures huddled at the corner. They had lost the scent. This was her chance. Her shoulders followed her head but, suddenly, both drew back. Directly over her, a pair of long spectral legs dangled from a limb. The body dropped quietly to the ground and lay in a knot before the door of the tree. After a second a head rose horizontally. The frightened childish eyes met hers.

"I'm coming out," Lucinda said. She wasn't afraid now. "You can hide in here," she said in a loud whisper.

She squirmed out, flattening her legs against the ground. Through the grass she felt the crawling as Cajy's long legs slid by her.

From inside the back porch Lucinda leaned against the lattice wall to watch. Because of what she knew, her eyes were able to see a movement from the length of legs the tree could not contain. With every minute the dark deepened its protection. But now the voices were coming back, belligerent again and yelping in mock imitation of hounds. They made a running attack on the tree. A tall boy swung himself up on the picket fence and reached for a branch. He shook it viciously.

"Better git on out of there or us'll come up," he called.

The boys below echoed him. One by one, they mounted the flimsy fence. They tugged at the lower branches and shouted. The din brought Mittie out of the kitchen in a mumbling rage. Lucinda caught at her skirt.

"Here I am, Mittie," she said. "Listen to those boys. They're after Cajy."

"Shake him out," a voice yelled. The stiff-leafed live oak rattled like a bean bag.

Mittie grabbed the knob and banged the lattice door back and forth to get the boys' attention. Her eyes strained through the dark, trying to see who they were.

"Whachu doin tryin to tear down folks's tree?" she called. "Git down offen our fench, ever lasten one of you. Git."

She reached for the cord to pull on the porch light, but Lucinda caught her arm. "Don't, Mittie," she begged. "They'll see Cajy. Cajy's out there. They'll see him."

The boys were jumping down, taking to their heels. Mittie turned to Lucinda. "Whachu mean, see Cajy?" she asked.

"Down there," Lucinda said. She poi..ted to the tree. There was the sound of a crawling movement along the ground. They couldn't see him, but they could hear him coming. On all fours, Cajy was creeping towards the porch.

"They'll git Cajy," he was whining. "Git Cajy. Git Cajy." He cowered by the steps, keeping the position of an animal.

"No sich," Mittie declared. "Ain't nobody wantin nothin like you. Whachu doin in our yard? Effen you ain't goin where you ain't got no business ain't nobody a-payin you no mind. Whachu doin in our yard?"

"Cajy find Pappy," he moaned. "Cajy go to he Pappy." He stood beside the steps. "Cajy go to he Pappy," he whined.

"No, you don't," Mittie said. Authority rang in her voice. "You go on back where you b'long to be. They ain't a-wantin you over where your pappy is. You go on back to Gander. Your pappy'll git off when he can and come and see you. You know what your pappy say, a-tellin you how they ain't a-wantin you up there. What ud they be a-wantin with you up there?"

"Cajy go to he Pappy," he repeated.

"You go on back and wait," Mittie said. "Some of these days he'll be a-comin home and a-doin for you like he used to be."

She turned to Lucinda, "You go in the kitchen, honey,

and git that pan of cold taters on the shelf and bring them
out to Cajy. Cajy just a leetle hongry. Ain't got he pappy
a-comin home to cook and do for him no more. He ain't
a-meanin to steal. He just a leetle hongry."

Lucinda brought the potatoes. Mittie took them from
her and opened the door. She dropped them, one by one,
into the long-fingered hands.

"Cajy spell," he offered.

"No, you don't never mind about spellin now. You go
on back home, and don't you bother nobody and won't
nobody bother you."

"He just ain't used to doin without his pappy," Mittie
explained to Lucinda as Cajy slunk away. "Since Miz
Reeves got him alltime mindin the picture he can't never
git off to look after Cajy and cook him up victuals like he
used to. Sometime Cajy git hongry and go round the creek
a-beggin and a-stealin tell folks git all wore out with him.
But he ain't a-meanin no harm, and they ain't neither.
They just sick them boys on him to scare him out of stealin
they victuals."

It was the time for making new dresses, and Miss Letha Holt came to help Lucinda's mother. They worked together cutting things out. Then Lucinda's mother did the handwork while Miss Letha ran the machine.

Miss Letha had been tired so long she couldn't stand up straight even when she had time to. She was always in a hurry. She walked, as the moss hung, a little on the slant, her heels trying to catch up with her head. Her neck was goosed from bending over the sewing machine, and when she wanted to look up she had to tilt her head sidewise. That made her head always in the right position for sewing, but when she sat at the machine her eyes were so close to her work she had to take off her glasses. Sometimes when she was in a hurry and used only one hand to take them off the little curved silver arm would catch a lock of black hair and lift it up so that the white hair underneath showed. Lucinda tried to think of ways to make Miss Letha take off her glasses in a hurry.

They worked at the sewing in Lucinda's room because her mother's room was too dark with the shutters closed. When she got home from school Lucinda worked with them, using the scraps to make dresses for Adelaide. Most of the time nobody talked. Miss Letha whirred the machine, and when she had to ask Lucinda's mother about something she crossed over to where she sat and talked so low she almost whispered.

The darkness across the hall made an excitement in Lucinda's room. The shutters of her mother's front window and the two windows on the Mimosa Street side were closed tight, the slats turned down and the shades drawn to the sills. It made the whole upstairs strange. Nobody ever spoke of the darkened room. Every now and then Miss Letha's eye would dart across the room and come back to Mrs. Darby. She would look as if she were about to say something, but if she spoke it was to ask a question about the sewing or to say, "Do tell."

Every day when Lucinda's father came home and went upstairs to get ready for supper there would be a great banging and slamming. Shades would be raised, windows would be flung up, shutters thrown open.

After her father came down again Lucinda would make an excuse to go up so that she could see what had happened. But if she didn't hurry it would be too late. Her mother would go up as soon as he went downstairs and, tipping about with the greatest care, manage to close everything again without making the slightest sound. Neither of them ever spoke of the shutters or the darkness.

Lucinda's father sang and whistled a great deal, and at supper time gave them long accounts of what had happened during the day. Her mother didn't pay much attention. She didn't smile or laugh, no matter how funny he was. Her mother saved most of her talk for Mrs. Graham. Even in the night Lucinda never heard the loud angry talk that used to boil up after silent days.

On Saturday morning Miss Letha came at nine o'clock. Lucinda saw her hurrying up Cass Avenue, leaning more than ever. It was the day for making a slip cover for the living-room sofa.

As soon as Mittie had cleared the breakfast things away the material was laid out on the dining table.

"It ud sure make handsome drapes," Miss Letha said.

"I thought of getting enough for curtains," Lucinda's mother said, "but when we move they'd probably have to be cut off. These windows are longer than most. I think we'll move to a newer house than this, and the newer houses don't have such high windows."

"Oh, you're fixing to move?" Miss Letha asked through a mouthful of pins. "Any time soon?"

"I don't know exactly," Mrs. Darby said. "You'd better watch, Miss Letha—you're not holding that line straight. We don't want to ruin this beautiful linen."

Miss Letha sucked at the pins, gathering them together with her tongue. She took them out of her mouth and stuck them in the little cushion she wore on her shoulder. When she had anything important to say she always got rid of the pins in her mouth.

"I've lived where I live going on forty years," she said. "I don't like to be always moving around. But I guess this neighborhood's not what it was," she added.

"Lucinda," her mother said, "I wish you would go up to your room and see if you can find the yardstick we had there yesterday."

When Lucinda came back with the yardstick her mother was sitting beside Miss Letha at the table, but neither she nor Miss Letha was sewing. They leaned together over the corner of the table and talked in whispers.

Miss Letha was saying: "Miss Tina told me she'd never thought but what he was picking it up to take on home with him. She said she'd been seeing him for goodness knows how long picking it up every day, after every train as soon as it run. After she heard he wasn't ever leaving the place any more she got to watching. And, sure enough, he'd still come sneaking out the back way with his gunny sack soon as the train run. He'd pick up every lump and scrap. Some of the pieces were so little she couldn't see a thing but him reaching over and picking up and putting his hand in the sack. And then she'd see him sneaking right back fast as he could make it, the way he came."

"It's a disgrace," Mrs. Darby said. "I knew it was bad, but it's worse even than I thought."

"Miss Tina says she's all the time missing something, a hen or maybe some eggs out of the nests and, all last summer, vegetables out of the garden. She says all the neighbors along Pine Street have been missing things like that. She says seeing him picking up the coal like that makes them wonder about the things they lose. Maybe it's him taking the other things, too. And not just for him and Cajy." Miss Letha gave her head the sidewise tilt so that she could look at Mrs. Darby.

"Nothing would surprise me," Mrs. Darby said, "after all I've seen."

"Miss Tina says many's the time since they've been so hard up that she's gone up there to call and took along a nice fresh basket of figs or maybe green beans out of her garden. But do you think she ever got in with them? She says sometimes she near about beat the door down, being dead sure they were there. But she never once got in with them. When the shoe was on the other foot, she said, Mrs.

Reeves would drive up to her door and sit there in her carriage while her driver took things in to her. Not once did she darken Miss Tina's door. She'd sit rared back in her carriage while he took them in. That was the way she'd do things for people, sitting back in her white gloves. But now they won't let anybody return a favor. Above that."

"But not above eating what their servant steals in the night," Mrs. Darby said.

"If they'd sell the picture," Miss Letha said, "I guess they'd go right back to their grand ways."

"You can't be very grand on the income of thirty thousand dollars," Mrs. Darby said. "It sounds like a lot of money, but it wouldn't even repair the house and restore the grounds, not to mention furnishing the place again."

"I reckon they see that," Miss Letha said. "I reckon that's why they figure they're grander the way they are, with the portrait there to remind them."

"Isn't Mittie putting us down to supper a little earlier every night?" Lucinda's father said. "Whose house is this, anyway?"

"Straighten your chair, Lucinda," her mother said, "and put both feet under the table."

"Having a revival down on the creek?"

"It's not straight yet, Lucinda. Use both hands. If you would use both hands you would get it straight to begin with."

"What I'm trying to find out is why I have to come home on the run every afternoon to eat my supper in the broad daylight."

"It's nearly six o'clock, Clifford."

"So it is." He took out his watch. "In fourteen minutes it will be six o'clock. It's exactly forty-four minutes until our usual suppertime."

"Butter your biscuit, Lucinda. You are growing so fast now you need lots of butter to make strong bones."

"What I'm trying to find out, Ethel, is the reason for this business of eating in the middle of the afternoon." His voice had gone louder with every word. Lucinda heard the wrench of the chair legs against the rug. He had pushed the chair back so that he could pound on the table. He pounded with both fists. "That's what I'm try-ing to find out," he cried.

"A little later, please, Clifford. This is no time—"

"This is no time for supper, if that's what you mean."

"You know very well what I mean."

The swinging door sang out hoarsely, and Mittie padded around the table with three fierce thrusts of the plate of hot biscuits. Mittie was mad, too.

"What's eating her?" he asked when the door had swung to behind Mittie.

Instead of an answer there was a look. Lucinda felt it crackling over her head.

"Well, speak out. What is it?"

Lucinda's swallowing was the only sound.

"I don't know what you're talking about, Clifford."

"Oh, yes, you do. You know damn well what I'm talk-ing about. I'm damn tired of living in a madhouse." He pushed back the chair again. "Are those shutters closed again?" he cried. He waited and looked. He brought his voice down and said it again very slowly. "Are those shutters closed again? Are they?"

"Clifford, will you please?"

"Are those shutters closed?" he shouted.

He leapt from his chair. He ran out of the room and up the stairs. Lucinda didn't dare look at her mother. Win-dows and shutters banged wildly. He came down, still on the run. From the hall he shouted into the kitchen, "Come to the dining room, Mittie."

He stood behind his chair. "It's well past time for a showdown," he declared.

Mittie came in, dragging her feet and mumbling.

"Lucinda," her mother said, "you may go to your room until we're ready to go on with the meal."

"No, she won't," her father cried. "She'll stay right here. We've got a few things to clear up, and Lucinda's as much concerned as any of us. More, probably." He sat down. "I want to know why those shutters are closed every day. I want to know why I have to leave my office in the middle of the afternoon unless I want to eat cold supper. I want to know why Mittie skulks around the side of the house when she starts home instead of going out Mimosa Street as she always did until a week or so ago. I want to know why Lucinda goes tipping around upstairs as if there were a ghost in the house."

Lucinda didn't know she had been tipping. She counted the beans left on her plate.

"Well, speak up," he said. His voice had come down as if he were less mad now. But he would be mad again if somebody didn't answer.

"Maybe it's the gun," Lucinda said. She could hardly hear her own voice.

"Ain't gonna have no nigger a-shootin at me," Mittie snapped. "Ain't a-catchin me a-hangin round tell dark so's I can't see what's a-goin on."

"So that's it," he cried. He was madder than ever. His hair was waving, and his face was red all over. "That's what you've made of a simple fact, is it, Ethel?"

"You told me yourself, Clifford. You told me they had given him a gun. You don't think I could be indifferent to a thing like that, do you, just because you don't get upset? You're never upset about anything. It's too much trouble. But somebody has to protect Lucinda. Somebody has to look after Mittie. I've seen him myself. I see him every day, peeping through the bushes, down by the fence. You don't think I'm going to let him shoot at us, do you? Not if I—" She broke off, crying. She put her face in both hands and sobbed.

He was up now, walking the floor. Back and forth, he strode. "So that's it," he cried, trying to believe his ears. "So that's it."

"He'd shoot anybody who so much as looked that way," the sobbing voice said. "You've never understood how hard it's always been on me, how that awful place has always got on my nerves. And now with that old man running in and out of the bushes with his gun, peeping through at people—"

Lucinda felt the limpness come into her father. He sat down. She heard him take a deep breath. Then he put out both hands. His right hand felt for Lucinda's hand. He squeezed it hard, as if he would break every bone. Then he held on to it with main strength until she clenched her teeth against the pain. His left hand was patting her mother's hand, trying to pass on to her the sudden calm that had come over him.

"Listen carefully," he said, "all of you. There is nothing to be afraid of over the way." He took a long, slow breath and started again. "I told your mother, Lucinda, about a letter I had from Mrs. Reeves a few weeks ago. But perhaps I didn't make it clear. I'm going to explain very carefully this time, and I want the three of you to listen. I suppose a great many people are saying things now that are not true about Mrs. Reeves and Castleton. You all have been hearing them, and that's why you are confused and frightened. I'm going to tell you just what is true, and then all of you will know there's nothing to be afraid of."

"I'm not afraid of anything," Lucinda said.

"No, of course not. Of course not. But Mittie seems to be. So we'll all get it straight."

Mittie's smoldering eyes turned towards Mrs. Darby, but she was staring at the cold food on her plate.

"Looks as if we've all been getting a little tense," Clifford Darby said. "Let's get it all straight now and keep it straight." He turned to Lucinda, but Lucinda knew he wasn't talking specially to her. "Several weeks ago Mrs. Reeves was offered thirty thousand dollars by a New York firm for that big portrait of theirs. They gave her until August to make up her mind. After the New York man went back he got to worrying about fire or something; so he wrote to Curtis Hardin, and Hardin came to see me about it. We'd talked about it in the winter when Hardin was thinking about taking out insurance on the picture, himself. But I guess he decided not to go into it. This time he got me to write to Mrs. Reeves in my own name and tell her that if the portrait was not insured the Griscom Gallery wanted to take out a policy that would cover it until August. Is all that clear?" he asked. "The reason I'm telling you this," he went on, "is to explain about the letter Mrs. Reeves wrote to me. In that letter she said that the picture is not insured. She said they had never felt that it was necessary because there is always somebody in the house. And she said that lately they have taken to guarding it day and night, that she and her daughter are in the room with it all day and their servant sleeps in the room with it at night, with a gun beside him." He looked from one face to the other. "And that's all there is to it."

"That's all I said," Ethel Darby said.

"Where does Mittie get the idea that the old man would

be shooting at people who are going about their own business? Don't you know, Mittie, that a great many people sleep with pistols or guns in their rooms?"

"I've seen him, myself. I've seen him peeping out," Ethel Darby cried. "Every day I see him. Down on all fours sometimes."

"But have you seen the gun?"

"But, Clifford, she told you, herself, he guards it with a gun."

"Have you seen a gun, Lucinda?"

"I haven't seen *him,*" Lucinda said. "Not for a long time."

"Have you seen the gun, Mittie?"

"I ain't to say seen it."

"What do you mean by that?" he asked. "Have you smelled it? Have you heard it?"

"No, sir, but I been a-seein Abe. He don't ack like hisself. He's out there now a-settin in the fench corner like he was—"

"Out there now?" Clifford Darby sprang to his feet. He sounded frightened himself. Lucinda began to shake.

Her mother said, "That is what—" Her voice stopped. She could not go on.

"I see him a-settin over there most ever day about this time," Mittie said. "Maybe after sundown he'll go to guardin, but he's most always over there along about this time. Most always, here lately."

"That's fine," Clifford Darby said. He was walking up and down again. "That's just fine. We'll go over and pay him a call. Right now, before dark. We'll see for ourselves. We'll have a talk with him. Come along, Lucinda. We'll go and bring back a report."

Lucinda's mother caught at her arm. "You'll do nothing of the kind," she cried. "Go, yourself, if you like. It's high time you took a little interest in what's going on. But you'll not take Lucy."

"Of course I'll take Lucy," he said, still being calm. "I'll take her to the fence so she can see for herself that the old man has no gun."

"Clifford!"

He caught Lucinda's hand and drew her after him. "We have to calm these excitable women," he said. "We're the riot squad, out to see what it's all about. Ready, officer?"

Lucinda managed a weak laugh, but she held tight to his hand. "I see him, now," she said as they started across the street. "I see him now," she repeated, trying to ease her voice.

His head was rising from the tangled bushes in the fence corner where he had been sitting. They heard dead twigs fall apart as he touched them.

"Looking for something?" Clifford Darby called.

"His name's Abe," Lucinda prompted.

He was a little man with white hair. His face was tan, like Cajy's; but rounder and old.

"Lost something, Abe?" he called again.

The old man turned. Lucinda saw that his hands hung empty at his sides.

"Evenin, mister; evenin, missy." He stood, looking vacantly at them.

"Trying to find something?" Clifford Darby asked. He and Lucinda were beside the fence now.

"No, sir," the old man said, "just a-waitin, just kinder waitin round."

"What are you waiting for?" Clifford Darby asked.

"Just a-waitin," he said. "Thinkin maybe I be a-seein Cajy. Maybe Cajy be a-goin by."

"So you're the fellow who taught Cajy to spell?" Lucinda's father asked. He laughed.

"Reckon not," Abe said. "Reckon didn't nobody learn Cajy."

"S'pose you haven't got one of those old guns of Colonel Cass's where you could show it to me?" Lucinda's father said, laughing as he talked. "I've heard a lot about those old Cass guns."

"No, sir, no, sir," the old man said. "It's up at the house." He pointed through the trees. "It's up there."

They were backing off. Lucinda's father said, "If I see Cajy I'll tell him you were looking for him."

"That's right," Abe said, absently. "I'm a-lookin."

"I told you," Lucinda's father said as they walked away. "That's the way it is with most of the things we're afraid of."

"I wasn't afraid," Lucinda said. "I told you I wasn't."

"Of course not. But now you can tell your mother and Mittie that he had no gun except up at the house, that there's nothing to be afraid of. You just stay on your side of the street and don't worry about what goes on across the way."

Mittie was still in the dining room, but Lucinda's mother had left the room.

"We asked Abe," Lucinda said. "He told us the gun was up at the house."

Mittie didn't look up.

"He told us he was looking for Cajy," Lucinda explained, feeling very important as she took over the job of setting Mittie right. "He won't do any harm to people who don't try to take the picture. He's just looking for Cajy."

Mittie crossed the hall to the screen door they had left unhooked. "Well, ain't nobody else a-lookin for Cajy," she said.

"Has she gone upstairs?" Clifford Darby asked, looking at his wife's chair.

Mittie nodded. But before she could speak his question was answered by a cry that split the air, a high, drawn-out cry that sent such a sickness through Lucinda she had to lean against the table. Surely her mother hadn't screamed like that just because she'd found the windows open again. Her father held on to the table, too, for a second. Then he ran out of the room. Lucinda had never heard him go upstairs so fast.

As soon as she came in sight of the house Lucinda knew that something had happened. It looked as if it had covered its face with its hands and drawn back a little from the street. The front door was closed, but that would not have been particularly strange if it had been the only different thing. It was her own windows that were most different. Both of the upper sashes had been lowered halfway—a position Lucinda had never seen before—and the shades had been drawn all the way to the sills.

The front door looked locked. Lucinda considered going around to the back door. She could not face the thought of turning the knob of the front door and finding that it was locked. But it seemed that it would be worse to have somebody see her walking around to the back. Whoever saw her might know there was a reason why she did not go in the front door; might even know what the reason was. She pulled herself together and set a foot on the first step. Each of the three shallow steps swam away, first from one foot, then from the other.

When, finally, she stood on the porch, confronted squarely by the door, she knew the thing had happened to her mother, not just to the house. The memory of last night surged up in her. She'd held it off as long as she could. There was no longer any pretending she had not known ever since last night that something was wrong. Her father had pretended to her, and she had pretended to Mittie. But she had known from the moment of the scream.

All evening, helping Mittie with the dishes and listening to the story of how Conjur Ann was ridden for a horse until she grew hooves on her hands and feet, she had known something was wrong upstairs. She had known it when her father told her to slip in bed like a mouse because her mother was tired and wanted to sleep. She had pretended then that that was all. And all day at school she had pretended there was nothing frightening about having eaten breakfast alone while strange feet scurried about overhead and in the kitchen, making sounds she had never heard before. The look of the front door had put an end to all the pretending.

What if her mother was dead? The fear plummeted through a channel of emptiness that reached from Lucinda's head to her feet. What if it was death that had happened to her mother last night? What if she was lying up there now, dead? What if that was the reason for the look of the house? Somebody who knew that her mother was dead might be looking out a window now, seeing her standing there, afraid to go in. Somebody might go by and see her standing there, acting as if her mother were dead. But her mother was dead. She knew it. The worst thing that could possibly happen had happened. But, so long as she didn't open the front door, there was still hope that it was something else. She flung herself against the door. The knob moved in her hand, turned from the inside.

"Sh!" her father said, and led her into the living room. He looked tired and sad.

"Your mother is sick, Lucinda," he said. "The doctor says it's a nervous breakdown—not a serious one, but she must have complete rest and quiet. There's no room in the hospital, so we must take care of her here. The doctor wants her to sleep as much as possible and, since our room is on the street corner, I thought she could be more quiet in your room. She's in your bed, and the nurse has moved your clothes into your mother's closet. I'll sleep down here on the sofa so I can hear the telephone."

"The nurse?" Lucinda echoed.

"Miss McCarver is here to give her massages and baths and make her comfortable so she'll get well faster. You must be Miss McCarver's assistant and do exactly as she tells you about everything. The doctor thinks you and Mittie and I had better not go into the room for a few days. He'll tell us when he thinks we can see her. I've been sitting here where I could hear people come up on the porch so I could open the door before they ring the bell. As soon as you've been to the bathroom and had your milk, I want you to come here and sit so I can go down to the office for a little while. I've muffled the telephone bell until it hardly sounds. You must keep a sharp ear out for that. Your mother has been losing a lot of sleep, and we want her to make up for lost time."

Lucinda sat midway between the two bells, but nothing happened. Everybody seemed to know they should not be rung. Day after day, it was the same. Sometimes when Lu-

cinda got home from school Mittie would tell her about
the bowl of custard Mrs. Carter had sent, or the basket of
strawberries Flora's mother had brought, or the box of
roses that had come from Mrs. Graham. But nobody ever
came after three o'clock. Lucinda sat between hall and living room, her elbows propped on her knees, her chin in
her hand, listening, waiting. If she had known nothing was
going to happen she could have read, but she was always
listening. Her book lay unopened on the floor beside her.
The sum of her senses was focused in her ears.

She began to know the secrets of the house. The third
step from the top whined whenever Miss McCarver's cautious foot was set upon it. It cried out under Mittie's
clumsy tread. Under Lucinda's foot it only winced, but,
nearly always, Lucinda remembered to step over it. She
wondered why she had never heard it before. Now that she
knew about it, she didn't see how she could ever play the
scale game again, bearing down on it as if it were like all
the other steps. The most important outside sounds came
from the big wisteria vine and the elaeagnus tent over at
Castleton. Even allowing for the difference made by the
new listening, and by the March winds, it seemed strange
that the wisteria could be so important now when it had
been nothing before but the biggest vine anybody had
ever seen, throwing out first one arm and then another,
then a foot and then a tail, like a monkey leaping from
tree to tree. In one place it ran to the top of a pine and
swooped down as steeply as the roof of a wigwam. Then
it rolled in and out of the elaeagnus, making a long tunnel
before it rose again to spread itself in all directions in
canopies and umbrellas that were beginning now to show
blobs of white. Lucinda could tell by the sound whether

the wind was in the tent part or the tunnel part or in the parts that were mostly open. The loud creaking sound was made by the tent straining against the tree ridgepole. The flapping was when the wind went under an open roof and batted it up and down. In the tunnel it wheezed and growled and moaned. The wind in the elaeagnus corner made the silence of the house more still.

It was on a windy day that Lucinda discovered about the clock. Sometimes it talked to things. The first time she noticed it, it was talking to the telephone. The clock had been her grandmother Darby's. Her father had brought it back when he went to Ohio for her grandmother's funeral. It sat on the living-room mantel and struck the hours and half-hours. At half past four it struck with deep resonance, and the long minute hand hitched over to the exact middle of the figure 6. In the next breath the telephone answered back, a high thin *ping*. Lucinda knew she had heard it. There was no question in her mind. She held on to her patience and waited until five o'clock. But when five o'clock came the clock droned out five slow *pungs* and that was all. There wasn't a sound from the telephone. At half past five it was the same. Before six, her father came home.

The next day a remarkable thing happened. At four o'clock when the first *pung* rang out, it was answered with a rich, mellow *pung* that was considerably more audible than the telephone voice had been the day before. *Pung,* the clock said again. And *pung* the low voice answered. Lucinda had not the slightest idea what it was that had spoken. She was sure it was not the telephone. Every piece of furniture, every object in the room, sat perfectly still with downcast eyes and folded hands, determined to give

nothing away. *Pung,* the clock said for the third time, and
the fourth, each time followed by the same soft echo. At
half past four it was just as it had been at four. At five
Lucinda knew she would have her best chance. She saved
all of her listening until then, shut out the creaking of the
vine, held her ears in check. After the first stroke and the
first reply she was as baffled as ever. But the second stroke
had no sooner sounded than Lucinda saw and heard the
answer. Her eyes happened to be fixed on the old pewter
inkwell that stood in a Chinese plate on the table. She
saw the inkwell move. The motion was so slight she would
hardly have known that she saw it if it had not been repeated each of the other times. Each time the clock struck,
the inkwell moved to make its gentle answer.

ONE AFTERNOON Miss McCarver came downstairs and leaned over Lucinda's chair. "It's been two weeks today," she said. "I'd like to try having you go up to see her for a few minutes."

"Right now?" Lucinda asked.

"Yes, now. Run along while I'm talking to Mittie about her supper." Miss McCarver hurried away before there was time to talk about it.

Lucinda pulled herself upstairs by the handrail. She wasn't ready for it yet. She hadn't let herself think about it, the shock of seeing her mother disguised by an illness that kept her in bed in a room that was not her own, that was not anybody's, really, now.

The door that had been shut for two weeks, except as Miss McCarver wormed herself in and out, stood halfway open. The five o'clock light, let in by the two lowered shades, made bright slits in the dark of the floor. Lucinda turned her back so that she would not see them, so that she would be conscious only of the dark. She was thinking what she could say to Miss McCarver. She could say her mother was asleep and she did not want to disturb her. But what if Miss McCarver thought she did not want to go in? What if she thought she did not love her mother? She put a hand on the facing of the door to steady herself and moved into the dark. One by one, the low pink dresser, the chairs and table, came out of the shadows. The next move was for her mother to make. Perhaps she really was asleep. Lucinda forced her eyes past the outline of the bed to the long mound that lay so still in the middle of it. It looked as if it could not possibly move. Lucinda's throat tightened. She clung to the door, suffocated by the silence that had gathered in the room like dust. She could not rally her voice. To make up for its failure, she took a step towards the bed. Then, another, and another, and towered over it. The littleness of her mother, tucked like a child into the narrow pink bed, thrilled through her.

"Mother," she said. Her voice hardly sounded, but the act of speech made her legs as light as air. She ran around the bed and dropped to the floor beside it.

"Lucy," her mother said. She opened her eyes. The fingers of her left hand moved against the sheet. "Where have you been, Lucy?"

"I've just come home from school," Lucinda said.

"You know I've always told you I'd much rather you'd wake me than go off to school without telling me good-bye. It makes the day so long when I don't see you."

"I won't any more," Lucinda said.

"It's been so long since I've seen you," her mother said. "I can't think when I went to bed in your room."

"I can't either," Lucinda said.

"It was a silly thing to go to bed in here," her mother said, "wasn't it?" She almost laughed.

"Not any sillier than for me to go to bed in your room," Lucinda said. She tried to laugh, too.

She heard Miss McCarver coming into the room and realized she had been standing in the hall, listening.

"Don't you think we could have a little ice cream together?" Miss McCarver asked. "It's been a long time since we've had a party around here." She carried a tray that held three dishes of ice cream.

"I really don't care for anything, thank you," Lucinda's mother said. "I don't feel hungry."

Miss McCarver looked at Lucinda.

"If I sit right here on the floor and hold it for you, then couldn't you eat?" Lucinda said.

Miss McCarver beamed approval on her.

"Well, I may be in a baby bed," her mother said, "but I guess surely I can feed myself." She drew herself up, and Miss McCarver piled pillows behind her. "Sit here on the side of the bed," she said to Lucinda, "and tell me about school while we eat our ice cream. Has your father been helping you with the arithmetic while I've been sick?"

"He did last night," Lucinda said.

Miss McCarver's eyes were dancing.

"We'll have to get him to give us a report on Lucinda's arithmetic when he comes home," Miss McCarver said.

"Mother can work the problems faster than anybody, faster than Miss Carley," Lucinda said.

"Maybe I can help you again in a day or two. Maybe not tonight, but pretty soon."

Miss McCarver returned the three empty dishes to the tray. She smoothed the sheet and raised the window shades. Then she leaned over Mrs. Darby's pillows.

"I may as well stay like this a little longer," Mrs. Darby said. "I like changing my position now and then."

FRIDAY NIGHT movies had become a habit. The doctor had said movies and drives and quiet diversions were the only treatment needed now. Tonight's picture was one Lucinda's mother and father thought she would not like. They thought she would rather stay with Betty. But Betty had gone to spend the night with her cousins on the other side of town.

"Why can't I go to Sue's?" Lucinda asked.

That was too far away, they told her. Going to Sue's wasn't like going to Betty's, anyway. She never went to Sue's unless she was definitely invited, the day and hour specified.

They wondered if it would do to let her go to Flora's.

"Please let me go to Flora's," Lucinda begged. "I haven't been to Flora's for such a long time."

Flora had had no time lately for little girls like Betty and Lucinda. Her friends now were boys and girls in High School.

"Go see if Mittie locked the kitchen door," Ethel Darby said.

Lucinda knew this was so they could talk about letting her go to Flora's. They didn't like her to go to Flora's any

more. They thought Flora was too pretty and too old.
They didn't like her because she was still in the Sixth
Grade when she should have been in High School.

Lucinda stayed in the kitchen a little longer than was
necessary, to give them plenty of time.

"Go ahead and telephone Flora," her father said when
she came back into the room. He was laughing. "Ask her
if she'd like you to help her with her Monday lessons," he
called as she gave the operator the number.

"You'll ask Flora no such thing," her mother cried.

But of course Lucinda knew he was joking.

"She says yes, to come on over," Lucinda reported. She
promised to stay right at Flora's house until they got home
from the movie.

Flora's mother and father had gone somewhere. Her
sister, Jean, was playing bridge in the living room. Flora
and Lucinda went upstairs.

"I'm going to try on Jean's new evening dress," Flora
said. "Maybe I can get her to lend it to me sometime.
You can watch while I put it on."

Lucinda sat by while Flora stepped out of her own dress
and slipped Jean's pink chiffon over her head. The shoulders fell into place. Less than an inch of skirt lay on the
floor around Flora's feet. She tightened the belt. It might
have been made for her.

"Isn't it grand!" Flora said. Her finger dragged at the
V of the blouse. She lifted her chest on a long breath.

Lucinda nodded, fascinated.

Flora was walking up and down before the long mirror,
twisting and turning, taking deep breaths, holding on to
the V.

"Jean's got another evening dress," Flora said. "Don't you want to put it on?"

"Oh, yes!" Lucinda said. She had a quick vision of herself, a match for Flora in magnificence.

"It's white and red," Flora said. She lifted a striped dress bag from the closet. "Take it out and put it on."

Lucinda held back. "Will Jean care?" she asked.

"What she doesn't know won't hurt her," Flora said. She pulled at the zipper in the side of the bag. "It's not new like this, anyway."

It was the color Lucinda liked best, red with tiny white flowers scattered over it. She reached for her buttons. She had to see herself in it. She turned her back to hide her thinness from Flora. The red and white satin slithered over her shoulders.

"You do look very nice," Flora said, surprised. "I guess it's because you're tall."

"I must be as tall as Jean," Lucinda said, looking down to see how neatly the skirt cleared the floor.

"Jean's not so very tall. She's really very short to be grown up."

"But I'm as tall as that," Lucinda said. She had looked in the mirror. Her beauty had given her the assurance she needed to defend her height. She pinned her long pigtails around her head.

"Having your braids around your head, like that, makes you look older," Flora said generously, "and shows that you'll probably be pretty when you're grown up."

Lucinda realized that hers was a milder kind of beauty than Flora's; but for the moment, at least, she preferred herself. She wished Flora would go out of the room so she could look in the mirror as long as she liked.

A tapping sound drew their eyes to a door that opened on the sleeping porch.

"What's that?" Lucinda asked.

"Hush," Flora hissed. She held up the skirt and took long strides to the door.

"Hey, Flo," a hoarse whisper called.

"Watch that door," Flora said to Lucinda. She pointed to the hall door.

"Well, blow me down," the deep voice said. It was one of the big boys.

"How about it?" the voice said. "I saw them drive off. How about coming along? I told Hugh and Nip we'd meet them over there."

Flora held the door half shut. "I don't know," she said. "Mother and Dad have gone, but Jean's here. Got some people playing bridge. If they'd go to a movie or somewhere, maybe I could come."

She slid out but didn't close the door. Lucinda could hear their voices whispering, but she couldn't hear their words. She couldn't listen for shaking. This was what Sue meant when she said: "I know things about Flora. She isn't *nice*." This was what the girls at school were thinking about when they looked at Flora and laughed in that frightened way behind her back. It was why the boys cleared their throats at each other when Flora passed where they were standing. The whispers had stopped coming into the room. The silence, pressing against the cracked door, made Lucinda remember what Anna May Thornton had said: "Flora sneaks off in the dark and kisses boys." Maybe that was what she was doing out there now on the dark porch. Lucinda strained her ears to the porch, at the same time closing her mind against the dreadful moment of knowing.

The whispers started again. Lucinda moved farther from the door, slipping her feet along the floor so that nobody could hear. The door opened. The boy's voice came through. "It's the safest place," he said. "It's the best one when I haven't got the car."

"I'll get out of this dress," Flora said. "It won't take a minute." She came back into the room.

"Well, make it snappy," the boy said.

Flora caught Lucinda's wrists. "Swear you'll never tell," she said. "Cross your heart and swear."

Lucinda crossed her heart. "I swear," she said.

"If you'll never tell, you can be the one I have secrets with," Flora promised.

"You never do tell me secrets," Lucinda said. "You say that you will, but you never do." Her voice had begun by being reproachful, but it weakened before she finished. She wanted Flora to tell her who it was, waiting out there on the porch. She wanted to know where they were going. But what if Flora should tell her about the kissing, too? Suddenly, the excitement had gone out of the thought of Flora's secrets.

"I can have a date with Glenn," Flora said, "if you'll walk around and make enough noise for Jean to think we're both here."

Already she was out of the pink dress and skinning on a red sweater. In another minute the porch door closed after her.

Lucinda turned the knob to be sure the door was shut tight. She heard muffled giggles as Flora and Glenn clambered down the outside steps. They were steps **that** had to be watched carefully even in daytime. They were as steep as a ladder and almost as bad for catching feet in their skeleton frame. What if Flora and Glenn should fall? They would go to the ground with crashing noise. The bridge players would rush out to see what had happened. Everybody would know about Flora then. If they fell and were caught Lucinda would be caught, too. Jean would see her in her dress. Jean's friends would see her. They would know that she had taken Jean's dress out of the bag and put it on. And they would know she had helped Flora sneak off. She would be the one who was to blame if Flora fell down the steps and got caught, because Flora could not have gone if she hadn't promised not to tell; if she hadn't agreed to walk around like two people. She hadn't walked any yet. She moved a chair to make a noise and let all her weight go into her feet as she turned from the door.

Then she saw herself in the mirror. She walked slowly towards it, backed away, and slowly approached it again. She was so tall she hardly needed to lift the skirt as she walked. She stopped a minute to listen. An indistinct patter of talk rose from the living room, but not a breath came in from the dark of the porch steps. The room was safely Lucinda's now; the mirror all for her. She took the track of Flora's parade up and down, giving wide play to the swish and swing of the skirt. Her feet remembered the rhythm of the march at school. Her private words for the march were:

> School is out and so are we,
> Me and Sue and Sue and me.
> We'll go off awhile and play
> And come back another day.

But a new set of words was fitting into the measure as she marched:

> I am beautiful and tall,
> I am not so very small.
> I am more like Miss Carley
> And Miss Jean and Emily.

She wished Miss Carley and Miss Emily could see her now, grown up and beautiful in the dress. She stopped before the mirror to drink the beauty in, holding the skirt out to its full width. It was like the skirts in the portrait. It was like the dresses in the portrait, red and white like both of them. She backed off gradually, holding out the skirt. The portrait was there in the mirror before her, and she was a part of it, a part of the red and white. She was in the little chair, her hand warm against the rounded back of the cat. But it was more than being in the portrait. It was being at Castleton with Miss Emily and Mrs. Reeves. It was being at the party when Miss Emily made her debut. Lucinda wasn't marching now. She was dancing. The portrait was there in the mirror. There were the two beautiful women with their surging skirts and jewels, the three tall men, the gold harp, herself in the little chair, painted into the portrait like all the others. She held out her skirt and closed her eyes and danced under the richness of the gold ceilings. From room to room she danced, into the ballroom where the twenty fiddlers played, into the dining room where the cake as big as a washtub sat in the middle of the table, back into the room where the portrait hung. While music flowed around them she danced with Mr. Curtis Hardin, her eyes on the portrait in which she herself sat.

Now THAT Miss McCarver had finished with old Mrs. Hardy she dropped in every day or two. When she was the nurse she had given an air to the house, with the little cap that made her pretty and the neat uniform and the quiet voice. It seemed strange that she should look less dressed up in her best clothes than in the uniform. She looked fat and uncomfortable.

Lucinda hoped Mrs. Brown wouldn't know how often Miss McCarver came to see them, how often they took her with them for drives and to the movies. Miss McCarver had nursed Sue's father for two weeks before he died, but she would never nurse anybody in that house again, she said. Mrs. Brown had treated her like a servant. She'd eaten every single meal from a tray, sitting by herself in the upstairs hall, while Mrs. Brown and Sue ate at the table in the dining room. She'd never been treated like that before or since, she said.

Miss McCarver was much more fun than when she was the nurse. When she came everybody talked and laughed. Lucinda wouldn't have missed a minute of one of her visits. This time Clifford Darby was working on a report that was spread out on the dining table, but Miss McCarver kept calling to him until he finally gave up and came, grumbling, into the living room.

"Why can't you women let a man work in peace?" he complained.

"Miss Mac says you've got a good story for us," Ethel Darby said.

"According to Bud," Miss McCarver threw out.

"Good story?" He didn't know what they were talking about.

"Bud said that meeting today was something," Miss McCarver said. "Sounds like the fur really flew."

"Yes," Clifford Darby said, "it was pretty hot."

"Bud came home just long enough to eat his supper, so I didn't have time to get it all. What I want to know is—"

"Clifford didn't tell me there was anything special about the meeting," Ethel Darby said.

Lucinda wished she hadn't said it in that voice. Miss McCarver would know she thought he didn't tell her things the way he ought to. Lucinda could see Miss McCarver trying to look as if she hadn't really heard what Mrs. Darby said.

"You men!" Miss McCarver moaned. "You make a lot of fun of women for their fights and gossip, but when the Monday Lunch Club puts on a fight it's time to call out the militia."

"Oh, I don't know about that," Clifford Darby said. He was trying to make it seem that it wasn't anything much that he had failed to report. "I reckon I've seen worse fights in my life."

"You've been in the club only a little while," Miss McCarver reminded him. "Just you wait. Bud brings me a tale as good as this every now and then."

Lucinda saw her mother look up quickly to see if he had heard that, if he had taken in what Miss McCarver said about how her brother told her things.

"I must say," Miss McCarver went on, "Sam Lewis is usually mixed up in it. He's got the courage to fight for his stands."

"Or the gall," Clifford Darby said. "But he came up against somebody who could outargue him this time."

"Think so?" Miss McCarver asked. "Bud wasn't so sure. He said Lewis gave him as good as he sent. And all Lewis needs to get going is to strike a snag. He'll show Hardin if he has to leave his business and work at the thing eight hours a day."

"That's just the trouble," Clifford Darby said. "It *is* his business."

"What's it all about, Miss Mac?" Ethel Darby made a point of turning to Miss McCarver, rather than to her husband.

"It was about the club's annual project," Miss McCarver began.

But Clifford Darby was ready to talk now. "You see, Ethel," he said, "the club has one major project each year. Curtis Hardin had one idea, and Lewis had another."

"Lewis wants the club to launch an Azalea Trail," Miss McCarver said, "but Hardin—" She threw up her hands.

"Yes," Clifford Darby said. "Lewis had a mighty fine map of his whole plan. A four-foot map showing where every tree would be, beginning half a mile out on each highway and coming on into town to connect with the streets where there are already azaleas. It showed how new trees would be put in to fill out the gaps on Palmetto and Magnolia and maybe a couple of other streets."

"I can't imagine why Curtis Hardin would oppose an idea like that," Ethel Darby said. "That's just what Macklin needs."

"I wouldn't say Hardin opposed it," Clifford Darby said. "He said he'd be all for such a plan except that he thought if we could do only one big job this year there was something else more important right now."

"Mrs. Graham is always talking about that kind of thing," Ethel Darby said. "She says what Macklin needs is to promote its good points. She says we ought to have some kind of pilgrimage, something that would attract people on the way to Natchez and New Orleans and Mobile. She told the Woman's Club last year she would give twenty-five dollars to start some sort of pilgrimage."

"Lewis spoke of that," Miss McCarver said. "He said he was sure the Woman's Club would go in with the men."

"Of course they would," Ethel Darby said. "We talked about it at the meeting when Mrs. Graham's offer was read. We talked about having an Open House Week at the time when tourists are visiting the larger places. Since there are no gardens here to speak of, the thing to do is to feature houses. Mrs. Brown has the only garden in town worth looking at, but lots of the old houses are interesting."

"Why didn't they go ahead with it?" her husband asked.

"They may yet," she said.

"It was Castleton that got them to arguing, wasn't it?" Miss McCarver asked. She knew she was saying the wrong thing, but she couldn't stop herself. "Somebody said Castleton was the only famous place in town, and people would come here expecting to see it. When they found they couldn't, they'd be sore. Some of the ladies thought it might give the visitors a bad taste in their mouths if they went away disappointed. After all, those places on Magnolia and Palmetto are not any different from the general type all through this section."

"But Mr. Lewis's azalea idea is something different," Ethel Darby said. "I don't see why an artist like Mr. Hardin couldn't cooperate on something like that." She talked in an easy natural voice as if she hadn't paid any attention to what Miss McCarver had said about Castleton. Everybody relaxed.

"Well, if you three women will give me the floor a minute," Clifford Darby said, "maybe I can tell you."

Ethel Darby and Miss McCarver bobbed quick smiles at Lucinda to include her in the audience. The sudden cheerfulness of Clifford Darby's voice had put everybody in a good humor.

"Hardin wasn't necessarily opposed to the azalea idea," Clifford Darby said. "In fact, he didn't say a word about it except that he thought, right now, that would be putting the cart before the horse. He said he knew some of the pilgrimages had been very helpful to the towns that promote them. But he said right now we have an emergency on our hands, and that unless we can undertake both he'd suggest we let the tourist business wait until we can clean up the mess on Gander Creek."

Miss McCarver laughed. "Bud said Lewis jumped straight up and shouted, 'What's so wrong with Gander Creek?'"

"Well, what is wrong?" Ethel Darby asked.

"A good deal, I guess," Clifford Darby said. "For one thing, it's never been taken into the city. It's not exactly a health resort, you know. Without waterworks and sewers—"

"You can't kill a nigger," Miss McCarver broke in. "You never hear of a case of typhoid down there. They thrive on filth."

"What makes you think they thrive on filth?" Clifford Darby cried. His good humor was gone. Lucinda could hear him holding on to his voice. He leaned over, resting his arms on his legs. The lock had fallen over his face.

"Oh, you know how they are," Miss McCarver was saying. "You can't kill them. They grow up like weeds, half a dozen in one room. You know how they are."

"I know they're not property any more," he said. "But what makes you think they thrive on filth—and you a nurse?"

"Well, you know we don't nurse them. They can't go to the hospital."

"I guess that's one reason you don't know how they thrive. Maybe you'd be interested in seeing the figures Hardin had on the death rate down there. I guess they're dying off faster down there than in any spot in the state. And that just about means on the map." He grinned as if to say he hadn't meant to be so cross about it. "You nurses!" he added, and grinned again.

"You know what I meant," Miss McCarver said, not entirely appeased by the grins. "You know, yourself, a nigger can stand ten times what one of us can. That's all I meant."

"Sure I know. We know Miss Mac's heart is in the right place, don't we, Lucinda?" He wanted to be sure Miss McCarver felt all right again.

"What does Mr. Hardin want us to do?" Ethel Darby asked. "Does he think we can take them into our homes?"

"No, only into our town."

"There've been movements before now to take Gander Creek into the town. But they always come up against the tax problem," Miss McCarver said.

"Sure. There are plenty of problems. That was what Hardin was talking about. He says we ought to tackle those problems right now and solve them before we undertake anything else. He says it's not simply a problem of decency or humanity. It's a matter of self-preservation."

"Bud said Lewis answered that by saying that if the town went in for the Azalea Trail we'd soon be prosperous enough to take care of the situation down on the Creek without working a hardship on anybody."

"Yes, and that was when Hardin said the chances are ten to one that before the first azalea blooms we'd have an epidemic down there that would call for an annex to their cemetery and ours, too."

"What was it you said, Mr. Darby? Bud said it was pretty cute."

"I didn't say enough. I just sat there like a damned piker, afraid to cross Sam Lewis."

"But apparently you said something," Ethel Darby said. "What was it?"

"I only said maybe it wouldn't help the town much if some of the tourists missed their way and found themselves down at Gander Creek or Dump Corner instead of on the trail."

Lucinda surprised herself by laughing out loud. Everybody looked at her and laughed, too.

"Bud said Lewis got mean before it was over. Threw Hardin's pictures up to him. Said they prove that it's only the worst side of things down here that interests him, and that it certainly looked as if he was out to give the community a black eye."

"When you think of that picture of his that took the prize in the New York exhibition," Ethel Darby said, "you have to admit he doesn't care what people think about things down here. If he's ever painted anything that's beautiful I don't know what it is. He's always on the other side about everything. Always painting ragged, barefoot cotton pickers and things like that."

"What other kind of cotton pickers are there to paint?" Clifford Darby asked.

"I can see you sided with him," she cried.

They all heard her voice. The subject would have to be changed; but gradually. She mustn't suspect.

"Bud says a committee was appointed to consider the two plans. But he says Lewis will have that trail or bust. Now that he's got the gas concession and the hotel, the next thing he needs is a boost in the tourist business."

"Yeah, I guess so," Clifford Darby agreed. But he was through with the subject. He went back to his papers.

Miss Carley had been running around the room faster than ever. She wasn't particularly in a hurry. It was rather that she was too happy or too excited about something to walk in a commonplace way. She had a new dress, too, and lately she'd been parting her hair in a new way and twisting it into a low roll from ear to ear in a way that made her look like a wide-awake little girl.

The morning had begun with singing twice as long as usual, and they had acted their history lesson instead of answering questions about it. Even arithmetic wasn't so bad, for Miss Carley had taken a little pasteboard room out of the cupboard and was measuring it to show them how to work the hard example.

"Who would like to help me measure another room?" Miss Carley asked.

As half a dozen hands waved in the air the door opened with such gusty suction that the window shades sprang straight out. Crutch Rubbers sailed into the room, blazing with angry authority. Sixth Grade shook in its shoes.

"Will you come to my office at once?" she said, shooting terrifying looks at Miss Carley.

"Of course," Miss Carley said. Her voice was quite calm,

but anybody could see she was scared to death. She always was when anything went wrong. She always thought she was to blame. She always began thinking how she might have kept it from happening.

She wasn't in a hurry now, but she knew what Miss Crutcher meant by "at once." She put the pasteboard room on the desk and took her pocketbook out of the top drawer. Then she half turned to the children. She didn't know whether it would be better to beg them to be quiet while she was gone or simply to trust them. The smile that wavered across her face carried more pleading, perhaps, than faith. She hesitated a second at the door, decided to leave it open, and crossed the hall to the door that was marked "Principal" in stern black letters.

Something was certainly wrong. It had been the darkest of all Crutch Rubbers' black looks. Her face had said it was the worst thing that had ever been wrong at Broad Street School. Worst things usually happened in other rooms. But, whatever it was, Sixth Grade was in it, too, this time.

The good girls and boys felt a little frightened and a little smug, but considerably excited. A drama was about to be staged for their entertainment. They waited with uneasy impatience for the next scene.

As they waited, another mood surged up around them. Troubled conscience was a part of the mood, but, with it, was a swaggering defiance. Fred Cane thrust his hands into his pockets and pursed his lips for whistling. Maybe old Crutch Rubbers had seen him going into the Supply Room, but if she dared accuse him of taking anything he'd show her.

Arch Coffee was remembering something, too. He'd been

sure for a week, now, that nobody had found out about the broken basement window. He hadn't broken it on purpose. He wasn'ᵗ going to let her do anything to him because the old window was broken. Anybody might have done it. He reached over and took a biting nick out of Lee Grady's fat neck. Anybody could see that his record was so clean that he dared this deliberate mischief in the very hour of a showdown. Lee let out a yelp, and the room began to crackle like a fire kindled with fat pine.

Through the open door commotion rolled in from the Seventh Grade. That meant Crutch Rubbers had called for Miss Mitchell, too. Muffled blows battered the separating wall. Wheeler Adams, on long tiptoed strides, went down the aisle and through the door to investigate. A low whoop greeted him. He came back, dusting chalk off his meddlesome nose. But he brought Seventh Grade's idea with him. As he returned down the aisle his hand slid along the blackboard, pushing the half-dozen erasers to the back of the room. From there he sent out a barrage. Immediately every eraser in the room was whirled into action. Choking dust fell whitely and impartially on the heads of just and unjust. Sixth Grade coughed and sneezed and giggled.

A tapping step crossed the hall, and the Seventh Grade door closed sharply. Miss Mitchell had gone back into the room. Sixth Grade subsided and waited. Five, ten, fifteen minutes passed. The erasers sailed across the room again. Spelling time had passed, and English time was almost gone. Miss Carley had never stayed out of the room so long.

James Givens popped up and rapped on his desk. "Very well, class, school is dismissed," he chirped in a high falsetto that set everybody to laughing.

Even the best little girls had to stuff handkerchiefs or fists into their mouths. Miss Carley could not have found a worse time to come back. She stood at the door, searching the forty-four faces for a single exception to the disorderly behavior. Not one head was bent studiously over a book. Not one pair of eyes met hers with unselfconscious light.

But everybody saw the sadness and redness of her eyes. She was too sad to reprove them for their faithlessness. Her look said what did it matter, anyway, when something so much worse had happened, something that had kept her for nearly an hour in Crutch Rubbers' office, something that had made her cry until her eyes were red.

She was sitting behind the desk now, holding a book in her hands. She had taken the book out of a row that stood on the desk. She had opened it just anywhere and was looking at it, but she was not reading. Every few minutes she blew her nose. There was no other sound in the room. Every now and then an eye looked up to see what she was doing now. But she wasn't doing anything. She only sat there. She didn't even turn a page. Everybody in Sixth Grade knew you could put up a better bluff by turning a page occasionally.

The door opened with another explosive crash, and there stood Crutch Rubbers again. This time her wrath was certainly directed at Miss Carley.

"Did you," she barked, "tell—"

"Not yet," Miss Carley said, rising and holding on to the desk. "In a minute I—"

Crutch Rubbers flung her look from Miss Carley to the south side of the room.

"Flora Denton," she said with searing command, "you

are to gather up all of your belongings and report to my office at once."

Her look said it again. Then her voice, louder and madder, repeated, "At once."

Flora had started with a shock that sent vibrations into every backbone in the room. Under Crutch Rubbers' eyes she fumbled in her desk. As she walked down the aisle and across the front of the room to the door her beautiful head, aureoled with curls, shook like the head of the green mandarin on Mrs. Brown's library table. Crutch Rubbers stood with her nose in the air and her hand on the knob until Flora's wobbly high heels had clicked into the hall. Then she hurled the look at Miss Carley again and charged after Flora.

"You'll never guess who I ran into, coming out of church," Lucinda's father said.

He had stayed only an hour with the organ. Now they were driving along the highway that followed Marsh Creek, sandwiched in at twenty miles an hour in the aimless Sunday procession.

"No, I suppose not," Ethel Darby said. "Who?"

He raised his voice for Lucinda, alone on the back seat. "Who'd you rather run into on Sunday afternoon at the corner of Cass and Magnolia than anybody?"

"Sue?"

"No, not Sue."

Lucinda thought about it. "Miss Carley?"

"Of course."

"She was pretty far from home," Ethel Darby said, "not to have a car."

"Pretty far. She was passing the church as I came out, and asked me which house was the Dentons'."

"Oh," Ethel Darby gasped.

"So I told her if she'd hop in my car I'd put her out at the Dentons' door."

"She was walking all the way from her house?"

"Guess so. She'd heard the organ, she said, as she crossed the Square; and she said some pretty nice things about it."

Lucinda leaned forward.

"I told her that I didn't really know anything about it, and that I'd always wanted to take lessons."

"Clifford!"

"Well, why not? You can say things like that to her. And I'm mighty glad I did. She told me about a man who may be here this summer, that maybe I can study with."

"But you'd have to begin at the very beginning. You can't even read."

Lucinda watched the red wash her father's cheek and spread into his neck.

"I know all about that, Ethel, but maybe I could learn."

"Who is the man?"

"His name's Ellis, Carl Ellis. He and Hardin have been friends ever since their student days in Paris. Hardin wants to get him out of New York, says the place is overcrowded with fine musicians. He's persuaded him to come down here for the summer and do a sort of circuit-riding job for this section."

"He surely doesn't think a man who's lived in Paris and New York could stand a place like this. If Mr. Hardin thinks this is such a fine place to live, why does he stay away half the time?"

"Looks like he's going to stay here more, now. He couldn't work here when his father and uncle were alive, always fighting his painting and trying to get him into that cutthroat business. He's built a studio on the second floor of the old house. I guess he's ready to settle down here, now. Miss Carley seems to think Ellis will like it here, too. She says once he gets the idea of the possibilities

he'll never want to leave. She says there's not even a third-
or fourth-rate pianist or teacher in a hundred-mile radius.
She thinks he'll find lots of talent. He's going to live at
Hardin's house if he comes. His wife has a job in a book-
store in New York so she can't come."

"Well, don't get your hopes up," Ethel Darby said.

The red had stopped running around his face, but little
cords of muscles were flickering along the line of his jaw
and standing in broken columns between the flesh and
skin of his neck.

"Shall we go see how the new houses are coming along?"
he asked, and turned the car towards Shadyside.

"You can breathe here," Ethel Darby said as they headed
into Rainbow Drive, "and you can see out."

"Shadyside's a funny name," Lucinda said, "when
there're not any trees."

"But there are trees," her mother said, "and they're the
kind that grow fast. What do you think about naming a
street Mimosa when there's not a mimosa tree anywhere
in sight?"

"There used to be," Lucinda said. "Mittie said they
used to be all up and down. You could smell them before
you'd see them."

"Used to be," her mother echoed. "I've had enough of
things that used to be. And of the smell of them."

Lucinda knew she had said the wrong thing. It would be
her fault if her mother got upset now.

"I forgot to tell you, Lucinda," she said, laying her arm
along the back of the seat and turning until she found
Lucinda's eyes, "what Mrs. Harris said this morning at
church. She said Mrs. Brown's taking Sue out of school.
Has Sue told you?"

"No," Lucinda said. She hardly heard what her mother had said. She was too busy thinking how fine it was that she was not upset.

"I suppose if you had gone up there yesterday Sue would have told you. Maybe that's why they went to New Orleans. Maybe she's going to put her in school there. Mrs. Harris was wondering why the rest of us are willing to leave our children in a school that's not good enough for Sue."

"She does a lot of wondering," Lucinda's father said.

"She heard a lot of children were expelled Friday but she hadn't heard why. I don't suppose Sue has been up to mischief, has she? She wasn't expelled, was she, Lucinda?"

"Oh, no," Lucinda cried, shocked at the idea.

"Did you know some of the children had been expelled?" her mother asked.

"I think it's mostly in High School," Lucinda said. "Betty told me there were just two in the Seventh Grade."

"Why didn't you tell us?" her mother asked. "You should tell us when such serious things happen at school."

"Any in the Sixth Grade?" her father asked before she had thought how to answer her mother's question.

"Yes," her mother said, "any in the Sixth Grade?"

"One," Lucinda said.

"Who was it?" her mother asked. "And what for?" Before Lucinda could answer she repeated, "Who was it, Lucinda, and what was it for?"

"Flora," Lucinda said.

"Flora," they said to each other. "Flora."

"I've never liked Flora," Lucinda's mother began. "It's exactly what—"

"Mrs. Brown is sadly mistaken if she thinks she can

always pick up Sue and run away from ugly things," Clifford Darby said.

"I've never liked Flora Denton," Ethel Darby said, "and I'm sorry we ever let you play with her, Lucinda. You must never under any circumstances go to her house again or ask her to come to yours. She's entirely too old for you."

"I wouldn't leap to conclusions, Ethel," Lucinda's father said.

"Whatever it is," her mother said, "she's no fit companion for Lucy."

Lucinda was relieved to see that they were not going to ask any more questions. She didn't want to have to tell them what Betty had told her. Betty had told her that one night a policeman had caught Flora and Sadie McClain and two boys hiding behind the big vine at Castleton.

"Did the policeman think they were going to steal the portrait?" Lucinda had asked her. But Betty didn't know. She had stood shaking her head back and forth, saying she didn't think it was that. But she didn't know what it was. She was frightened, and she couldn't talk for crying. She said her mother wouldn't let her go to see Flora. Nobody had seen Flora since she walked out of the Sixth Grade in front of Miss Crutcher.

"Those poor Dentons," Ethel Darby said. "My heart aches for them."

SIXTH GRADE bulged with mothers and flowers. Some of the small, thin mothers sat in desks with the children. Others sat in chairs that had been placed in side aisles and across the back of the room. Vases, pitchers, fruit jars, and buckets, crammed with flowers, stood in a line along the window sills. Miss Carley's books had to be stacked on the floor to make room on her desk for sweet peas, spice pinks, and nasturtiums. A scrub bucket, crowded with lilies, stood on the floor beside the desk. Near the door another scrub bucket held magnolia blossoms almost as big as the heads of the children.

Not a breath of the fragrance of the flowers moved outward through the windows. Instead, the steaming heat that pushed into the room bound the fragrances together and distilled an essence so dripping-sweet that mothers and children, floor and desks and walls were saturated with it.

At last the play was finished. Nobody had come in at the wrong time. Nobody had forgotten his lines. The trouble was that everything had been buried under the hot smells. Neither actors nor audience had cared what happened to the fairy princess or anybody else.

But Miss Carley had a special look as she came from

behind her desk. "The next number on our program," she said, "is the singing of the Marseillaise." Her voice was low, but it made everybody listen. It cut through the drowsy pall of flowers. She moved to the piano where Betty was waiting. "Betty and I are going to give you a duet accompaniment," she said, "and Mrs. Saunders will lead you in singing the song of the brave French people." She waited a minute. "A few hours ago," she said, "King Leopold surrendered to the Nazis. The Belgian soldiers have turned their backs on the French army. The hearts of the French are baffled and torn, but they have risen with new courage to defend their beloved land. The song we are going to sing is in their hearts today as they march against the invaders, offering their lives for their country. We'll play it through once before you sing."

She sat beside Betty on the piano bench, and their four hands cried out,

> Ye sons of France, awake to glory!
> Hark! hark! what myriads bid you rise!
> Your children, wives, and grandsires hoary . . .

The hands slowed down, then leapt forward with such soaring volume that it was as if strings and brasses had been added to the piano.

> To arms! to arms! ye brave! [the piano cried]
> The avenging sword unsheathe!
> March on! march on! all hearts resolved
> On victory or death!

Miss Carley turned to the room. "Mrs. Saunders," she said, "won't you sing it in French? I wish you would sing the French as the children sing the English words."

Mrs. Saunders nodded, and Miss Carley turned back to the piano.

"Marchons, marchons! Qu'un sang impur abreuve nos sillons!" Mrs. Saunders' high quivery soprano sang while the children's voices rang in parallel translation, "March on! march on! all hearts resolved," the French and the English moving side by side.

Miss Carley left the piano and came to stand beside Hilda's desk. "After our closing song we hope our guests will stay and look at our maps and drawing books and other samples of our work. But, before we sing, I have a very important message for the Sixth Grade."

Mrs. Potter and Mrs. Sill sat at the desk that had been Sue's. They whispered to each other whenever there was a lull. Mrs. Sill said: "She's sometimy, isn't she? Nearly always I'd say she's plain, but sometimes—"

"I know what you mean," Mrs. Potter buzzed. "This is one of her good days. You'd never dream she was nearly forty."

"How many of you have ever painted a picture?" Miss Carley asked. Her eyes swept the room.

There was a shifting of feet here and there. Lucinda could see from Miss Carley's face that no hands were raised. Lucinda's left hand held on to her right to keep it from going up. You woudn't call it painting pictures when you had nothing but a play-set of water colors from the five-and-ten-cent store. Lucinda was sure that would not count. It was the other kind of painting that made the hand want to go up.

It was the painting she felt herself doing sometimes when she didn't have even a play-set brush in her hand.

She would be thinking of Castleton or the picture, and all of a sudden she would be painting the picture, herself. She would feel her arms stretching up and swinging out into space, sweeping the air with the red of one billowing skirt, the white of the other. She would feel her hand shaping chairs of red and gold, shaping the gold harp and the men and women, setting the round ball of the cat beside the little chair, a quick pointing for an ear and a swerving curl for a tail. The painter stayed at Castleton nearly two years, people said, while he painted the portrait. But often Lucinda painted it before she went to sleep at night.

"Not anybody?" Miss Carley said.

Left hand held hard to right.

"I wonder how many of you would like to paint a picture this summer?"

Lucinda's hand shot up.

"There's one," Miss Carley said. Lucinda didn't dare look at Miss Carley, but she could feel the smiling in her voice as she counted slowly, "And two-oo, three-ee, fo-ur," drawing it out to coax the uncertain ones along. She waited a minute. "And now music. Not just taking piano lessons, but learning about the music that can come out of the piano and violin and other instruments; singing, too, and listening to records and making up tunes of your own to play or sing. How many of you would like to be in that kind of music class this summer?"

More hands went up this time. And all at once. They had learned from the painters not to be timid.

"Seven," Miss Carley cried. "That's grand. And probably there'll soon be more of you feeling the same way about both the painting and the music."

She would paint the cat first, Lucinda thought: a gray and white one curled up beside a little chair.

". . . a free school," Miss Carley was saying, "with Mr. Hardin himself teaching the painting and his friend, Mr. Carl Ellis from New York, teaching the music."

*Mr. Hardin himself.* Mr. Hardin of the pianos, the painter of the picture that won the prize. Mr. Hardin himself teaching the painting, showing her how to paint a cat that was gray and white like a real one.

"So Mr. Hardin has asked the Board of Education for the use of one of our school buildings for the three summer months," Miss Carley was saying. "As soon as he knows which building we may have, the time and place for the classes will be announced. In the meantime some of you may want to talk to me and to your parents about joining the classes."

People had begun talking to each other all over the room, mostly mothers talking in whispers, but three or four mothers were asking Miss Carley questions. Miss Carley tried to sort them out and take each in her turn, just as she had to do every day with the children.

"Maybe they won't find any great talent," she was saying, "but what of it? It's the children's right. In working sincerely at an art one is concerned with the essence of goodness. We owe our children a chance at this kind of experience. Some of them won't want it. But others, whether they realized it or not, have been wanting it. Some of them have been needing it. I only wish there were somebody to teach the other arts, too, and gardening and some of the crafts."

Mrs. Dodd couldn't wait for Miss Carley to get to her. She'd tried twice to break into the talk. Now she was getting to her feet. As she stood up, the room went quiet as suddenly as a snapped-off radio.

"Nobody can be more interested in this idea than I am," she said, " but I wonder if this tragic summer of 1940 is the time for Macklin to set up a school of this sort."

"I think, Mrs. Dodd," Miss Carley said, "that this tragic summer is exactly the right time for a school of this sort—"

Mrs. Porter and Mrs. Sill turned to each other and smiled. Cator, seeing Miss Carley had a mind for nothing but what she was saying, punched Lucinda in the back. "Slip it to James," he whispered. A folded note, marked *Jas.*, came through the crack. Lucinda fixed her eyes on Miss Carley to watch for a safe minute for passing the note across the aisle.

Something had happened to Miss Carley. Sixth Grade had never seen her like this. Either she was going to manage it this time or she was going to give way altogether right there in the middle of what she was saying. There was no cautious backing away towards the protection of her desk. Her tension spread over the room. Nobody moved or breathed. The note lay on the seat beside Lucinda, forgotten even by Cator. Every child was watching with all his might to see if Miss Carley would be able to hold on.

"We've made only a beginning at what we'll have to do for our own defense, not to mention what we must do to help the British defend the rights of free nations and free souls. We're hearing a lot of talk lately about how much too soft we are. It's true that we need more stamina and harder bodies. But we also need sharper sensibilities and deeper insight so that we can see past the material threat to nations and property into the moral threat to the human soul. The philosophy of Hitler is more deadly than his armies. It travels faster, too."

She was safe now. Her voice was strong and steady. Her eyes were dry. She was making everybody keep still, making everybody hear every word she said.

"Hitler's boast is that in Nazi Germany a youth will grow up that will make all the rest of the world shrink back, a violently active, dominating, intrepid, brutal youth. Even if we wanted to, there would be no use in trying to match that plan. We hate bullies. There's nothing for us but to move in exactly the opposite direction. We must teach our children to care more about the differences between things that are right and wrong and ugly and beautiful. While we're making them strong in mind and hard in body and building guns to protect them, we must think more than we've been thinking of their spirits. We must look to a generation whose hearts will dare to be gentle, to a democracy that is really a brotherhood of Christians. The arts feed the spirit. And they're its voice. That's why we need their leavening qualities now more than we've ever needed them. Our schools must recognize this and give them an equal chance with the sciences. In a world where hearts have grown hard and cold enough to pave the way for Hitler's brutal philosophy we are learning how desperately we need to draw on every resource God has given us for lifting spirits and warming hearts. When we have the courage to take a bolder stand for the development of these resources we'll find that our social and political reforms have sprung from an impetus that goes deep enough to be powerful."

Applause rippled across the room. Miss Carley backed away from Hilda's desk.

"I'll probably be able to tell you in a day or two which building will be used for the classes," she said, "but if we don't know before school closes on Friday you can watch the *Sentinel* for the announcement." She was standing by the piano. "Now if Betty will come back to the piano," she said, "we'll sing our own 'America' and that will close the last Visitors Day for this Sixth Grade, which is just about the most precious of all the Sixth Grades I have taught in this room."

"I think it's fifteen," one of the whisperers in front of Lucinda said.

"And probably as many as five hundred children," the other groaned.

As they drove home together Lucinda's mother said to her, "I suppose this Mr. Ellis is the musician your father wants to study with."

"I guess he is," Lucinda said.

"Do you think you would like Mr. Ellis' classes?"

"Maybe," Lucinda said. The word palpitated as if it had been spoken by an accordion. She waited a minute. It was better to have it over now while they were sitting side by side and didn't have to look at each other. "But I think I'd rather be in Mr. Hardin's class," she added.

"I doubt if you have enough talent for painting," her mother said, "and there's nothing much you can do with pictures after they're painted. You sing such a lot around the house. You probably have a talent for music. You seem to like music."

"I like painting, too," Lucinda said.

"You don't really know about that, Lucinda. You don't really know what painting is. If you think coloring those little pictures in your workbook—"

"My drawing book always gets A," Lucinda said.

"That's a different matter. I expect half the children in your grade could say that. Your father's always talking about buying a piano. Don't you think it would make him happy for you to go into the music class?"

"He's the one that wants to take music lessons," Lucinda said.

As Lucinda got out of the car after her last day at Sue's, Mrs. Brown said, "You must keep a good eye on Castleton for me, Lucinda."

Lucinda knew she didn't really mean anything by that, but the words rang in her ears as she went into the house. The dreaded hurt of the good-bye to Sue was forgotten in the new closeness suggested by the carelessly spoken words. She dallied on the steps to let the good eye wander across the way. If Miss Emily should come walking down the avenue now, she would wave to her. Remembering Mrs. Brown's words, she wanted to wave, anyway. But if Miss Emily were there she would surely wave back. And then Lucinda would run over to the gates and they would talk. After that it would be so easy for things to happen. They would walk up the avenue together, and when they got to the house Miss Emily would ask her to come in, and—

"Lucy," her mother called, "why don't you come on back to the porch? Your father fixed some lemonade for you. It's getting hot."

They were talking hard and kept right on as she leaned over to kiss them.

"Scott Hughes said the meeting started at ten o'clock and went straight through to three. He said the whole trouble went back to that day at the club when **Hardin** bucked Lewis about the Azalea Trail."

"Maybe Hardin wouldn't have fought the Azalea **Trail** if he had known Lewis was on the Board," Ethel **Darby** said.

"The hell he wouldn't. What did that have to do with it? You don't know Hardin."

They were talking about Mr. Hardin. The new thinking about herself and Castleton and becoming Miss Emily's friend made a feeling of closeness between herself and Mr. Hardin, too. Maybe he would know when she went to the painting class that she was Miss Emily's nearest neighbor. Maybe he would know about Mrs. Brown's asking her to keep a good eye on the place. Mrs. Brown and Mr. Hardin and herself were bound together as the friends of Miss Emily. She would have a special place in the painting class—

"Mrs. Carter said the meeting didn't even stop for lunch. They sent over to the Elite for sandwiches and coffee and went right on with it."

"Of all the nerve for a set of men to take out their spite like that—"

"Well, you know Mrs. Graham always said he isn't a very good painter. The day before she left she told me she had written to the other trustees of her museum. She heard they were about to buy one of his pictures. She said she told them they would be making a mistake. It was a picture called 'Fat of the Land' the trustees were considering. She said it was nothing but a lot of dirty Negroes eating out of a garbage can. She told them things down here are not like that at all. All his pictures give the wrong ideas about things down here."

"Don't quote that fool woman to me any more, Ethel. I don't care what she said. I guess she was quoted plenty in the meeting. Lewis had a gem from the old lady to illustrate all his points. He'd tell them Hardin wouldn't teach the children right, anyway, and then he'd say what Mrs. Graham said about painters and how she ought to know since she was a trustee of a museum."

Lucinda was almost sure they were talking about the painting class, but it was too mixed up with other things. She waited for a chance to ask if they knew when the school would begin. But her father was too excited to stop talking. His voice was getting faster and louder as it always did when he was angry about something.

"What does that fool woman know about pictures?" he shouted.

"She knows a lot," her mother said. She held her voice down to remind him not to talk so loud. "She's given thousands of dollars' worth of pictures to their museum. When Ralph first wrote me about her he told me what a great patron of art she is. She's been to Europe eleven times, and she always went to the galleries and museums everywhere. She said she felt it her duty to keep her museum from buying a picture that gives such a false idea about things down here. She said people who saw it wouldn't realize that the Negroes want to go barefoot down here because it's so warm, and that if they eat out of garbage cans it's because they are too lazy to make a garden. She said that 'Fat of the Land' picture is a libel, just as all of his pictures of the South are."

"I could give her a few addresses," Clifford Darby began, leaping in again before Lucinda's slow tongue could get going.

But her mother stopped him. "Judy Means said the Board had plenty of reasons why they didn't want him to use the buildings. One was the nudes."

That made him madder than ever. "Good heavens! Don't tell me they thought he was planning to set up a life class for the children."

"I guess not that," her mother said. "They talked about how many nudes he's painted, and somebody said no man who sat in a studio painting naked women was a fit teacher for innocent children."

"For God's sake, Ethel!" He jumped up and began charging up and down the porch.

"I'm only telling you what they said."

"Well, don't tell me any more such tripe. I don't want to hear it. I suppose Judy didn't tell you what Dr. Frazier said?"

"About religion? She said it was sacrilegious. He said religion and art come from the same source. He was the only man on the Board who tried to talk them into lending a building. It's the first time, Judy said, he ever opened his mouth in a meeting of the Board, so naturally they didn't pay much attention to him."

Lucinda gave up. Her thoughts went back to what Mrs. Brown had said. It moved across her memory, word for word, tone for tone; but nothing happened. She went through the whole experience of getting out of the car and lingering at the steps while her eyes turned towards Castleton. But it was not the same. She could not feel how it would be with Miss Emily walking down the avenue, herself waving and running across the street to walk up the avenue and into the house. In all the months Miss Emily never had walked down the avenue. She wouldn't now. She would always stay up there behind the trees. Lucinda would never see her or the house or the picture. She knew it now. It didn't matter whether the picture went or stayed; she would never see it. It was the way Mrs. Brown had talked about keeping a good eye on Castleton that had set her to thinking about being Miss Emily's friend. It had made the feeling that they were all friends together. But they were not, and there wasn't any way for them to begin to be. She heard her father's words again, forced by his anger through the insulation of her daydreaming.

"Frazier's the one man on the Board who's not a crook or a politician or a nitwit, but he spends all his time in the clouds. He shuts his eyes and spouts high-flown notions without trying to do anything about them. He can't even put them into words people will understand. What burns me up is that nobody, not even Frazier, reminded them that the school buildings don't belong to them. I'd like to rub every one of their noses in the inscription on the cornerstone of the Roseland school. Do you know what it says? *Macklin's Gift to the Children.* And the children locked out now. If they don't look out Lewis' next project will be putting up filling stations in the school grounds."

"Eva Carley will be upset, I expect," Ethel Darby said.

*The children locked out now. The children locked out.*

"If we had realized in time the lengths Lewis would go to, maybe we could have brought pressure," Clifford Darby said. "But who could imagine anybody—"

"Don't forget, Clifford, there are plenty of people on his side."

"Of course there are. And all lined up ready to fight. It's the same thing we're seeing all over the world today.

Too many of us who see the right are too damned indifferent or lazy or selfish to do anything about it. And now the devils have the upper hand. If we'd been working as hard for what's right as they have for what's—"

In a minute, Lucinda knew, her mother and father would notice and ask her what was the matter. If she went too fast they would surely know something was wrong. They would call her back and ask her questions. She sneaked her feet into position. Her eyes measured the distance to the door. She held her breath and made it in three steps. By pushing down on the screen door she kept it from squeaking. She got inside just in time.

"If you're going upstairs, Lucy," her mother called, "you'd better wash your hands before you come down. It's almost time for supper."

# THREE

JUST ANY Saturday was better than the first two days of summer vacation had been. As soon as school was out on Friday, Betty had left to spend a month with her grandmother. Flora didn't count any more now than Sue, who, everybody said, was gone for good. Lucinda settled herself on the front steps to watch for her father's car. When she saw it coming up the street she would run out to meet it so that she could drive around to the garage. Sometimes her father sat in the garage to listen to the news from the car radio. Lucinda liked the coziness of sitting beside him in the car in the half-dark garage. Sometimes he would squeeze her hand if the radio said things that were very bad.

He listened to the radio in the garage because Lucinda's mother didn't like to hear the war news. She said it made her hot to hear it. She asked what was the use in being disturbed over the terrible things that were happening in Europe when there was nothing to do about them.

It was when she said things like that that he forgot about not exciting her. He would talk loud and beat the table with his fist as he used to do before she was sick. It was when she said there was nothing to do about things that he was most likely to forget. He would say, "There are plenty of things we can do." And he would talk about taking our heads out of the sand.

Last night both of them had been excited. He had sat in the garage a long time after he got home in the afternoon, but that hadn't kept him from turning on the radio in the living room as soon as supper was over. Lucinda had seen her mother waiting for her chance. When he seemed to be reading the paper she thought he wouldn't notice. She reached out and snapped it off. But it was the paper he hadn't been paying attention to. Lucinda had known that.

"My God, Ethel," he cried, "do you know what's happening? Do you know the Nazis are bombing Paris? Can you sit here with cotton in your ears while that is happening?"

"Well, what are you going to do about it?" she asked. The way her voice sounded made him remember. Lucinda could tell by the cords in his neck that he was remembering. But he had to say one more thing.

"It's our world as much as if it were the Carters' house," he said. But he didn't sound mad this time. He got up as he said it and left the room. Lucinda knew where he was going, but she didn't dare follow him. A minute later she heard the sound coming in from the garage. Her mother heard it too, but they couldn't hear the radio words. They sat with their eyes on their books as if there had been nothing to hear.

All day a threatening staccato from the Carter and Denton radios had beat on the heat-padded air around Lucinda's house. All day she had waited for her father to come home and make the connecting link with the something that was happening somewhere and knocking at the emptiness of Macklin. But he didn't come. Cass Avenue looked as if there would never again be a car moving along the burning, dusty pavement under the weighted branches and dry-curled leaves of the water oaks.

Lucinda looked to see if Abe was down by the fence, but he was not in sight. He hadn't been coming of late. It had been more than a week since Lucinda had seen him looking over the fence to see if Cajy was coming to talk to him.

The trees were meshed together now by the summer growth of shrubs and vines. Elaeagnus, wisteria, jasmine, smilax, and honeysuckle wove in and out, up and down, throttling limbs and branches, making the screen into a wall as impenetrable as bronze. Nowhere was there a keyhole for the eye. No matter how long one looked or waited, there was never a movement. The moss hung in grizzled cylinders against the motionless air, as fixed as the sturdiest tree. Even the elaeagnus corner was silent. Nothing less than a cyclone could get a word out of the elaeagnus corner now.

Every day people said, "It hasn't rained a drop since March." And when they said it they pulled their lips into the shape they made when they talked about Hitler.

Lucinda's father talked about the drouth, but it was the heat that bothered her mother. "Another day without a sign of a breeze," she would say. And a tightness would pucker Lucinda as if she were to blame.

Sometimes in the hot days you would think a breeze had come. You would hear a stiff rattling that made your eyes run to the magnolia tree, but as soon as you looked it would stop stock-still. Or you would hear a whisper in the pines and listen again. But that would be all—only a single word, one secret movement of long pliant fingers pressing against each other, and, immediately, they were prickly bristles again, piercing the solid sun.

As she sat on the steps Lucinda felt herself being absorbed by silence and emptiness and heat. Her bones were giving in to it. She was a part of the boards she sat upon, the post she leaned against. A mosquito settled on her bare leg. Her eyes knew it was there, but her hands could not exert themselves. She watched the red welt rise without feeling the sting.

The familiar cackle of Judge Redd's voice broke the silence, and she craned her neck lazily to see if he was in sight. When Judge Redd started home you knew it almost as soon as he left the Square. He was so deaf he had to scream to hear himself. He had something to say to everybody he met and to everybody he saw sitting on the Cass Avenue porches. Some of them didn't want to go to the trouble of shouting back to him; but they usually got the worst of it in the end, for the Judge would hang on until he figured out what it was they'd tried—or hadn't tried—to say.

Nobody knew why they called the old man Judge. Nobody could remember when he had ever done anything but hang around the Court House, visiting from office to office, spitting tobacco juice into one little fireplace after another or playing checkers under the water oaks in the Court House yard.

The Judge had spotted Mrs. Carter and Miss Winnie. They were bringing the little radio, sputtering in Miss Winnie's hand, out to the porch. They pulled up rocking chairs, and Mrs. Carter opened a paper fan. She rocked and fanned, fanning twice as fast as she rocked. Miss Winnie bent over the radio as she placed it on a small table.

"Reckon you carry that contraption ever'where you go?" the Judge called.

Miss Winnie shook her head, turned it as far as she could to right and left to tell him she was trying to listen to something.

"Trying to get the war news?" he shouted to Mrs. Carter.

"Trying to find out about Dunkerque," Mrs. Carter said, but she didn't really try to make him hear.

"Well, you can just keep your war news," he yelled. "Keep it all. If you want to know what I think, I'd say let 'em all go. Drop the French and British before they back down on you the way those Belgians did. We got all we can do here at home without puttering around, trying to pull Europe's chestnuts out of the fire."

He didn't hear the radio voice saying, "And at Dunkerque we saw the miracle by which the spirit conquers where the body, in all reason, could only fail."

"What I say," the Judge went on, "is all we need to do is tighten up on the Monroe Doctrine and put Jack Garner in the White House." He pushed his browned straw hat to the back of his head and stood waiting for them to turn from the radio.

Miss Winnie half turned. "That's right, General, you tell them," she sneered. "You've got the answers. But you'd better look out, or you'll miss the bus."

"What's that?" the Judge yelled. "What's that you're saying?" He had taken a couple of steps from the sidewalk into the Carters' yard. "I don't just get you," he yelled.

"Oh, go to hell," Miss Winnie said, not quite so loud.

The Judge stood waiting for her to repeat what she had said, waiting to see if he was going to be invited to come in and air his views. Mrs. Carter and Miss Winnie kept their eyes, as well as their ears, on the radio. The Judge stepped back into the street. Lucinda clung to the post behind the japonica so that he wouldn't see her. He carried his black alpaca coat over his left arm. His right hand held a big palm-leaf fan that stirred the air under his whisk broom of tobacco-stained beard. A dingy white cotton handkerchief trailed limply from the stem of the fan.

"The old fool," Miss Winnie said. "He's one the Nazis can have. They'd grab him off the gravy train before you could say Neville Chamberlain, and feed him to the Polish prisoners."

"Now, Winnie," Mrs. Carter began.

Lucinda didn't hear any more. She had seen the car coming up the street, coming more slowly than ever, barely creeping along. She moved to the banister rail and waited for her father to look up. Then she waved. He saw her and motioned. She ran out to the car.

"How about riding around the corner and opening the garage door for me?" he said.

She got in beside him. He had something to tell her. She could see that. His hands gripped the wheel as hard as if he were driving fast.

"Did you know they're out?" he asked.

Lucinda didn't know what he was talking about, but he wasn't waiting for an answer.

"Those poor, wonderful devils got out. Think about it, jumping into that English Channel, setting out in canoes, rowboats, on foot, any way at all."

"Oh, yes," Lucinda said. She thought maybe she knew.

"Without guns; without clothes, some of them; without

anything but guts, just plain guts." He turned to Lucinda. "You know, courage."

"Yes, sir," Lucinda said.

"Now if only the French can hold out. I'm afraid there's no hope for Norway, but I'll bet those French will last."

The garage door was already open. She didn't have to get out. The car slid into the darkness. He reached for the dial of the radio but held the knob without turning it.

"Can you keep a secret?" he asked. He didn't look at her.

"Yes," Lucinda said.

"Lately I've been stopping in at Mr. Hardin's studio on my way home—to talk about the war—and things."

"At his house?"

"Yes, at his house. A friend of his from New York is there. Carl Ellis. Came to help Mr. Hardin put on a sort of school."

"The school Miss Carley told us about?" Lucinda asked.

"That's right. Mr. Hardin had big plans, he and Miss Carley, but they've had a raw deal from the School Board. When that blow came, along with the way he was already feeling about the war, he just about gave up. But Miss Carley and Ellis and I were all there at his house this afternoon, and we all listened together to the news about Dunkerque, and after that Miss Carley got to talking, and I guess I did, too, and—" He turned to Lucinda. "It's a secret, you know."

"Yes," Lucinda said. She had been trembling from head to foot as he talked, and barely had breath enough to get the word out.

"I'm going to take music lessons."

"Oh."

"Piano lessons."

"Oh. Piano?"

"I'll have organ later. But first I'll learn what it's all about. I didn't exactly mean to, but Miss Carley kept telling them how much people here need what they can do and—well, I got to saying things, too, and first thing I knew I was telling them how I'd always wanted to know about music and didn't see how it would hurt the insurance business much for me to learn a little, nights—"

Lucinda couldn't think of anything to say but *oh* and she couldn't keep from saying that, although he was laughing now and seemed happy and easy.

"—so that sort of started things and Miss Carley kept talking about there being nobody to teach music here but those two women who don't know the difference between a major and minor scale. And nobody at all teaching painting." He stopped for breath.

"Are we going to have a piano?" Lucinda asked.

"Later. When I can play a little better. I'll practice this summer at Mr. Hardin's house. You won't forget, will you, that it's our secret? We won't tell your mother until I can play a little better, play something with the music."

"Practice at Mr. Curtis Hardin's house?" Lucinda asked, just to be sure.

"Yes. You see, they're going to have the school there. That's what we decided this afternoon. The Board of Education won't let them use a school building, so Mr. Hardin's going to clear out three or four rooms and use his own house. We looked at the rooms and decided which would be best. He'll put the furniture in storage and get in another piano and have some easels knocked together. It will all be in the paper. The classes will be free for the children but, of course, grown people like me will pay for lessons."

"Maybe I could go to the classes," Lucinda said, but she couldn't make her voice very loud. He didn't hear her.

"It'll take a few days to get going," he said. "You'll want to take lessons, too, don't you think?"

"From Mr. Hardin," Lucinda said. She tried to make her voice louder.

"But he teaches painting," her father said. "It's Mr. Ellis who teaches music."

As Lucinda crossed the Square she remembered about the knocker with Two PALMETTO STREET engraved on it, like the writing paper. It would be nice if "On the Square" were engraved on the knocker, too, but this, she felt, might be impossible, considering the knocker was a long narrow hand.

Both sides of the double front door stood open. As Lucinda came nearer the house she could see straight through the door to a high window, and through the window to an iron balcony rail. The sunshine of Mr. Hardin's back yard shone through the rail. The window let in so much sunshine that there was no seeing anything or anybody in the hall.

Almost too late, Lucinda realized that her eyes, dazed by the sun, were about to overlook a problem that had to be solved before she could be in the house. Five or six iron-railed steps curved from right and left of the walk to the front door. She would have to decide which flight was for her. She slowed her pace and fumbled with the latch of the low iron gate that opened on the ivy-carpeted yard. It was a shallow yard that offered little opportunity for the slow-moving act of choice to express itself. She would have to think fast. But before Lucinda's hand left the gate her eyes fell on Miss Carley. She sat at a small table, just outside the strip of sun, picked out of the shadows by her white dress and the band of white ribbon around her short black hair. She saw Lucinda and waved. The next thing Lucinda knew, she was standing beside the table waiting for Miss Carley to finish writing down things about Anna May Thornton. She didn't know which flight of steps she had taken.

Miss Carley was writing on a big sheet of white cardboard. "Music" was printed across the top in square black letters. "Be sure to bring your violin," Miss Carley was saying to Anna May. "Mr. Ellis hopes he can get together a little orchestra."

Lucinda saw through the back door of the hall to the brick pavement that covered the ground under a mimosa tree. Mr. Hardin was setting up an easel in the shade, trying to find a level place for it on the pavement. Two other easels were already there.

Ruth Hubbard and Jennie Cate came in and stood behind Lucinda.

"What are you going to take?" Jennie whispered, but before Lucinda could answer Anna May moved on and Miss Carley was saying: "I'm so glad you came, Lucinda. I was expecting you." Without waiting for Lucinda to tell her, she pushed aside the "Music" sheet and took out one marked "Painting."

"The Monday-Thursday morning class is already full," Miss Carley said, "but there's a place left in the afternoon group. Or you could come in the Tuesday-Friday morning group. Wednesdays are being saved for a special class."

"I'd like to come Monday afternoon," Lucinda said. She watched Miss Carley write her name under "M-T PM."

"Maybe you'll make the Wednesday class," Miss Carley said, as she wrote "12 years old" after Lucinda's name. "Come back at two o'clock Monday. And you'd better wear an old dress, or bring a smock, until you get used to mixing your paint. The painting class will meet upstairs."

The hall was filling with children. There were a few mothers, too. Miss Carley motioned Lucinda on. "Next," she said, and was ready for Jennie. Lucinda had forgotten to ask if there was anything to do today. It seemed a long time until Monday. She decided to wait until Miss Carley finished with Jennie and Ruth. Then she could ask her.

"Look at those steps," somebody said, and Lucinda's eyes started up them. She had heard about circular stairs. Now, she knew, she was seeing them. They made a long, lovely curl from the top of the house to the bottom like one of Mittie's best apple peelings. They hung as lightly as if Mittie were up there, on the third floor, holding the highest step by the crook of her finger.

Lucinda saw the Eaton twins in the room on the other side of the hall. She could talk to them while she waited for Miss Carley. But the way was blocked by the children standing around Miss Carley's table. Jennie's and Ruth's mothers had come with them. They were moving to the back of the hall. Lucinda found herself being pushed, willy-nilly, into the path they made through the waiting children.

"Well, thank goodness, he's taken up those wonderful old carpets and put away the draperies," Mrs. Hubbard said, just loud enough for Lucinda to hear. "I was worried about them when I heard about the furniture he'd left here."

"Look in the dining room," Mrs. Cate said. "He's left the sideboard and corner cupboard, but I guess he put the table and chairs in storage. It'll be like going to school in a museum for the children, won't it?"

"His mother will turn in her grave if they put a scratch on that Sheraton," Mrs. Hubbard said. Lucinda wished she knew which way to look to see the Sheraton. The way Mrs. Hubbard said the word made it sound like something beautiful. "You'd think he would have taken out the best pieces, wouldn't you?" she said.

"Wouldn't you?" Mrs. Cate agreed. "But, after all, he had to leave the wallpaper and mantels and the cupboards. If it were mine I could see a nick out of the Sheraton sideboard better than I could bear a scratch on this cabinetwork or wallpaper."

Lucinda thought the wallpaper was gaudy with such big flowers, even if they were faded.

"I've never cared for those marbelized mantels," Mrs. Cate said. "I think they're tacky. Why would you want to disguise such beautifully carved wood?"

Mrs. Hubbard didn't bother to answer. "I wonder where they'll eat," she asked, "Curtis and his guest, without a dining table?"

"Oh, on the terrace, I guess, or the side porch," Mrs. Cate said. "After all, this is a fourteen-room house, and it's still pretty well furnished with tables," she whispered. "I'll bet Curtis is paying Mr. Ellis a salary, as well as putting him up in the house. I hear his wife couldn't come because of her job in New York. So, of course, he couldn't afford to give his time like Curtis can."

They had pushed Lucinda along as they talked until she found herself directly beside a placard that said, "This Way Out." It seemed put there for her. She couldn't bring herself to turn her back on it. Anyway, Miss Carley was still surrounded.

Lucinda followed the direction through a hall back of the dining room and came out on a side porch. The steps were lower than those in front and were not divided. The walk to the side gate was twice the length of the front walk. From the steps Lucinda saw James Givens, leaning on his bicycle, talking to Johnny Fowler. Johnny was sitting on the edge of an old stone block that had been used for mounting horses in the days before the stable at the back of the garden had been made into a garage.

"How come you're back in town when school's out?" James called to Johnny.

Johnny looked away from him. One leg slid off the block. "I've got some things to do," he said carelessly. "Got to buy some things."

"Yeah, I bet," James said. He laughed with a noisy burst and hopped onto his bicycle. He stood balancing and laughing. "Why don't you go buy them?" he cried. "What you hanging round here for?"

Johnny didn't say anything. He couldn't look up. He was screwing his face into a knot.

"Well, why don't you go buy them, then?"

No answer.

"Hee-ee," James yipped. "I bet I know why. I bet I know where you're going." He sailed off, then turned and circled the mounting block where Johnny sat. "I bet I know, I bet I know," he cried as he circled. He brought his bicycle to a stop beside the block and began again the clever business of balancing. "Did you have to hitch?" he asked.

"I got here all right," Johnny said. He got off the block and thrust his hands into his pockets. He looked almost as if he'd stopped caring what James said.

"How far did you have to walk before you caught a ride?" James asked.

"Oh, not so far, I guess," Johnny said. "I guess I'll be going on, now." His hands, pushing at his pockets, propelled him for three or four steps.

James bent over his handle bars and circled again. "Sissy britches," he hissed. "Sissy britches, Sissy britches." As he circled faster, he sang louder, "Sissy britches artist, Sissy britches artist, Johnny is a artist, Sissy britches artist." He got so good at the circling that he just missed touching Johnny as he rode around and around. Johnny was trapped. With head down and cheeks flaming, he turned this way and that, but James was too fast for him. As he shortened the radius of his circle his chant shrilled and sharpened. "Johnny is a artist, Sissy britches artist," he sang over and over, twanging his bell.

Dizzy at last, he let the bicycle swerve. Johnny bolted. But he didn't have a chance. James quickly overtook him and pedaled along at his side, singing in a lower, but more threatening tone, "Sissy britches artist, Sissy britches Johnny."

Lucinda didn't dare let herself reach the street. She pretended to be waiting for somebody in the house. She wished Miss Carley would hear James. She always knew how to make him stop bullying the other children. James had begun circling again. Suddenly Johnny stopped trying to break away. A shudder caught him up. He flung his arms across his face and stood nailed to the spot, but shaking with a paroxysm that was sickening to see. Even James quailed before it. His bicycle surged briefly and dashed away. But still Johnny stood there, his head thrown back, his arms hugging his face, his legs and shoulders quaking.

She knew she could not pass Johnny while he was like that. She leaned over, looking for four-leaf clovers where only ivy was growing. When she looked up again Johnny was plodding along towards the corner. There was no further need for holding back. At the corner Johnny turned suddenly, and they were face to face.

"Hello," Lucinda said.

Johnny's eyes dropped. "Hello," he said. His voice was surly.

Lucinda wanted to say something else, but she didn't know what. The things she wanted to say tugged at her as they walked away from each other. When she got to Cass Avenue she looked back. Johnny's hand was on the Hardin gate. Lucinda's eyes scanned the Square. The coast was clear. The bicycle had carried James out of sight.

THE DINING ROOM was square, but Lucinda was painting it without corners. That made her picture round, except for the fern that stood out from one of the rounded sides. Inside the brown circle of the room was the bright yellow circle of the table. Lucinda laid on brown for the outer circle until it was dark enough to suit her. She added green to green until the fern she was painting was greener than the fern in the room. Its fronds were stiffer, too, more sharply pointed. She held the paper at arm's length and admired her fern.

The door opened, and Mittie came in. "Here 'tis Sattiday and you up here all day messin," she said.

"I'm painting a picture," Lucinda said.

"Ain't no piccher 'at I can see," Mittie said. She sidled closer and squinted.

"It's the dining room," Lucinda explained. "We'll all be in it. You'll be in it, too, maybe."

"No, sir. Ain't gettin me mix up with no Parish green. Ain't ketchin me a-messin round with nothin like that."

"I'll put you in, and there you'll be. I'll just take some—" Lucinda hesitated and looked at the brown arm hanging against the blue apron. "I'll just take some brown paint and some blue paint and put it on and there you'll be."

"No, sir. Ain't no paint in Mittie. That ain't what the Book say. It's dirt and spit and Adam rib, but ain't no paint." She squinted again at the paper, leaning over Lucinda. "Howcome you settin down a yellow apple?" she asked.

"That's not an apple. That's the table, our dining-room table." Lucinda's brush strengthened a leg.

Mittie grunted. "That little old wobbledy thing?"

"It's not wobbledy."

"All lobsided."

"It's not lopsided. Mr. Hardin said round didn't have to be just exactly round."

"Ain't yellow, noway."

"But the cloth is. The new cloth's yellow."

"Just messin," Mittie declared. "And them nuts ain't pick out."

Lucinda was mixing more yellow.

"When you gonna pick em?"

"Pick what?"

"Pick what? Ain't this Sattiday? Ain't I got ever'thing ready to make them teacakes, cepen nuts?"

"Mother said I could stay in here and paint all morning."

"Ain't nobody gonna call that paintin."

"Mr. Hardin gave me these things so I could practice," Lucinda said.

"Reckon you don't want no teacakes." Mittie was backing towards the door.

It seemed better to say nothing.

She waited beside the door. "Guess you don't want to hear no stories." Her voice deepened and drew the words out.

Lucinda was painting circles all over the sheet, crazily ringing them in. The idea had seized her, and she couldn't paint them fast enough: big blue circles for plates on the yellow cloth; little blue circles for saucers, and smaller ones for teacups. The quicker the stroke, the better the circle. Three more blue rings for bread-and-butter plates. All lopsided; all wobbledy. But beautiful. The faces would be next. They would be circles, too. Lucinda's head whirled with excitement and circles.

"I can tell while you're a-pickin," Mittie said.

The faces shouldn't be exactly circles, and they shouldn't be exactly white. Lucinda held the brush over the little colored jars, wondering about the color to be added to the white.

She didn't know Mittie was gone until she heard the screech of the third step.

On the second Monday Mr. Hardin said, "If you'd like to put in some extra time, Lucinda, why don't you come Wednesdays?"

She couldn't look at him. She had to go on cleaning her brushes as if nobody had said anything.

"There will be only five or six in the Wednesday class," he said, "so come in the morning if you like. Or afternoon. Doesn't matter."

He walked away. She hadn't said a word. She wanted to follow him out to the back yard to thank him. But she couldn't swallow. There was no use to try to speak. She thanked Jesus instead. She had been saying prayers about the Wednesday class. They hadn't been quick, dutiful prayers thrown out into the dark after she was in bed. She had got down on her knees every night and made a careful prayer about the Wednesday class, offering every inducement she could think of, even the promise to stop telling lies.

Now, as she crossed the Square, she thanked God for answering the prayers. She couldn't feel that it mattered a great deal about thanking Mr. Hardin. It was hard for him to say things, too. He could say almost anything about

a picture by just standing beside an easel or a table, saying
"H'm" or "M'm." When he took the brush into his own
hand he said even more. Sometimes, though, Miss Carley
had to say things for him. Not all of the children understood what he meant when he didn't say words.

Mr. Hardin and Mr. Ellis kept Miss Carley running
up and down stairs all day. She couldn't exactly teach
music or painting, but she knew about the children and
what to do about all kinds of things. Sometimes Mr.
Hardin would stand behind Clarice and shake his head
and look as if he didn't know what in the world to do
about a picture as bad as that. Then Miss Carley would
come along and send Clarice one of her loving looks and
say something that would help Clarice and Mr. Hardin,
too.

Almost as soon as she came in sight of Flora's house,
Lucinda heard the commotion in the yard. Cajy was standing in front of the house, spelling against a chorus of
laughter and prompting that came from Flora and the two
boys sitting beside her on the steps.

"All right now. That's *chim* enough for us. Get on to
the *pan*," Thad Elder called out.

"Or into it," Frank added. "Just get going."

"Chimpanzee," Flora cried, and pointed to Cajy.
"Chimpanzee."

They broke into peals of laughter. Cajy's eyes were
fixed on a distant tree. He neither saw nor heard them.
The song came out as if he had nothing to do with it.
But he took his good time, more time than his audience
could spare. Thad threw a penny to him. Cajy stooped to

pick it up, and the string that held his galluses together snapped. They laughed harder than ever. Cajy twisted and tied until the galluses were repaired.

"Spell 'pickaninny,'" Frank ordered. He reached behind Flora to dig Thad in the ribs.

Cajy began to sing. He strained and squirmed for every note. It would have been easier if he had had a tree or a fence to lean against. He was too tall and thin to stand in the open like that. His clothes looked as unsupported as he did. His khaki shirt hung in rags, but that hardly mattered for his skin and the shirt were the same color. His arms and face were deeply scratched and smeared with oily black mud. The blue corduroy pants were too full for him but so short they barely covered his knees. There was a fringe of beard that looked funny on his little-boy face.

Frank threw out a penny as Cajy finished spelling "pickaninny." "Spell 'mulatto,'" he said.

Cajy bent over, his hands against his knees, to rest a minute before he began again.

"Hee-hee," Thad cried. "Spell 'kangaroo.' Kangaroohoo," he sang, imitating Cajy's tone.

But in the dark cavern of Cajy's throat the *m* had already begun to be a song.

Each boy whispered against Flora's curls. Flora giggled. Cajy did not see them. He looked at nothing, singing the *u* and the *l*, for the most part, in the cavern; moving his eyes rather than his lips. But when he came to the *a* he opened his mouth wide and his hit-or-miss teeth shone. For a minute their whiteness and the clear open music of the *a* gave his face the look of a smile.

As Cajy sang the *a* he saw Lucinda. She had stopped by

the tree in front of the McCalls' house. He looked at her until the *a* was finished, but when he got to the *t* the song returned to the cavern and his eyes rolled.

"Come on, now, Cajy," Thad said, "let's have that kangaroo-hoo." He stood on the grass in front of Flora and Frank and bent over, hands on knees, as Cajy had bent for his rest. "Kangaroo-hoo Cajy," he sang. He loped stiffly about, keeping his hands on his knees. "Kangaroo-hoo Cajy."

Flora and Frank screamed and howled. Cajy made a sound that was a sort of imitation of their laughter. Frank threw out a nickel. Cajy groped in the grass until he found it. Lucinda wished she were on the other side of the street. She could not cross over without seeming to avoid the group at Flora's but, as she thought about passing them, she felt herself stumbling over the looks from their eyes. She would wait to see if Cajy was going to spell "kangaroo." When he finished she would pretend she had suddenly remembered something important. She would cross the street then, running as fast as she could go.

Cajy had begun on a high shrill note and was slowly coming down the pentatonic scale. Over and over, he sang the oo-oo, up and down, high and low. Thad wouldn't find it quite so easy to imitate this. It seemed to Lucinda that Cajy was singing for her, rather than the group on the steps. She decided to stay with him as long as he spelled. As she watched him, she thought she would try to paint a picture of him some time. He wasn't so much like a man, anyway, as the picture of a man.

"I know a word I bet you can't spell," Flora said. But before she said the word, Sam Gardiner's cut-down car came tearing up the street, Sam's fist beating strident honks

from the horn. The three tumbled down the steps and
into the car. They rattled off without a word for Cajy or
a look for Lucinda. Cajy paid no attention to their going.
He finished the song. Lucinda could go home now.

As she passed Cajy she said, "Hello, Cajy."

"How-do," Cajy muttered absently. He went on down
the street droning, "How-do, how-do." His bare feet
padded softly on the uneven bricks. He walked slowly and
so did Lucinda. She kept an ear cocked until his voice
faded away.

Mittie's song came out in the street to meet her:

> "Oh, Lord, Oh-oh, Lo-or-rd,
>     Whachu gonna do about me?"

Lucinda ran through the door, into the happy mood.
This would be a good time to tell Mittie about the Wednesday class.

"Oh, Mittie," she cried.

Mittie scowled when she saw Lucinda.

"Were you looking for somebody?" Lucinda asked.

"Ain't a-lookin for you," Mittie said. She poured a glass
of milk for Lucinda and started the song again. In spite
of Mittie, the ecstasy of the song flowed over Lucinda.
She sank into the kitchen chair. Mittie ignored her as she
sang:

> "Oh, Lo-ord, oh, Lo-o-ord,
>     Whachu gonna do about me?"

She tilted her head and waited, as if for an answer,
then went on:

"Is you got me a chair a-waitin up there?
Whachu gonna do about me?"

Lucinda drank the milk, loving Mittie and waiting for
a good chance. Mittie was cutting okra into thin slices.
Every slice was even, though her eyes were somewhere far
outside the window. Like the song, they were bathed in
happiness.

"Effen you don't know, don't nobody know
Whachu gonna do about me."

Mittie took a deep breath.

"Mittie," Lucinda began, "want me to tell you something good?"

Mittie reached into a drawer and rummaged noisily.

"I'll let you be the first one to know," Lucinda offered.

Mittie grasped the granite bowl in both hands and
turned the blinding glory of her face full on Lucinda.
"Honey," she said, "Mittie ain't got no room right now
for knowin nothin moren what's in here." She tapped
with her finger somewhere to the left of her stomach. Her
voice was solemn, but she couldn't keep her face from
spreading. Her thick red lips stretched and stretched until
they reached the breaking point. She let out a high shrill
*hee-ee-ee*. It was a voice and a language Lucinda had never
heard before.

Mittie went to the refrigerator, took out a bowl of
butter, spooned deeply and dropped a yellow lump into
the hot skillet. The pungent brown smell popped and
cracked as it rose into the room. She changed its tune with
glistening rings of onion. The smells came together. Mittie

stirred and added this and that. She took three big red tomatoes from the refrigerator and cut them, dripping, into the skillet. The smell changed again. Then she slid the dimes of okra in, stirred mightily, clapped on the lid and mopped her face with the bottom of her apron.

"When will supper be ready?" Lucinda asked.

"Skillet say one hour fum now," Mittie said. She went into the pantry. She was determined to be alone.

Lucinda heard the front screen door open and shut. Her mother called her name. She would tell her about the class. They met in the hall, ran into each other's arms. Her mother was happy, too.

"It's all settled. We're going to move into the house as soon as it's finished. By October, surely. And look. I found the loveliest blue hat for you, the exact shade of the blue in your new dress." She held out a paper bag. "Let's try it now." She had started upstairs.

"With the dress, too?"

"If you like," her mother said.

Arm in arm, they went up the steps. "Up, up, up," the scale rose in Lucinda. She felt it swelling inside her as her mother's voice said on the outside, "They're going to tint the plaster for us, and I picked out—"

She would save the Wednesday class for her father. He was the one who would like it best, anyway. Lucinda's arm tightened in her mother's. They mounted lightly on the rising scale.

MORNING BEGAN now with the grinding of the Carters' cistern. Little by little, cupful by cupful, the metallic singsong dragged Lucinda's consciousness up from the well of sleep. Then the Dentons' cistern began its rasping yelps. That brought her wide awake and made her remember about the drouth. Everybody who had a good cistern was using it now. In a minute the gulping and sputtering would begin at the bathroom faucets. Then she would know it was seven o'clock. For ten or fifteen minutes the water would gurgle and choke until it began to come freely.

At the first sound from the bathroom Lucinda's mother and father would run to fill pans and buckets because at eight o'clock another gurgling would begin and the water would be turned off again until five. The drouth was blotting up the river. Between five and six in the afternoon Lucinda helped with the water, but in the morning she lay and listened to the others. It was better, her mother said, not to have too many sleepyheads underfoot.

There were no more tub baths. The bathtub was darkly stained from the water that stood in it from day to day. A long-handled saucepan hung on a hook in the bath-

room so the water could be easily dipped from the tub.
The tub was the reservoir. They didn't dare empty it, so
the sediment and stain could not be scrubbed away.

First, there had been the precaution of cutting off the
water from nine at night until six in the morning. Then
it had been cut off at six in the evening. After a week the
hours were reduced again. Macklin suffocated and thirsted
and blinked in the glare of a sun so persistent it could
not be thought of as absent, even in the night. It gave way
grudgingly, just long enough for you to get to sleep, and
promptly came forth again to shine all night. No matter
how early you were awake it was already busy, looking as
if it had always been there and always would be.

There was no more calling out to Lucinda to hurry
about her bath. Everybody knew sponge baths took longer,
particularly when you had to make a little water go a
long way. At first it was fun to stand and scrub but after
a few days it was a dull and tedious job. When Lucinda
couldn't manage to go over her entire body, first with a
soapy cloth, then with clear water, she left off the soap
and slapped at herself with a cloth dipped in cool water.
She liked that.

One of the most exciting things the drouth had done
was bringing Mittie to live in the house. Gander Creek
was nothing but a slimy trickle. Lucinda's mother and
father were shocked that some people were willing to let
servants, who lived down there, continue to work for them,
going back and forth each day. Trunks and boxes were
moved about in the Darby storeroom, and a cot was set
up for Mittie. It made the house seem happy and cozy
to have her there, with the songs coming out of the room
that nobody had slept in before she came.

At first Mittie hadn't wanted to come. But now she liked being there. Lucinda heard her calling from the back porch to friends who walked along Mimosa Street.

"My white folks ain't a-lettin me take no chanceties," she would say proudly. "They ain't a-lettin me take no chanceties with that dirty old water."

People talked about the drouth now more than they talked about the war. They talked about how long the city's reservoir could hold out without rain, and how long the drinking water should be boiled. They said, "Looks like we'll dry up and blow away." They drove out in the late afternoon to see what was left of the river. "That must be what the Red Sea was like when the Israelites marched through," somebody said.

At Mr. Hardin's the bathrooms had been locked. Class periods were cut in half. Pupils carried their own drinking water in bottles of all kinds and shapes. The painting pupils poured water out of their drinking supply for mixing water colors. One of the things Miss Carley did was to see that everybody had his own bottle of water. She always saw to it that the children were started at their work before Mr. Hardin came out of his own studio. She wanted him to have plenty of time to work on his sketches for the mural he was going to paint somewhere away.

There was no particular stopping time on Wednesday, and sometimes Lucinda was the last to finish. Miss Carley liked for her to be slow because, so long as she stayed on, Miss Carley did not have to go home. She and Mr. Hardin talked a lot about the commission. Lucinda liked it when they talked back in Mr. Hardin's studio with the door open. Usually then she heard their voices without hearing their words. It was easy to paint when she was alone in the big room, wrapped in the happy comfortable feeling their voices made.

Today Lucinda and Mr. Hardin were working at the easels in the back yard. Miss Carley stood in the door. "I can see you two painters are going to work late," she said. "I am going to leave you to finish in peace."

"It goes better when you are here," Mr. Hardin said in his slow voice. He didn't look up from his work.

Miss Carley came out to pick up some brushes that had been left on the long table. She straightened an easel that was on its side.

"I wish you wouldn't go," Mr. Hardin said. "It seems clearer when you're here."

Lucinda saw the look come into Miss Carley's face. She put a hand out to the table. The ends of her fingers were white where they pressed against the table top.

"I think I'd better go," she said. Lucinda could see she wanted to stay.

"Wait until the car comes back, and I'll run you home." Mr. Hardin looked up as he said that, and smiled all over his face.

"But that will be six o'clock. Maybe later."

"So much the better. By then I can show you the sketch for the third panel. Bring your book and sit here," he said. He got up and moved the canvas deck chair out of the sun, nearer his easel. He took the book from under her arm and put it on the chair. "You can't leave Lucinda and me here without our teacher," he said. He laughed and sent a broad grin to Lucinda.

Miss Carley laughed and looked at Lucinda, too. Then

she stretched herself on the long chair and opened the book.

Lucinda touched her leaf with a streak of yellow. It moved on the page, ready to fly away to nowhere. She was painting the song that Mr. Ellis's class had sung Monday morning.

"He's trying to lower the temperature by giving them an October song," Miss Carley had said to Mr. Hardin Monday morning as the children's voices sent the song upstairs. "I'm glad to hear the tune I learned in the Second Grade instead of the one the children have been singing the last few years."

"I sang it, too," Mr. Hardin had said. "In the Second or Third Grade, I think. Miss Lulie Hart was the teacher."

"Yes. She was my teacher, too," Miss Carley had said. "It was the Second Grade. She taught Second Grade for more than thirty years."

"Think of them," Mr. Hardin said. "Miss Lulie, Miss Sarah Cole, Miss Nellie Blitch, Miss Lacey Loftin, Miss Cynthia Legg—"

"Miss Eva Carley," Miss Carley said.

"But a little different, thank God."

"Not so very, I'm afraid," Miss Carley said.

"Listen," Mr. Hardin had said. "Lord, how it takes you back!"

He and Miss Carley had stood listening as the children sang:

"Come, little leaves, said the wind one day.
Come over the meadow with me and play,
Put on your dresses of red and gold,
For summer has gone and the days grow cold."

"Good heavens," Mr. Hardin said. "Silly how it gets you, isn't it? Why doesn't he let them sing something gay and cheerful, like 'Danny Boy' or 'Long, Long Ago'?" Lucinda didn't understand why Miss Carley had laughed when he said that.

They were always laughing when nobody else did. Lucinda didn't know why in the world they were laughing now as Miss Carley looked for her place in the book.

Lucinda went on painting leaves, nothing but leaves; some on the tree, some on the ground, some floating on the wind, like the leaves in the song.

Nobody in the Wednesday class was as slow as Lucinda. Johnny had painted a field full of cows, eight or nine of them, while she had painted nothing but one tree and some leaves. Lester Hill had painted a filling station with three automobiles beside it. Ann Snyder had painted a street full of houses. Lucinda was ashamed of being so slow, but there were nice things about it, too. If she had been as fast as the others she wouldn't have been here now, alone with Miss Carley and Mr. Hardin.

All of a sudden Mr. Hardin threw down his pencil and sprang to his feet.

"I can't do it, Eva," he cried. "I can't do it. I won't try. My heart isn't in it. I can't let myself in for spending the whole fall and winter smearing up eighty square yards of wall space while the world's falling to pieces around me."

Lucinda put out her foot to stop Mr. Hardin's pencil that was rolling towards her on the brick floor of the terrace. She would have stooped to pick it up, but she was afraid to move with Mr. Hardin raging around like that. She looked across to see why Miss Carley didn't say something. Miss Carley had closed her book. She looked as if she were waiting to be sure Mr. Hardin had finished before she said anything.

"I can't do it," Mr. Hardin kept saying, "and you can't expect me to. Nobody can." He stopped in front of Miss Carley and stood looking down at her. "It's all different since France fell. I can't think of anything else."

"Only a few weeks ago," Miss Carley began, "you were saying wonderful things about fighting the enemies of the spirit with the weapons of the spirit. But now, when you have a chance to paint a mural that can say for our day what Michelangelo said for his day, you talk of turning down the commission."

"Of course I do," he cried. "Did the Sistine frescoes save Italy? Don't quote now what I said two months ago about weapons of the spirit. It's too late for that now. It's too late for anything but guns."

"Perhaps it is," Miss Carley agreed. "But aren't you talking as if this were like any other war in history? The English know better than that. Besieged as they are this minute, they know guns are not enough. Think how Myra Hess's concerts are gathering them into the National Gallery while air-raid sirens scream over their heads. When your country is ready for you to take up a gun or try your hand at designing bombers you will be told. But in the meantime—"

Mr. Hardin walked across the terrace and picked up the pencil. He didn't know Lucinda was there. He almost bumped into her as he bent down.

"If you will go ahead with this mural as you're planning it," Miss Carley said, "you will make a call to arms that our artists and scholars cannot resist. A call to their own arms. If you can get some of them to cut a few more windows in their ivory towers, to join the company of Michel-angelo and Dante and Voltaire and Beethoven and Milton, maybe you will help cancel some of the brutality that is set on devouring the world. This mural would tell them that they can make our dead hearts live again, that if they had been taking their gifts more seriously all along maybe we wouldn't be up to our necks in materialism now."

This was almost like the way Miss Carley talked to the Sixth Grade. Lucinda almost knew what she was talking about. Mr. Hardin had sat down in the chair beside Miss Carley.

"Do you remember," she was saying, "how, after Ceburn Robb was here wailing about the lot of the misunderstood artist, you said he had it all turned around? You said it was the business of the artist to do the understanding, to know and to care so much about the world he lives in that his work with words or pictures or music will have to be illuminating?"

"Sounds damned arrogant," Mr. Hardin muttered, barely loud enough for Lucinda to hear.

"No, Curtis," Miss Carley said. "It sounds like you—before the things that are happening in Europe broke your heart."

Lucinda heard the catch in Miss Carley's voice, saw her turn her head away, saw her leave her hand on the arm of the chair to be covered by Mr. Hardin's hand. Before his hand went back to the sketch, he said in his gentlest voice, "It's you who are the artist, Eva."

MR. HARDIN was pointing to Lucinda's picture with the end of his brush. "Don't be afraid, Lucinda," he said, "of making this as good as the picture you're seeing inside you. Don't you think you cheat a little sometimes, keep back the best for yourself?"

Lucinda knew what he meant.

"Don't be afraid," he repeated, "of making your picture as good as it can be." He leaned over her, using his brush to mix a new color. He left the sample on the side of her picture and moved on to Jennie's picture.

Downstairs the instruments were working on a new piece. They started and stopped, and started and stopped until the painters looked at one another a little desperately. It was easier to paint when the music downstairs moved smoothly forward.

*Da-dee-da-dum,* the fiddlers sang, and Mr. Ellis' baton rapped against the music stand, stopping them again. The painting class sighed. Then they pricked up their ears. Another strain was floating in on them, but not up the stairs. It was coming in through the back and side windows. There was no lagging or limping about it. With a brisk, syncopated rhythm the strange-toned instruments were turning a humble prayer into a dance tune:

"It's a me, it's a me, it's a me, oh, Lord,
Standin in the need of prayer."

There was no resisting it. Shoulders swayed, and feet
shifted. One by one, every painter left his easel and
crowded to the windows.

"It's the little jug band," Anna May cried. "Come and
look. It's the little jug Papa told us about. It's the dancing
dolls he saw in the alley, back behind the store the other
day."

Lucinda pushed into an opening along a window sill.
She saw the five little boys about her age, and younger,
gathered around a soapbox wagon beside Mr. Hardin's
yard. The boys were singing and dancing and making
music on crazy-looking instruments. They could have stood
in the shadow of the water oaks just as easy as not, but
they stood outside it, not minding the sun. They didn't
mind the dust either. It was easier for their bare feet to
dance in the dust.

" 'Tain't my sister, 'tain't my brother,
It's a me, oh, Lord,"

the drummer sang.

His drums were tin cans, half a dozen of all sizes,
mounted on the wagon: a big lard can, coffee cans, baking-
powder cans, a little snuffbox. He made a great to-do with
his stick, beating first on one can and then on another,
running around the wagon with dancing steps, twirling
the stick as it traveled from can to can. When he was not
too busy with the drums he joined in the song.

Another boy sawed on a cigar-box fiddle. Another played

a real ukulele. The smallest, blackest boy tooted into the
jug, swelling his cheeks and rolling his eyes as he blew
into the little-necked half-gallon jug, holding it now
against his lips, now at arm's length.

The fifth boy played on a mouth harp, sliding it back
and forth with his left hand. His back was turned to the
windows. No one could see what his right hand was doing.
It seemed to be beating time. He waved the harp for a
minute and sang,

> " 'Tain't my father, 'tain't my mother,
>     It's a me, oh, Lord,
>     Standin in the need of prayer."

Without stopping for a deep breath, they went into
"Yes, Sir, That's My Baby."

The drummer beat the cans for all he was worth. The
music downstairs was drowned out. The painters, leaning
from the windows, saw Mr. Ellis' class standing on the
side porch. They saw Mr. Ellis run out to the group in
the street. He was so excited he ran from boy to boy,
watching first one and then another, beating time for them.
The boys went on with their music as if they didn't know
he was there. Everybody at the windows moved with the
music, a foot, a head, a voice.

The boys finished the song. Mr. Ellis was talking to
them and looking at their instruments. In another minute
they were trailing up the walk, ushered by Mr. Ellis. He
was smiling from ear to ear. The painters could see what
the mouth-harp boy had been doing with his right hand.
A tray-size stage was swung around his neck by a piece of
clothesline. It bobbed against his stomach as he walked

along. Three dirty-looking, loose-jointed wooden dolls, strung on wires, stood on the stage. The stick in the boy's right hand beat on the wires to make the dolls dance. It was funny to see the dolls dancing against his stomach as he walked along the path.

Clarice squeezed Lucinda's arm. "Aren't they cute?" she said.

"Shucks," Lester said. "I've seen them lots of times. The jug one's mother's our washwoman. I see them lots of times when we go after the clothes."

Jocile's heavy tread was pounding up the stairs. Miss Carley came out of the room across the hall and spoke to her. "Do you want something, Jocile?" she asked.

"Yes'm," Jocile said. "I want Mist' Curtis." She was mad. She didn't care who knew it.

"I wonder if I could help?" Miss Carley asked. "Mr. Curtis is busy in the studio. He asked me to look after the class this morning."

"He's got niggers down there," Jocile growled. "Got em in the parlor. Little old dirty niggers off the Creek."

"I don't understand," Miss Carley said.

"Mist' Ellis," Jocile said. "He went out and brung them dirty niggers in. Got em playin white folkses' music in the parlor."

The door of the studio opened, and Mr. Hardin came out. "What's this you're stewing about, Jocile?" he asked.

"Got niggers in the parlor," Jocile snapped. Beads of sweat stood out on her slick, black face.

"Good Lord, but you're a snob, Jocie," Mr. Hardin said. He grinned at Jocile as he said it, but she didn't smile back.

The music started downstairs. Mr. Hardin went down

a few steps and leaned over the banister. "Look, Eva," he said. "He seems to have dug up those little boys we've been hearing about, the children from the Creek."

"That's them down there now," Jocile cried. "In the parlor."

"You run on back to your work, Jocie," Mr. Hardin said. "We won't let them hurt anything."

"Got 'em settin in with white folkses' children," Jocile complained. "Got 'em—"

Mr. Ellis' voice broke in from the lower hall. "Eva," he called. "Can you come down? Get Curtis, and come see what I've found."

"In a minute," Miss Carley said.

"They can play any instrument in the band. Every blessed one of them." His voice rang with excitement. "Get Curtis and come here."

"Poor damn Yankee," Mr. Hardin said to Miss Carley. "He's forgotten where he is."

"I know," Miss Carley said. "He hasn't any idea—"

The painters heard Miss Carley and Mr. Hardin go down the steps. They tiptoed to the hall. Some of them huddled on the upper steps. Some leaned over the banisters.

Mr. Ellis was at the piano. The little Negro boys were gathered around him. Two of them were playing violins, one played a clarinet, one the drums, one the piccolo. Mr. Ellis played the tune through for them to hear, singing as he played,

"Jesu, joy of man's desiring . . ."

The drummer, finding little to do with his stick, added his voice to Mr. Ellis'. The children of Mr. Ellis' class sat by, big-eyed.

Lucinda stopped hearing. The music went on. The children whispered. But Lucinda was seeing her next picture, the one she would paint for the exhibition. It would be the jug band. She would paint the little boys under the tree as she had first seen them. But she would turn the mouth-harp boy so the dolls would show. She would paint the dolls dancing and the jug moving back and forth and the drummer's stick twirling over the cans. She would paint them playing "It's a Me."

THE PAPER was stuck under the screen door. Lucinda picked it up. Across the top was printed, "Notice to Water Users." Lucinda read: "Beginning today, and until further notice, water will be turned on only in the morning between seven and eight o'clock. In the afternoon trucks or wagons will drive through the streets distributing artesian well water from the Jenks Mills at Caraway. Each house in the city limits may receive as much as one gallon per occupant. Drivers will not be allowed to leave vehicles. Those requiring water will carry vessels to the vehicle to have them filled." The mayor's name was signed at the bottom and, under it, the date.

Lucinda stood in the hall and read the notice a second time. Then she saw the date. Once her eyes were fastened on it, she could not move them. The matter of the portrait was settled. She had forgotten about the first of August. Now August was nearly gone. The consciousness of Castleton surged in her. It seemed she had only to turn her head and, there in the hall, directly behind her, would be the deep green masses of the trees, making her know about the house that was shut into them and the portrait that was shut into the house.

234

She heard steps in the hall above her. As her mother came downstairs, Lucinda held out the paper.

"Yes, I know," her mother said. "A boy came around this morning with the notices. One was left at the back door, too. I don't see how we can stand it much longer."

Mittie was pouring water out of small buckets into large ones, getting ready to carry in the supply from the street.

"Four gallon ain't nothin moren a drop," she said. "A little old pail of well water ain't no way stoppin a drout. Lessen youall's churches goes to prayin us'll all be a-spittin cotton and a-dryin up to blow away."

"I expect a great many people are praying," Lucinda's mother said.

"Many ain't 'nough," Mittie said. "Look like many ain't hardly enough to do no good a tall."

"Hear that bell," Lucinda's mother cried. "Maybe that's the water."

The three of them listened. A bell clanged somewhere out of sight. It was on Mimosa Street. A lean gray horse drew a rickety wagon into view. Each of the wobbling, steel-tired wheels creaked in its own key and rhythm. Three barrels were mounted on the rough board bed of the wagon. The Negro driver waved his voice over the street like windy banners. He sat high on a slanting seat. In one hand he held driving lines made of rope. The other shook a big dinner bell between phrases of the song.

"Ain't nobody but old Speckleface, hissef," Mittie said.

"It's the water wagon," Lucinda cried.

"Speckleface a-drivin," Mittie said. "He'll sing ever' drop of water out of that there barrel 'fore he'll lift a hand to tote."

Speckleface was singing:

"Here yo water,
Cool and fine,
Sweet like wine,
Here yo water comes."

"Best water you ever seed, Miss Mittie," he called out.

"Don't know what anybody's a-wantin with a measly little old gallon," Mittie grumbled. She trotted out, a bucket in each hand.

Lucinda looked for the speckles, but Speckleface was solid shiny black, without so much as a freckle to explain his name.

He dipped the water out of the barrels with a cool splashing and sloshing.

Mittie shouted proud commands. "Mind out where you're a-pourin. This here street don't git no sprinklin tell the Lord send rain. An don't you be a-givin us no moren our share. Ain't enough to do no good noway. Don't you be a-givin us what b'longs to go to them." She pointed to Castleton.

"Ain't a-gettin none," Speckleface said. "This here water's for them 'at comes and gits it, them 'at totes they buckets out and gits it. You ain't gittin Spec offen this here wagon." He slapped the rope against the back of the horse and lifted his voice again,

"Oo-ee-ee, oo-oo-oo,
Heah yo water comes."

"Aren't they going to have any water?" Lucinda asked Mittie.

"Look like ain't," Mittie said.

"Bring yo buckets,
Bring yo pans,
Wash yo hans.
Here yo water comes,"

Speckleface sang as he turned into Cass Avenue.

"Looks like they'd want water, too," Lucinda said.

"Look like," Mittie agreed.

"That's the first clear water I've seen for weeks," Mrs. Darby said as she took the bucket from Lucinda. "This will be good drinking water," she said. "But of course we must boil it, too," she added.

Mittie sniffed her disgust. She dragged her feet with stubborn resistance to the pace set by Mrs. Darby.

Lucinda considered the vessels of water on the porch table. There were two preserving kettles, two small tin buckets, six Mason jars. Under the table was a washtub full of water. The kitchen table was covered with full buckets, and there was the half-filled tub in the bathroom. One of the small buckets could be spared. Soon her mother would go back upstairs and Mittie would be busy in the kitchen. Lucinda sat on the back steps and waited until the kitchen became safely quiet. Then she picked up the bucket she had decided on and carried it around the house to the oleander corner. She set it behind the trees and walked carelessly back to the porch. Mittie had brought a pan of potatoes out to the porch.

"You can git a knife and hep," she said to Lucinda.

"I told Betty I'd come down there a minute," Lucinda said, backing gradually towards the hall door.

Mittie paid no attention to Lucinda. She was talking to the potatoes. "Don't know why they can't eat you bake," she said. "Got enough to do 'thout peelin you. Totin water all day."

Lucinda tipped through the hall and through the front door. She looked along Mimosa Street and down Cass Avenue. It would never do for somebody to see her and ask where she was going with the water. Anybody would think it strange for anybody to be going to Castleton. Nobody was in sight. An automobile was crawling along almost two blocks away. She would wait for it to pass. It came slowly. It was the Baskin car. It was never in a hurry. The Baskin girls lived in their car, people said. Sometimes they slept in it on hot nights. All day and until late at night Mary Sue and Alice drove up and down the streets of Macklin. They never got out and went in anywhere. Everybody came out to the car. Their friends came out and sat in the back seat and talked and laughed. The drug-stores sent their ice-cream sodas out to them. Half the stock of the shoe shop was carried out to the street while they sat in the car, trying pair after pair of shoes. Whenever they slept too late for breakfast at home they drove to town and sat in front of the Elite where the waiter brought out orange juice and scrambled eggs and bacon, toast and coffee, served properly in courses.

Mary Sue drove with one hand on the wheel. Alice was stretched out on the back seat. Her head rested on the arm of the seat, and she held the magazine high to read aloud from it. Suddenly, Mary Sue laughed out. Then Alice laughed. They laughed until they were whooping. Lucinda, peering from behind the oleanders, laughed too. Mary Sue had to stop the car and put her head down on the steering wheel. Her laughter was focused on the floor of the car. But Alice's laughing popped out in all directions.

Now and then they leaned out and looked into the Castleton trees. It was not what they were reading that had made them laugh. It was something one of them had said about Castleton. Lucinda wondered what it was. She had never heard anybody say anything funny about Castleton. At last they were able to drive on. Lucinda set out with the bucket.

Before she got as far as the chained gates Lucinda had to shift her load from her right to her left hand and back again. She could not think about what she was doing, about the end of her journey. She was simply Lucinda carrying a bucket, that had become very heavy, along the gravel path beside Castleton's overgrown fence. The gravels burned like coals through the thin soles of her sandals. At the Pine Street corner she shifted the weight again. A spiciness had fallen across the air. Lucinda looked for the cause of the smell in the crowding shrubs and bushes, but there wasn't a flower in sight.

From the narrow gate—the box gate—she looked down the path. With the bucket there could hardly be room for her to walk between the walls. They rose above her head. She remembered how they had closed behind Sue's mother and aunt. She thought it might be better not to go in. She could leave the bucket inside the gate. Maybe Abe would see it there and take it to the house.

Another perfume was in the air. The boxwood path was a river of fragrance. "Drink it in, drink it in," Mrs. Bogart had cried that day so long ago. Lucinda remembered and swelled now with deep breaths of it. Her eyes followed her nose. The path ended in a patch of sunshine. She went in. The boxwood moved back with soft rustling. Showers of little leaves, turned yellow by the drouth, fell to the ground. A few of them fell into the water. They were the smallest leaves Lucinda had ever seen. *Come, little leaves—*

She was not prepared to find herself entirely exposed as soon as she reached the sunshine. The trees and shrubs stood back to leave a widely rounded opening before the house, making the semicircle where, in Miss Carley's photograph, the horse and trap had stood waiting to take the ladies for a drive.

A soft glow lay on the face of the house, silvering to the same dull tone the bricks that had been pink and the columns that had been white. The steps, spreading and swirling like the steps in the photograph, like the skirts in the portrait, drew Lucinda. She had only to set her foot on the first step. They would do the rest. They would take her up and up to the line of the tree-tall columns, across the portico, and into the place of the portrait.

Miss Emily would meet her at the door and take the bucket and thank her for bringing the water. Then there would be her mother (like a tree of white japonicas), and the room bigger than the schoolroom, and the portrait reaching from wall to wall, from floor to ceiling. There would be the red and white and gold of the five painted people (with necklaces and bracelets and rings) and the gold of the harp. There would be the little empty chair and the round gray cat waiting to be touched. She would sit with Mrs. Reeves and Miss Emily and the portrait people in the room of the all-night dancing (fiddles sounding through the trees)—

But maybe the portrait was not there now. Maybe it was already gone, already on the new wall. If she went in she would know. If she went in now she would have to know.

If it was gone there couldn't be even the wondering any more.

The house grew bigger as she thought about it. She stared upward, a diminishing dot of a girl. The closed door and shuttered windows canceled the invitation of the steps. The columns, marshaled like a military escort, stood guard between her and the house. The house looked down its nose at her. There was no need of water in a house so definitely closed and barred, so haughtily withdrawn. She was a trespasser. She knew she must get away before somebody saw her.

She had set the bucket on the ground to rest her arm. She lifted it to the fourth step. The first three steps were too insecure-looking. On the step it looked more like good water than when it stood carelessly on the ground.

All at once the sun that had shone in the opening was not there. The ribbons of the ivy-wrapped palmetto slithered sharply over her head. The wind had come. A fringed curtain of moss swept out at her, like Mittie's apron shooing off the Carter chickens.

Lucinda turned to go, but the boxwood path had become a tunnel of boiling shadows. She could neither go nor stay. She was caught between the looming house and the threatening path. She remembered about Flora and the High-School girls and boys. What if the dreadful thing that had happened to Flora should happen now to her? What if a policeman should find her here? Policemen could be hidden behind the columns, behind the boxwood wall, behind the trees. As she thought of policemen, the place became alive with them, all watching her, waiting to see what she was going to do, ready to reach out for her.

Maybe Abe was looking at her too. He might be standing behind the shutters with his gun. He would rush out with the gun if she started up the steps.

The treetops reared, and the trunks groaned as they strained to tear their feet out of the ground. But they were too deeply buried, too tied down with twisted, knotted ivy and periwinkle.

In spite of the commotion, the trees were less frightening than the house and the path. They had a familiarity. From the inside, they looked much the same as from Lucinda's house and yard. She plunged into them and made blindly for the direction of home. The driveway would have made an easier route for her feet, but at its end would be the chained gates. By keeping to the right she should come out at the corner nearest her own side gate. She could worm her way through one of the holes in the fence on that side.

She had to give up trying to run. She hadn't expected to find so many vines trailing on the ground. Every step was a battle. A sickening odor welled up. The smell went through her. It was this that her mother had smelled. It made a sickness and weakness in Lucinda. She coughed and pinched her nostrils to shut out the smell, but she needed both hands to fight back the scratching bushes. The wind had a million hands, and every one held an angry whip. The wind made the heat worse, too.

Lucinda had lost all sense of direction by the time she stumbled through to a small area of bare ground. She was in the house the elaeagnus and wisteria made under the clump of cedars. On every side the wall was unbroken. She couldn't even find the door that had let her in. There was no opening but one at the ground. She made a frantic dip to it and crawled six or eight feet, saving first her dress, then her hair, until she came out of the darkness to a hole in the fence. She crawled through and scrambled to her feet.

There, under her eyes, was home but, from this new angle, a place strange and different. She could not think of taking herself into it with scratched arms and hands and stained dress. She tried to think of an excuse for the way she looked.

Black mountains of clouds tumbled about on the high wind. The heat flared up with a zigzag frenzy and burned its way across the sky. Thunder leapt out of the gash and bellowed at Lucinda. It caught her up and tossed her sky-high, rolled her over and over on the wheeling clouds and let her down with a thud. She ran for her life. Tepid water in drops as big as saucers splashed her face and arms and drew the smell of suffocation from the dust of Mimosa Street.

Not until the next night, when Mittie discovered the long scratch on her left arm, did Lucinda run into real difficulty. Her mother had been easily sidetracked.

"Some bobwire rubbed against me over in Betty's yard," she had told her mother.

"You mean you rubbed against it," her mother had said. "You must learn to walk straight, darling. You look careless and lazy wandering all over the sidewalk when you go down the street. It's the same way in the house. You're always running into things. You haven't learned yet that a straight line is the shortest distance between two points, have you?"

"I guess not," Lucinda had said, thinking how fine it was to be let off so easily. "I'll try to walk straighter," she had said as she held her arm up for mercurochrome, and her father had saved the day by coming in to announce that the storm was only another false alarm. There hadn't been enough rain to lay a spoonful of dust, he said, but the air was much cooler.

Lucinda was so surprised at Mittie's delayed investigation that she blurted out the first thing that came into her head, forgetting that she had already told her mother a different story.

"I caught it on the hedge at Mr. Hardin's," she said.

"Ain't no hedge round Mr. Hardin's. It's just a fench."

"There's a hedge out in the back," Lucinda said. "We paint out there sometimes."

"Ain't no stickers in hedge," Mittie said.

"There are in Mr. Hardin's," Lucinda said, knowing Mittie was not likely to have a chance to examine Mr. Hardin's hedges.

Mittie had finished the supper dishes. She took off her dishwashing apron and wound the clock.

"Are you going upstairs now?" Lucinda asked.

"Got to cool off first," Mittie said. "Got to set on the step tell I cool off."

"I'll cool off, too," Lucinda said. Mittie wasn't listening. She had taken out the yellow soda box and the vinegar bottle. She was mixing soda and vinegar in a glass.

"What are you doing?" Lucinda asked.

"I'm a-stirrin it up," Mittie said.

"What's it for?"

"For Mittie."

"But what for?" Lucinda insisted.

"To take," Mittie said. She turned up the foaming glass and drained it. "Long as you can belch it off you ain't comin down with the fever or nothin," she said.

"I guess I'll cool off, too," Lucinda said.

"You cool off out in front," Mittie said. "This out here's my coolin-off place. Alltime wantin to set out back when you oughta be a-settin out front like a lady."

Lucinda knew something was up. "I'd rather stay with you," she said.

"Lookee there," Mittie said. "Ain't that your mother a-callin you?"

"No. She's talking on the telephone. She's got to call a lot of people."

"Your daddy alltime wantin you in with him in the evenins."

"He's not here," Lucinda said. "He's gone back to the office. Mother's talking to Mrs. Coomb. That takes a long time."

There was a gentle shaking at the lattice door.

"Viney's come to set a little," Mittie whispered. "You go on out in front."

"Mother told you not to let people from the Creek come here now," Lucinda whispered.

"Viney ain't to say from the Creek," Mittie said in her normal voice. "She ain't no moren on the aidge."

"Miss Mittie Belle," a rich voice called guardedly from the steps.

" 'At you, Viney?" Mittie called in a hoarse whisper. "I'm a-comin. Just have you a seat in the cool. I'm a-comin out."

Lucinda disappeared into the back hall until Mittie was settled beside Viney on the steps. Then she slid back to the porch and into the chair nearest the hall door.

"I most about give you out," Mittie was saying.

"I always wus a-comin," Viney said. "Just wanted to go down to Henry's first."

"Reckon he's bad?" Mittie asked.

"Dead," Viney said.

"Is anybody else?"

"Cajy took down."

"Cajy."

"Found him a-layin on the ground a-lappin like a dog.

Ben found him at the creek place along about sundown."

"Where they ain't no water."

"Ain't even so much as mud."

"Reckon he didn't know."

"Reckon he didn't. Some say he just had one of them fits of hissen and fell down by the creek. And some say he done been sick in the shack and didn't have nobody to tote him a drink, so he just crawl out and try to git him some. They toted him back. He wus a-spellin when they toted him back. Singin his letters."

"Reckon he's right bad off?"

"Annie say he gonna die. She say that old clock of Abe's 'at ain't never run a lick all these years wus a-strikin alltime they wus totin him in. She say she reckon it strike a hunderd times, strikin alltime they totin him in and puttin him on the bed. She say the strikin's a sure sign. After all them years. She say it's a-strikin now to call the time for Cajy."

"Who's a-doin for Cajy?" Mittie asked.

"Annie is," Viney said. "Her and Jim's a-takin turns. I'll be a-goin in to hep."

"Look like Abe oughta know about Cajy bein sick," Mittie said. "Look like somebody oughta go up there and tell him about his boy."

"Come daylight they'll be some to go," Viney said. She lowered her voice. "Ain't nobody a-goin up in there at night. He hadn't oughta be a-leavin Cajy alltime by hissef, a-bein like he is."

Lucinda had to strain her ears now to hear. She wondered if she dared risk moving to another chair.

"They got him a-guardin," Mittie said. "He can't git off

no more while he's a-guardin the piccher. But reckon he'd find some way to go effen he knowed his boy wus sick. They oughta go and tell him."

"Ain't nobody a-goin to go in there at night." Viney was firm. "Up in that place. Come day and some'll go and tell him. Ain't nobody a-goin to go at night. I done heared 'em say."

"Look like Abe ud been a-makin out to go some way. Been a-hangin round evenins at the fench all summer a-waitin for Cajy to go by. Ever' evenin he wus hangin round tell here lately. Here lately I ain't been a-seein him atall."

"And him a-knowin Cajy couldn't do for hissef."

The Denton piano sent a burst of music across the street, such a gay, ringing blend of piano and three or four voices that every note and every word of the song made its way through the Darby house to the back porch.

"A tisket, a tasket, I lost my yellow basket."

Under cover of the music Lucinda moved to the rocking chair. She was so close now she could have touched Mittie's shoulder by sticking a finger through the lattice.

"Look like Cajy didn't never have no good times or nothin," Mittie said.

"He had spellin. Singin them words like anybody else a-singin Glory-to-God. Sometimes nights you'd hear him a-singin down on Gander, and fore you knowed it you'd be a-wantin to let out a Bless-Jesus like you wus in meetin."

"Didn't spell no Jesus names and sing no Jesus songs," Mittie reminded her.

"Howcome you sayin he didn't? Howcome anybody

know what Cajy spell and him off in the marsh? Or him so
fur off all anybody could hear wus him a-singin? Howcome
anybody know he wusn't singin ever' one the preacher's
words? I bet he could a spell ever' word the preacher could
preach."

"He might could," Mittie agreed, "but he ain't never
had no learnin. Reckon spellin's for some just like talkin
is or singin."

"Reckon."

"Look like a body wouldn't be a-needin spellin effen he
couldn't write. Just a-walkin round a-singin letters ain't
a-doin nobody no good."

"Folks ud give him money."

" 'At's right. They give him money. He just stand
there and sing them letters, and they give him money to
go off and buy hissef a loaf of bread. Couldn't do nothin
with his spellin, but they give him money."

"Look like folks like listenin," Viney said.

The two women on the steps sighed long sighs. Lucinda
wished she dared get rid of her own extra breath.

"It's nighttime when he do the guardin with the gun,"
Mittie said.

" 'At's right," Viney said.

Through the hall Lucinda heard her mother's voice at
the telephone.

"If you could get in the Thursday crowd you'd like it
better," she said. "The Monday crowd's not half so nice.
The Lesters come Thursdays, and Mrs. Raymond and Ella
Rainey. We're making dresses for children now, and
there's nothing I love more. They're not attractive like
Lucinda's. They have to be so warm. But they're not bad
a bit. The Red Cross sends the patterns and—"

"Reckon I wouldn't mind a-goin to tell Abe effen you didn't mind to go," Mittie said.

"I done told you I ain't a-goin," Viney said. "They's folks a-doin for Cajy, and I'm a-goin to do. Come daylight they'll be plenty won't mind to go."

The steps creaked. First one woman, then the other stood.

"I reckon you ain't a-comin for Henry's funral?" Viney asked.

"Reckon not," Mittie said. "I sure would like to go, but my folks is lookin after me. They ain't a-lettin me go off down where people's sick. But look like us could go up there and tell Abe about his boy."

The voices passed beyond earshot. Mittie had followed Viney to the gate. Lucinda knew that good nights said over the gate were long ones. Her mother was still talking on the telephone. "Some of the girls think our bridge club ought to do nothing but knit," Ethel Darby was saying. "Some of them have been bringing their work and knitting while they're dummy. But Loulie says—"

Lucinda decided to go upstairs and wait for Mittie to come up to bed. She took out the practice paper and began to draw the faces of the little boys in the band. But they didn't look right. She didn't have her mind on the boys. She was thinking about Mittie and Viney and Cajy and Abe. Viney was the one who liked Cajy best, but Mittie was the one who wanted to go tell Abe. Maybe by now she had persuaded Viney to go with her. She decided to see if they had left the gate. From the side windows of her mother's room she could see the gate if it wasn't too dark. She crossed the hall. It would be better not to turn on the lights in her mother's room. She held her hands around her face and pressed her nose against the screen. They were still leaning on the gate.

The longer she looked, the easier it was to see them. The moon was coming up. The light grew whiter and spread up and down Mimosa Street, making shadows under the trees. It reached across the street to the Castleton trees.

The night chorus of katydids and crickets flowed up to the window and ebbed away. It came and went in waves until it seemed to be no more than a ringing in the ears. Through the ringing, Lucinda heard Mittie say, "Look like I can't think about a-goin in and goin to sleep and him not a-knowin." Lucinda couldn't hear what Viney said in reply. The same thing she'd been saying, probably. Maybe after Viney left, Lucinda was thinking, she could offer to go with Mittie. If Viney didn't stay too late maybe Mittie would be willing to go with only her. As soon as Viney left she would watch for a chance when her mother wouldn't know. Then she would go back downstairs and tell Mittie she would go with her. All day she had pushed back the frightened thoughts about her trip with the water. It seemed now that if she could go with Mittie's warm bigness close beside her she wouldn't be afraid at all. She would know this time how things would be, and that would make it all right.

She went to the front window to see if the moonlight reached all the way along Mimosa Street to Pine Street. She pressed against the screen, again cupping her hands around her eyes. For a second she thought the gates were standing open. Then she looked again and realized that instead of one pair of gates she saw two. The moonlight fell, bright and full, directly on the tall posts and panels of curled and twisted iron. She stood looking as the moonlight spread and included the triangular valance over the gates where a giant's pen had written, with indelible metal, a flourishing *R* and *C* and, below the entwined letters, the date, 1802.

It seemed that never in broad daylight could the elaborate detail have shone more clearly. There was the emptiness where half of a big iron *fleur-de-lis* had fallen away. There were gaps where scrolls or rods should be. There were the breaks made by the missing bars that once had paralleled the posts. But Lucinda had never before seen the look of two pairs of gates. She sat on her feet and leaned on the sill and stared. The shadow gates slanted away in front of the real gates and reached across the approach to the avenue. They were taller, narrower, finer than the real gates. The chain was on the shadow gates, too.

The longer Lucinda looked, the sharper her eyes became, the farther they were able to see. She was seeing farther, she thought, than ever before, even by day. A little more growing of the moon was all she needed to be able to see all the way. She wondered why she had never before looked at Castleton from that window. As she waited to see farther she realized that the light was growing dimmer. A gust of wind, dry and cool, brushed her face and lifted her hair. The shadows made sudden, darting movements, shrank little by little, and were lost in the dark.

By the time the light was gone Lucinda had the eyes of a cat. She did not need the moon to show her the automobile that was standing at the left of the gates, drawn up until it seemed to touch the Castleton fence. It was no more than the black shape of an automobile, drawn away from the street, crouching beside the fence. She hadn't seen it in the moonlight, but it looked as if it had been there a long time.

Her mother and father were moving about downstairs, locking doors and closing windows and turning off lights. She barely had time to get to her own room and into her nightgown. Not until she was safely in bed did she think again of Mittie. She hadn't heard her come upstairs. Her mother and father were upstairs now, tipping about, talking quietly. They thought she was asleep. What if they had locked Mittie out? What if Mittie had gone, finally, to tell Abe and should come back after everybody was asleep? The longer she thought about it, the more sure she was that Mittie had not come in. Mittie would come back from Castleton and find the doors locked. She would try first one door and then the other. Then she would know she was locked out. She would have to go back to her house down on the Creek. Then she would take the fever and maybe she would die. If that should happen Lucinda knew it would be her fault. She was the one who knew Mittie was locked out. She would be a murderer if Mittie died.

She heard the patting sounds in the bathroom. Her mother was brushing her hair. That meant her father had gone to bed. In a few minutes her mother would be in bed, too.

Lucinda got out of bed and put her ear against the keyhole of the door. She would wait until after the door across the hall was closed. Then she would go to Mittie's room and see if she was there.

She listened to the clap of the little mules against the tile of the bathroom floor. They were trying not to make a noise, but now and then a heel struck as sharply as a tap dancer's. The sound of the patting stopped. After a few minutes the door closed behind the little heels.

Lucinda's feet and legs ached from squatting by the keyhole. She sat on the floor. She would have to allow time for her mother to go to sleep. She was sure that at least half an hour must have passed when she put her hand on the door knob. She turned it so slowly and carefully that it made no sound. Keeping her hand against the wall for guidance, she made her way down the hall to the door at the end. She hoped Mittie wouldn't be frightened by the opening of the door. She found the knob of the door and turned it.

"Mittie," she whispered. "Mittie."

There was no answer.

The room was heavy with heat that bore down from the exposed rafters. There was the smell, almost musty, almost sour, that had been in the room since Mittie had been sleeping there. But Lucinda knew Mittie was not there. She reached wildly above her head until she found the string tied to the cord that pulled on the light.

Mittie was not there. The new little cot, already sagging in the middle like the seat of the kitchen chair, stood untouched against the wall. It looked as if Mittie would never be in it again. The tears burned Lucinda's eyes.

Music was coming again from the Dentons' piano, but it was hardly more than a breath. Only two voices were left, Jean's and her young man's. They were half singing, half humming:

> "Dum dee dee dum-m, da dee dum-m,
> Me and my little banjo."

The words trailed off vaguely into unbearable sadness. Lucinda had to stop looking at the bed that Mittie might never sleep in again.

Maybe, Lucinda thought, there was still time to save her. If she went downstairs and unlocked the door she might find Mittie there, just coming back from telling Abe. The thought of seeing her standing on the back steps was so comforting she could not wait to go down. She pulled out the light. Just as she stepped into the hall the other door opened, and her father in his blue pajamas came out.

"Why, Lucinda," he said.

Instantly her mother was beside him.

"Did you want Mittie for something?" her mother asked.

"She's not there," Lucinda said. Hearing the words coming out of her own mouth was too much for her. "She's gone. She went to tell Abe about Cajy being sick." Words and tears poured out together.

"What's this?" her father asked.

"Come into your room," her mother said, "and tell us what's the matter." She put an arm around Lucinda's shoulder and guided her into the room. "Get into bed and tell us quietly."

"We've got to unlock the door," Lucinda sobbed. "We've got to fix it so she can get in."

"The door's not locked, Lucinda," her father said. He was stroking her back.

Her mother was holding out a paper handkerchief to her. "Take this," she said, "and blow your nose. And you must stop crying if you expect us to understand what you are trying to say. Mittie's right out in the yard, Lucinda. One of her friends came to see her and they've been talking over the back gate for hours. We didn't lock

the back door. We called to her to lock it when she comes
in. But she's slow about coming. Your father was going to
call down to her that she would have to talk more quietly
or come in. He was going to tell her they were keeping
us awake."

Lucinda's father had left her to turn off the overhead
light. He didn't want to see her crying. He drew a chair
to the side of her bed so he could take her hand. Her
mother sat on the foot of the bed on the other side.

"Good night, dear, sweet dreams, dear,"

the voices were singing over at the Dentons'.

The tears came with a fresh gush.

"What is it Mittie was going to tell Abe?" her father
asked.

"Viney told Mittie Cajy's sick," Lucinda said. "Mittie
thought his papa ought to know but Viney wouldn't go
with her."

"Well, Mittie didn't go," Lucinda's mother said.
"They've been hanging over the gate since long before we
came upstairs. I'm going to call to her now that she must
come to bed and let us all get to sleep. There's nothing
to worry about, darling." She had got up from the bed and
was leaning over Lucinda to kiss her good night.

"Mittie's trying to get Viney to go with her," Lucinda
said. "That's why she doesn't want to come in."

"Viney doesn't want to go?" her father asked.

"She said people would go in the morning. She said she
wouldn't go at night and nobody else would. But Mittie
said she wouldn't be afraid if she didn't have to go by
herself."

"Good old Mittie," Lucinda's father said.

"Viney said Cajy's going to die," Lucinda said.

Her mother turned with a jerk. "The idea. What talk!"

"They think Abe doesn't know about Cajy?" her father asked.

"Viney said he doesn't."

"Of course Abe ought to know," her father said.

"Come on to bed, Clifford," her mother said. "Come on and let Lucinda go to sleep."

"Bless her soul," he said. "If she wants to go over there tonight, I'll go with her."

Before he could move Lucinda's mother cried, "Clifford Darby, what are you talking about? Of course you'll do nothing of the kind."

She had swung around so fast she had to hold on to the bedpost. Lucinda felt the tremors her hand sent into the bed.

"I think it's pretty damned humane of Mittie," he said. "If that's what's keeping her out of bed I guess I can do that much to help, go with her to tell the old man."

"Go with her where?" Ethel Darby asked. Her voice was high and charged. "And what would you tell him, here in the middle of the night? You know how Negroes are about death. Viney probably made the whole thing up, just to have a big tale to tell Mittie. You know how dramatic they are about death. Cajy's probably no more sick than you are." She talked fast and held onto the bedpost.

"On the other hand—" he began. He was taking out his watch.

"Clifford," she cried. The bed shook as she clutched the post with her two hands.

The look fell like a curtain over his face.

"You'd do this to me," Ethel Darby said, "do this to Lucinda and me? For those Negroes?"

The words sprang to his lips. But he managed to bite them back. The look spread downward. His shoulders drooped. His fingers uncurled and hung, disjointed, limp like the lock of hair.

"At this hour of the night," Ethel Darby said.

"Of course it's bedtime," he said, "time for Lucy to kick us out."

"There's Mittie now," Lucinda's mother said. "Hear her? She's decided it's not necessary to go tonight after all. She's locking the back door. Now we can all go to sleep."

"Hear her?" her father asked.

"Yes," Lucinda said.

"Everything's all right now," he said. But he didn't look at her. "In the morning we'll see—"

"Turn over now and go to sleep," Lucinda's mother said.

"If anything else troubles you," her father said, "better come directly to headquarters. I'll leave both our doors open." He turned off the table lamp.

In the hall they said good night to Mittie. "Hurry and get to bed, Mittie," Ethel Darby said. "You've kept us all awake long enough."

LUCINDA AND JOHNNY were the only ones left. Jocile wanted to clean the painting room, so they were working downstairs in the music room. Twice, already, Miss Carley had reminded Johnny that it was getting late and he must not forget about being at home in time. "In time" meant in time to help with the milking. Johnny thought he could finish his picture. Now that he and Mr. Hardin understood each other, Johnny was having a fine time with his animal pictures. Mr. Hardin knew, now, that Johnny didn't want his mules and horses to be running or even walking. He wanted them to be standing still. But not, of course, like dead mules and horses. This one was going to show what he'd had in mind all along, a horse that was standing still because he was too tired to take another step. There was something about tired animals that Johnny wanted in every one of his pictures.

Mr. Hardin stood behind Johnny, stroking him with the gentle *Hm*'s, saying nothing else. Then he crossed over to Lucinda's easel. She could feel him looking, but he didn't say anything. Lucinda wished he would say the *Hm*'s for her, too. They always seemed to flow straight down her arm, into her hand and brush, and into the picture. But this time he stood behind her and said nothing at all. After a minute or two he left the room and went back to the terrace, where his easel stood and where Miss Carley and Mr. Ellis were copying music at the long table.

Miss Carley and Mr. Ellis were getting ready for the trip the jug-band boys were going to make to play on the radio. Miss Carley had bought new clothes for them, and Mr. Ellis had got their instruments in shape. Some of those were new, too. Mr. Ellis was going to make a speech on the radio and the little boys were going to play. They were going to play "It's a Me" and "Jesu, Joy" and a piece they had made up themselves about the drouth, called "Down Where Gander Used to Be." Mr. Ellis had talked a lot to Miss Carley lately about what he was going to say in his speech. Lucinda liked to hear them talk because they got so excited whenever one of them thought of another good thing to put into the speech. Miss Carley and Mr. Hardin would tease Mr. Ellis and tell him he had to sign a pledge not to say anything in his speech that he hadn't tried out on them. Lucinda loved to hear him practicing the things he was going to say.

"I'll tell them that if a few of those would-be virtuosi, hanging around New York, waiting for somebody to stake them to a Town Hall recital, would take a little trek west or south maybe they'd get an idea of what American music is," he was saying out on the terrace now.

"No, you won't," Mr. Hardin cried. "Just slow down a minute. Be a shade gentler about it. Think back a little. Remember how long it took me to get you out of that New York trap."

"Well, I'm out, now. It makes me sick to think of the

hundreds of grand guys, good as buried up there, confused by managers and critics and the congestion they're making worse. Think what they could do for this country—and this country could do for them—if thev'd scatter themselves over the map."

"All right, all right," Mr. Hardin said, "but don't take a big stick to them. Remember how tactful I was with you." This was the teasing kind of talk Lucinda liked to hear, whether she could understand it or not.

"Sure, but think how long it took you to get anywhere," Mr. Ellis said. "Tell me," he cried, "where do our American symphonies come from? Do they come from New York? No, sir. They come from Oklahoma. Oklahoma! Who ever heard of Oklahoma? And where do our pictures come from? From little old Macklin! A thousand miles from nowhere."

"Not quite all of them," Mr. Hardin said. He was really laughing now.

"Why, when I think I might have gone on forever," Mr. Ellis said, "without knowing the kind of things these five little bastards can do, the kind of leaders and stabilizers they're capable of being for their race; for all of us—"

"Off again," Miss Carley said. "He's as gone on his little nigs, Curtis, as you are on the Wednesday children."

"It's not just what those little boys can do. That's exciting enough, God knows, but it's the things they've opened my eyes to about the qualities of their race. I've been thinking for weeks about the great American music that's stirring deep down under this two-race society of yours and that will be smothered until there's more honesty in your relationships with each other. But lately I've been thinking in much the same terms of their whole status as human

beings. It's down here that the solution of the Negro problem should really get under way. With a strange mixture
of kindness and cruelty, you're holding them to a level
worse, often, than that of slavery. But, just the same, you
understand them better than we do in the East. In your
hearts you know what's under the good and the bad in
them. You know their emotional richness, their capacity
for loyalty, their patience for hardships. You trust your
children, your food, your property to their care. If you
weren't so smug and selfish you'd think more about the
fine contributing citizens they could be if they had the
chance. Why, in God's name, don't you wake up? This
country can't afford to leave undeveloped such enormous
resources of mind and talent."

"Surely the things that are happening now in Europe
will teach us to take our responsibilities more seriously,"
Miss Carley said. "Here in Macklin I think a few of us are
beginning to come to our senses. And now that Curtis—"

"By the way, Eva," Mr. Hardin said, "I went in a few
minutes ago to look. You're right, dead right. It's just
what we've been expecting." He didn't want the talk to be
about himself.

"Yes?" Miss Carley said.

"Go in this minute, Carl," Mr. Hardin said, "and you'll
see what we've been talking about. The child is painting
a beautiful picture."

The words had hardly been words. Lucinda's eyes slid
sidewise to see if Johnny had heard them, and met his
eyes slanting up from the big, drooping roan. His look
changed suddenly to a wide-open grin.

"Gosh," he snorted, "youghta see your nose." He held
his hand over his mouth, but that didn't keep him from

shaking. "Honest," he said, "I can't help laughing. Go and look."

Lucinda went to the gold-framed pier glass that filled the wall between the back windows. The tip of her nose was as red as the paint she had daubed on one of the tin-can drums.

"How did I ever?" she began, but in that breath she saw the foolish look the red smear gave to her whole face. It was as funny as if she were looking at another person. As soon as she got the laughing in hand she looked at Johnny, and they both went off again. "Good thing it's just water color," she said between gasps.

The sound of steps in the hall made them draw their faces in. Lucinda went back to her easel, scrubbing her nose with all her might. She didn't dare look up, but she knew Mr. Ellis was coming into the room. She pretended to concentrate on something at the bottom of the picture. That kept her nose so low he surely could not see it. Dread of having Mr. Ellis see her face sobered Lucinda, but she could feel Johnny smoldering across the room. He gulped back a snort and turned it into a silly kind of sneeze.

Mr. Ellis was walking along her side of the room. He stood behind her. Under his eyes Lucinda's wavering backbone tried to steady itself. Finally he walked out as he had come in, without going around to look at Johnny's picture.

The words began to pour in from all sides, amplified by silence, until the room and herself and the picture before her were as light as cork, bobbing against the sea of words, *"The child is painting a beautiful picture . . . a beautiful picture . . . a beautiful picture . . ."*

"Well, I guess I better go," Johnny said. He was wiping

his brushes. "I'd give you some of my water for your nose," he said, "but it's all gone." He turned the milk bottle upside down to show Lucinda that it was dry. He'd got over having to laugh.

"I've got a little more," Lucinda said. She held up her bottle to show him he needn't worry about that. "I think most of it's off now, anyway," she said, still scrubbing at her nose.

"It wouldn't show hardly at all," Johnny said, "if it wasn't for rubbing it so much."

Mr. Hardin stood at the door. "You're pretty late, John," he said. "I have an errand out at Dump Corner. Hop in my car, and I'll run you out that far."

Lucinda settled down to finish the drummer. He was the hardest one. *The child is painting a beautiful picture. The child is painting a beautiful picture* . . . The words were rolling, over and over, giving her the feeling of the *Hm*'s, only much more.

"You mustn't think that," Miss Carley was saying out on the terrace. "You're being unfair. It was stupid and childish of me to let you see. Now you're blaming him. And you mustn't. You know how much your loyalty and friendship mean to him. You must not blame him for something that's not his fault."

"I'm not blaming him for anything," Mr. Ellis said. "I'm simply stating that the man is a blind and selfish fool."

Miss Carley stopped him. "He's never thought of anything except that we like to talk to each other, that we have the same ideas about a great many things. If I've been hurt, as of course I was when you found me dissolved, it's because sometimes I don't use my own intelligence. I haven't the sense to stop hoping he'll feel differently—some time."

"I wonder if he's capable of realizing that he'd never have finished those sketches without you. He'd never have accepted the commission. He'd never have set up this school, or made it go. For that matter, he'd never have pulled himself together and become the person, the painter, he is today. For the first ten years I knew him he was a divided soul. He came back to New York three years ago a different person. He was full of the talks he'd been having with you. He rattled off your ideas day and night. It was Eva Carley says this and Eva Carley thinks that. Mary noticed it at once. His work suddenly began to make sense. Came to life. Before I ever saw you I knew it was you who had healed him from those years when everything and everybody who touched his life down here worked together to destroy him. This was where he had to be to paint. But when he came back the three of them began all over to torture him. I don't know which was worst for him, his father's nagging about that cutthroat Hardin Brothers business, or his mother's two-faced maneuvers, or—well, the other thing. Thank God, he's through with them all now. And, thanks chiefly to you, his work is on the right track at last. But I wonder if he stops to think what he would do if he couldn't show his plans to you—or, to be more honest, take his plans from you. And what would he have done this morning if you had refused to leave your own breakfast and dash over here because he wanted you to help us eat those figs?"

"I'm foolish, I know, to come running whenever he calls."

"Exactly. Whether it's figs or murals. You spoil him. Let him try doing without you now and then. Flash another man in his face."

Lucinda couldn't keep from hearing the voices on the terrace. The words came and went in the way of grown-up talk, but some of them spread a film of thinking and wondering between her eyes and the round black face under her brush.

"I'll never cheat myself of any minute I can have with him, on any terms," Miss Carley was saying. "I'm not an eighteen-year-old girl, playing at a flirtation. I'm a thirty-seven-year-old woman in love for the first time. I expect I'll go right on being underfoot as long as I'm wanted. Surely you don't think I could—or would—turn my back on the things that are going on here now, the work he's doing with the Wednesday children, the things you're doing evenings with the darling little nigs, the way the mural plans are growing."

Sometimes they sounded as if they were mad at Mr. Hardin. But it seemed, too, that it was Mr. Hardin she was talking about when Miss Carley said she was in love.

"He needs you more than you need him. Give the fool a chance to realize it," Mr. Ellis said, so crossly that Lucinda hated him for a minute. But she couldn't go on hating him while Miss Carley was talking so gently to him.

"Oh, Carl, he'd have to know it if it were like that. I think I'm saying the right things to myself. I have it all worked out pretty well in my mind. I'll never forgive myself if you hold this against him."

"I know him too well for that," Mr. Ellis said. "Mary and I saw him through those hellish years when you hardly knew him. But this is one of the times when I'd like to—"

"There's one thing you're forgetting," Miss Carley broke in, "and I've been forgetting it, too. You saw Curtis always after he had given Emily up again. But year after year I saw the other side. I know how happy they were together —when they were happy. I know about those years when they expected some day to be married. Her beauty was incredible, Carl. If you had ever seen her you would realize what he has to remember—"

Sometimes Lucinda had heard people telling her mother things like this about Curtis Hardin and Emily Reeves. Sometimes, when people talked about the beauty of Emily Reeves, Lucinda would shut her eyes and try to see it. Now she did see it. For half a second it stood out clearly between her and the five little boys on the paper.

"To remember," Mr. Ellis said, scornfully. "He's served his time at that. One thing, at least, we can be thankful for; he didn't come back to her this time. He came back to his work."

There was a scraping of chairs on the terrace. "We've forgotten Lucinda," Miss Carley said, in her teacher voice. "She'll put her eyes out in that room. Lucinda," she called.

Lucinda went to the window. "Yes, Miss Carley," she said.

"Haven't you done enough for today?"

Lucinda nodded. Something was happening to her nose. She held the paint-streaked handkerchief to it. A trickling warmth came through. She ran to the bathroom, forgetting that the door was locked, now that there was no water.

Miss Carley met her in the hall.

"I guess I rubbed too hard," Lucinda explained into the muffling handkerchief.

"Wait a minute," Miss Carley said, "I'll unlock the door and bring some hot water from the kitchen."

At first Miss Carley didn't understand about the stained handkerchief. It made it seem that the nosebleed had been much worse. As soon as Lucinda could, she told her about the paint. Miss Carley got an ice bag from Jocile and made Lucinda sit quietly in the hall. The bleeding had stopped by the time Mr. Hardin came back, but he thought it would be better for Lucinda not to walk home.

"I'm running a taxicab, today," he said, "and you're my next passenger."

As they walked out to the car the thought occurred to Lucinda that the bleeding might begin again. It would be dreadful to have such a thing happen as she sat beside Mr. Hardin. She reached for the back door. "I guess I'll just get in here," she said.

She saw Mr. Hardin look back at Miss Carley and Mr. Ellis, who were standing in the doorway. He was trying not to smile about something. She realized that she had done the wrong thing but there was nothing to do now but to sit there shrinking and burning with shame and holding her nose with the paper handkerchiefs to keep the bleeding from starting again.

"It's somewhere on Cass Avenue, isn't it, Lucinda?" Mr. Hardin said as the car moved away from the curb.

"It's the last house," Lucinda said. "On the corner of Mimosa."

"That's right," Mr. Hardin said. "I remember. Your father told me—"

What her father had told him was swallowed up in the scream of a siren. The red fire engine had leapt into the street. It lunged forward, roaring for the right of way.

Mr. Hardin drew his car over to the side of the street. "We heard them the first time, didn't we?" he said, smiling back at Lucinda.

The siren cut their ears as the engine charged past them and into Cass Avenue. Lucinda held her breath and prayed for it not to be her house. The Square was suddenly full of cars and bicycles, following the engine, pell-mell, speed limits forgotten.

Mr. Hardin brought his car to life. He waited to let two, three, four more of the followers pass before he pulled back into the street.

Lucinda sat on the edge of the seat and leaned forward, straining for the first glimpse of the corner of Cass and Mimosa. The engine was well ahead, racing wildly against the hysteria of the siren and the fury of the bell.

It was a strange time to be remembering the words. She wasn't remembering them, really. They were simply there, saying themselves inside her, under the tumult of wailing siren, clanging bell, and honking horns. *The child is painting a beautiful picture. The child is painting a beautiful picture. The child is painting—* The noise and terror blurred the pattern of the words, elided them into a shaft of happiness that was ashamed before the panic of the moment, but not broken by it. Lucinda shuddered to feel herself speeding to the sight of her house in flames while this overwhelming happiness spread itself over her face, regardless of the dreadful thing that was happening.

"Please, God," she prayed, "don't let it be our house."

The car sprang forward with a leap that threw Lucinda against the back of the seat. Mr. Hardin had joined the race. He bent over the wheel, the farther to see, and drove like the wind.

Lucinda recovered her perch on the edge of the seat but she had to hold hard to keep it. The engine was paying no attention to Lucinda's house. It streaked ahead, pointed straight at Castleton's gates. It was bent on breaking the chains and crashing through with its own power and speed. There was no room left in Lucinda for anything but terror. The rampant engine plunged at the gates. Then, just in time, it stopped short. The siren caught its breath. The bell slowed down. "Bang . . . bang . . . bang," it went so that nobody could forget for a minute that something was wrong. Two giants tumbled off the engine. One of them braced the gates while the other brought down an axe with a mighty blow. Each man seized a gate, shook it, and dragged it open. Almost before they were on again the engine tore into the avenue, the siren wilder than ever. A train of cars followed, as geared to the speed and purpose of the engine as if they had been hitched to it.

Mr. Hardin's car was a part of the train. It had forgotten about Lucinda, peering and clinging in the back. It was a part of the headlong assault on Castleton, part of the smoldering impatience, unleashed at last. And Lucinda, a part of the car, was swept through the gates and up the avenue. They passed one car after another, brushing aside the interlopers, to make their way knowingly to the point where the avenue ended at the circle, and the circle widened to form the driveway to the back of the house. Only the engine and the policeman's car had reached the circle ahead of Lucinda and Mr. Hardin. Two firemen ran up the steps, followed by a policeman. Lucinda could see nothing more than the steps without leaning out, and she was afraid to budge from her corner. There was no sign of fire, not even the smell or feel of it.

A voice was singing in the car in front of Lucinda. The policeman had forgotten to turn off his radio.

As Mr. Hardin jerked on the brake Lucinda saw that a woman was running along the boxwood path, directly to their right. Mr. Hardin, seeing how close the cars came as they rolled into the circle, was not getting out of the door by the wheel. He was sliding along the seat to get out on the side by the path. He had forgotten about Lucinda. He didn't see the woman. The pale, heavy braids, wound around her head, had slipped, making her look as if she had on a hat much too big for her. Her dress seemed too big, too, and so long that it gave her a funny look. Lucinda thought she might be somebody from Pine Street who had followed the siren, as the cars and bicycles had followed it. She was close enough now for Lucinda to see that she was crying.

Mr. Hardin got out of the car, still not remembering Lucinda. He slammed the door and turned. The woman came out of the walled path. They stopped short, staring at each other, unable to move. Then Lucinda heard their voices meet in a cry. Their arms went out to each other. They stood together a minute, and all that side of Castleton was quiet while cars and voices poured into the circle. Lucinda shrank in to the farthest corner of the car.

"It's Abe," the woman was saying. "No, not a fire. No. He's wild. Crazy. He's shot the portrait to pieces. No, my precious darling, it's not a fire. Look at the house, Curtis. There it stands. No, it's the portrait, Curtis; the portrait. I locked Mother into one of the back rooms and ran out to telephone for help. I couldn't think of anything but the fire department. Nobody was at home in the little Pine Street houses. I had to break into one of them. After I'd got the fire department I tried to call a doctor. But all of the doctors were out. It took so long to find one. Nothing will stop Abe. Two of his friends had come from the Creek to see him. I left them hiding in the kitchen, waiting to tell us what it was that happened. But anybody can see he's crazy. Absolutely wild." Mr. Hardin was letting her talk. He stood, holding one of her hands, listening, looking at her.

> "In summertime on Bredon
> The bells they sound so clear . . ."

the radio voice was singing.

"Mother's back there," she said. "I got her as far away as possible and locked the door."

"Shall we go to her?" Mr. Hardin said.

They were moving together along the ivy-bordered path, under the pointed ribbons of palmetto. They walked along the aisle darkened by shiny-leafed trees, their arms around each other. They passed out of sight, and still Lucinda didn't dare leave her corner. She didn't know what to do with herself.

People were coming down the steps. A policeman stood at the top, ordering them away. Paul, from the filling station, and another man came down first. They looked straight at Lucinda as they passed, without seeing her. "I call it a good joke on the old girl," Paul was saying. "Reckon if she'd known what was going to happen she'd not been so quick to turn down thirty thousand bucks."

"I'll say," his friend agreed. "Well, she ain't got neither one now. Reckon what she's got now's just about nothing minus."

"Guess they musta told the old man a little sudden," Paul said. "Took him sorta by surprise so's he—"

The radio voice now was familiar. It was the one they listened to sometimes in the garage. "He said the fronts are everywhere, the trenches dug in towns and streets. Not only soldiers are involved, he said, but women and children, too."

Lucinda saw the Carter boys coming. She bent over, pretending to tie her shoestring as they passed.

"Guess he didn't know he was sick until he knew he was dead," Andy Carter said.

Maybe it was Cajy that was dead, and maybe if she and Mittie had gone to tell Abe last night—

"When you think about him being with it all the time like that," a strange voice said as it passed, "and always having that gun. And them big as life like that. I guess it's not a wonder."

Lucinda was dizzy from half standing on her head. The radio voice was holding the center of the stage for the minute. " 'Two or three years are not a long time,' the Prime Minister said, 'even in our short, precarious lives—' "

It didn't matter now whether Lucinda was seen or not. Most of the people coming down the steps were strangers —too excited, she could see, to pay any attention to her.

"Boy, did he shoot em down!" a big man in overalls said. "I swear to God it seems a lot more like murder than —whatever it is. Them being so big, and all. Looks more like just standing there shooting five people to pieces."

"Not standing, Buddy. I got there in time to see. That nigger was running wild. Running in circles. I bet he filled that gun and fired her forty times."

As soon as they passed Mr. Hardin's car their voices

were drowned out by the steady clarity of the radio speaker. His voice had taken on a ringing sound as if it could not hold itself in, as if soon the speaker himself would have to step out of the policeman's car and let his words cry out until they filled Castleton all the way down to the gates. " 'Since we have the honor to be the sole champion of the liberty of all Europe,' the Prime Minister said, 'we must not grudge these years or weary as we toil and struggle through them.' "

"Ever notice how things get to going till they're so bad it looks like you can't stop em?" It was the man from the five-and-ten. He and another man had reached Mr. Hardin's car. Two others came up and stood with them. "Take the way things are now," he went on. "Take the war and the drouth and all those people over at Jenks out of work."

"And the fever."

"And this up here."

"One thing kinder brings on another. Kinder scares you when you ain't doing nothing about it."

Two of the men moved on. They got into a car, rounded the circle and were gone. The five-and-ten man and his friend stood talking. Lucinda could see they didn't want to go.

"Think how it would be to have a place like this to come home to nights. Ain't a God's scrap of anything left inside but—"

"It's sure a fine house. Would a been if they hadn't let it go."

"Yeah. You wouldn't a thought, riding by, there was a thing like this in here."

The radio voice was ringing again: ". . . said he has no

misgivings as he views the process. He said no one can stop it. 'Like the Mississippi,' said Mr. Churchill, 'it just keeps rolling along—' "

*Like the Mississippi,* Cajy's song had taken over the word. It was spelling itself to Cajy's tune with Cajy's arms making it into the river. *M-i-s*—Lucinda heard it above everything, above the voices of the men and boys walking by to get into their cars, riding by on their bicycles, rolling along, on down the avenue.

" 'Let it roll on,' Mr. Churchill said, 'in full flood—to broader lands and better days.' "

The cars were trickling away, driving down the avenue as if it had been something they did every day, rolling along— The two firemen came out and stood between the columns. They were the right size to be standing there. They strode down the steps and climbed onto the engine.

"They'll bring him along when the doctor comes," one of the firemen said. "Jail's the only place we've got to put him."

The engine heaved. Stiff and lumbering, it made the turn of the circle. It didn't seem possible that it had traveled so fast a few minutes ago. Only the policeman's car was left.

It was not right to be sitting there when everybody was gone but the policeman and Mr. Hardin. Lucinda dreaded the shock she would give Mr. Hardin when he came out and realized that he had forgotten her. And she wouldn't like the policeman to see her and wonder what she was doing there. Maybe he would ask her. It was his business to know about things like that. Flora had been at Castleton when the policeman had seen her and all the trouble had started. If she didn't go home soon it would be dark and there would be questions. It didn't seem possible that she would be able to think of good answers today.

She made a quick survey of the circle and the portico. It was almost as dark as when she had left the water on the steps. The steps were swaying now with shadows. They were like a paper fan turned upside down. The columns were as dim as the columns in the photograph Miss Carley had. As she got out of the car she thought it might be better to go through the trees as she had done before. It seemed safer than to walk openly down the avenue. But she was already in the avenue. She stuck to it. She trudged along, afraid to make herself conspicuous by walking either slow or fast. She decided to try stepping only on shadows. But they shilly-shallied too much. She was soon too dizzy to look. The dark was coming fast, just as it had yesterday, rolling along, the river rolling, herself rolling down the avenue, rolling along, rolling, rolling—a rolling word.

"Where in the world have you been, Lucy?" her mother would ask. She couldn't hope to get off every time.

She would look as if she didn't mind the question at all and say: "Not anywhere. Just to Mr. Hardin's."

"But what kept you so late?" her mother would say.

And she would answer, easy-like, "Just painting—"

That started it. It came back, streaming through her and around her: *The child is painting a beautiful picture. The child is paint—* There was no room for thinking about the questions that were coming or the things up there behind her or anything else. The words were coming from everywhere, filling everything, filling her; but making her so light she seemed to be floating. If she hurried there would be time to practice the jug boy's face before supper. His face was not brown like the jug, but black. When he puckered up his mouth to blow, his head was almost the shape of the jug. If she could figure out the right places for the eyes and nose tonight, maybe she could finish tomorrow at Mr. Hardin's. With Mr. Hardin beside her saying the *Hm*'s, and thinking *the child is painting a beautiful picture,* it would be easy to finish. She broke into a kind of run, rolling faster. Her pace matched the way the words were racing inside her, and made running easier than walking.